A French Pilot in Gaitford

JAMES DE LA BOULLAYE

ISBN-978-2-9552270-0-8

For my Father

Who commanded squadron 346 Guyenne and the heavy bomber
base at Elvington (Yorkshire, UK) in 1944-45

.

CONTENTS

JAMES DE LA BOULLAYE

JAMES DE LA BOULLAYE

Translated from the French by JULIE SAPPA

Cover by MARC RASSIAT

1

BOIS-COLOMBES, NEAR PARIS, FRANCE, JUNE 1937

A large, fragrant rose bush in flower to the right of the church, the sweet warmth of the end of June, a cloud-free blue sky, a procession beginning to leave the church in Bois-Colombes. The start of the summer of 1937 is magnificent, but Anne won't be able to enjoy it. Lots of people have come, her childhood friends, those of her husband, relations and neighbors, all accompanying her to her last resting place. Anne has succumbed to the heart disease that turned her life upside down. She was 29 years old.

At the head of the funeral procession, Father Vauban, who has known Anne all her life, wearing a white chasuble covered in embroidery over a black cassock. He is followed by Philippe Destivel, better known as Phil, Anne's husband, carrying a rose in his hand and looking dignified in his flight lieutenant's uniform. At his side, his two children, Paul and Claire, aged eight and six. They are finding it hard to take it all in and to understand that their mom won't be there to look after them anymore. Maggy, Phil's mother, is dressed in black, and has a hardened air of tough times ahead. Next in the procession are officers in their brightly colored uniforms decorated with medals, contrasting with the somber suits of the civilians.

Whilst walking, Phil thinks about Anne, two years ago at Chartres. They'd just got back from shopping and she was having trouble walking up the stairs to their apartment. Completely out of breath, she'd had her first fainting fit and had remained unconscious for several minutes. The doctor they saw said she had anemia, too few red blood cells.

"She needs to increase her iron intake" he had pronounced.

A treatment was prescribed, but she didn't improve. Nothing worked and she had more fits. Phil took her to Paris to consult a professor of cardiology at Hôtel Dieu.

"It's mitral valve stenosis. I can hear the characteristic murmur. No doubt about it" he had concluded with an air of certainty.

There was no effective treatment and Anne needed, above all, to take it easy. She had rested, but her condition had gradually worsened and she was soon too weak to look after Paul and Claire and the house.

Phil had rapidly found a satisfactory solution. He had invited his mother, who had been widowed the year before, to come and live with them, to look after his sick wife and his children. Anne had continued to deteriorate. The doctors were not optimistic and envisaged the worst. They were all hotshots in cardiology, but there was nothing they could do for her apart from make predictions about cardiac insufficiency, which was beginning to become apparent, and the number of months that she had left.

Phil is finding it very hard to be widowed at 32, with two children to bring up and his mother at home. Anne was his childhood sweetheart. She lived next door to him in Bois Colombes. They had known and loved each other since childhood. For Paul and Claire, their mother's story doesn't end the way they always imagined it would. They always thought she would get better, because that was what everyone told them, right from the start of her illness.

The procession arrives at the cemetery and everyone gathers around the family tomb where Anne is being laid to rest.

"*Requiescat in pace!* Rest in peace" chants the priest, who blesses the coffin one last time by sprinkling holy water over it.

When the undertaker's staff begin to lower the coffin into the vault, Phil can't hold back his tears. Maggy can't help but notice and makes her disapproval felt.

"Phil, men don't cry, especially if they are officers! Behave yourself!"

2

PARIS, FRANCE, RUE LECOURBE, MARCH 1938

Maggy admires her son in his smart air force uniform as he goes off to a lecture on "Changes in strategy during the great battles of the first empire".

"I've made a *pot-au-feu*[1] for tonight, with some nice rich stock. There will be salt and gherkins to go with it", says Maggy proudly to Phil and the children, who are about to leave for school.

The kids aren't the greatest fans, but Phil loves it. It's great having his mother at home, because she rarely goes out. She's there to look after the kids, do the shopping and cook for everyone.

Now that he's been selected for training at the "War School", the final step to becoming a highly graded superior officer, he goes to the *Ecole Militaire,* which is just around the corner. He rents a four-bedroom apartment in an old building on rue Lecourbe, next to the Metro line, which runs aboveground in this part of Paris. The apartment isn't too expensive and it boasts molded ceilings and fireplaces everywhere. It doesn't have central heating, but the coal stoves burn continually, although he has to feed them with coal every

---

[1] A traditional French dish, a bit like a stew, consisting of beef boiled with vegetables. The meat and vegetables are generally served with salt grains and pickles, and the cooking liquid is often served separately, as a soup.

morning and evening to ensure that the temperature in the room remains comfortable, even in the middle of winter.

The children go to school nearby. Paul has just started at Lycée Buffon on Boulevard Pasteur, and Claire attends the primary school in rue Blomet, five minutes from home.

Phil often finds the time to come home for lunch and he is always there in the evening. He follows his children's progress at school attentively. A real mother hen during this time.

Maggy takes good care of the children, but she knows how to get to her son. She often does exactly what she feels like. If her son says he wants to go to Bon Marché next week to buy some new clothes for his children, she takes the initiative and goes with them before he gets the chance, so that she can buy them what she likes.

If he buys some new clothes for Paul, she tackles him head-on.

"Why on earth did you buy those new trousers for Paul? This material is really hard to iron. You don't know anything about clothes do you? I was brought up in the country. I can see when cloth is solid and hard-wearing. Please don't go buying things without asking me first in future. OK?"

Phil doesn't agree and he won't let her walk all over him.

"Mom, they're my children and I can buy them whatever I like. What you choose for them doesn't look very nice. In fact, some of what you choose is very ugly. It's not just the strength of the material that counts."

Phil expresses himself calmly but with authority, in a tone of voice that it's impossible to argue with. After exchanges like these, Maggy stays silent, even though, deep inside, she knows that she will continue to act in exactly the same way.

She had rapidly asked her son for a monthly budget, so that she could spend money however she saw fit. Phil realizes that his mother still sees him as her little boy who needs her to run every aspect of his daily life. She likes this state of affairs, because it's a bit like having a husband again, as Phil works and is the family breadwinner. She has found herself a new home, and she has a whole new world to manage and boss around. Nevertheless, although she doesn't choose to show it, she admires her only son Philippe, who has been her pride and joy since his birth.

Nothing in Phil's family history predestined him for a career in the air force. His parents had led a life that was far from adventurous. Having left the Beauce for the Parisian region, they had set up a modest greengrocers in Bois-Colombes. It was not until Phil finished primary school that Maggy began to make plans for her son, who was always first in his class. She applied all her energy to convincing her husband to allow Phil to continue to study. He had wanted Phil to take over their family business, and saw no reason for his son to follow long and costly studies. Maggy won out in the end, through her insistence and by calling her husband an "ignorant peasant"!

After finishing his *baccalauréat*, Phil, who was very patriotic and seduced by the idea of a military life, took the preparatory course at Lycée Condorcet for entrance into the military academy at Saint Cyr. He rapidly became interested in joining the air force, much to the despair of his mother.

"The Air Force! Why not the cavalry? You'd look wonderful on a horse!"

"The cavalry is so old hat Mom! It's still there, but not for much longer in my opinion. All the fighting is going to happen in the air!"

The flying aces had made a great stir during the Great War.

Everyone had heard of Guynemer! Aviation was scary, but fascinating, particularly for Phil, who had no other family traditions to get in the way, and didn't belong to a family of officers, engineers or priests. His dreams increasingly focused on aviation, but he had to wait until he finished his education at St. Cyr to experience it for real.

He went to Avord, close to Bourges, where there was an air force flying school, and he rapidly learnt to assemble and take apart airplane motors, to find his location in the air from geographic maps, to take off and land his plane and to use his plane's machine gun with ease. He qualified as an observation balloon operator and then as a pilot, both with the highest grades awarded by his instructors, thanks to sheer hard work and the luck that often accompanied him in his professional life. During the test for his pilot's license, he was told to fly a triangular route, first flying over Saint Etienne and then passing by Niort on his way back to his starting point close to Bourges. During the second leg of his journey, he got lost and panicked, but then came up with an ingenious solution. He flew at very low altitude until he spotted a farmer working in a large, otherwise deserted field. He landed on the grass and jumped out of his plane, leaving the engine running, and ran over to the farmer to ask his way.

"Excuse me, I'm lost. Could you please tell me where we are? What is the nearest town?"

The farmer, who was rather old, looked somewhat dumbfounded and didn't answer, cupping his hand behind his ear, indicating that he was hard of hearing. Phil asked him the same questions, at the top of his voice, but it was no use. No response. Unfortunately, the man really was deaf! Phil noticed a signpost on the road running along the edge of the field. He ran as fast as he could to the signpost, which told him that he was about 12 miles south of Angoulême, meaning that he had deviated from his initial flight plan. He ran back to his plane, breathless, and took off, managing to arrive back at his starting point within the time allowed, as if nothing had happened and with no-one any the wiser. Two days later, the same thing happened to his friend, Yves du Manoir, a trainee pilot like himself, educated at one of the finest schools in France, a rugby international and even captain of the French team. But he wasn't so lucky. During the test for his pilot's license, du Manoir also managed to get lost. He descended in altitude close to Reuilly station, in the hope of reading the name of the station, but flew straight into a copse of poplar trees. His plane crashed and the young Yves, glory of the French nation, departed from this life at the tender age of 23. Phil was badly affected by the loss of his friend.

After Avord, Phil was sent to the airbase at Chartres. He rapidly ascended to the rank of squadron leader. He was in charge of other men and took to this role with ease. He found a natural authority much appreciated by the lower ranked officers he commanded. When there was a decision to be taken, he began by discussing the issue with the principal players involved, and then weighed up the arguments they each put forward. Then, calmly, he made the decision, explaining his reasons if necessary, but never changing his mind. His firm placidity was reassuring for those he worked with.

Phil became one of the first French specialists in instrument flight rules, a skill that would serve him well in times of war. One night, while he was flying with his crew over the Beauce, both his motors failed. No alternative, he had to land! He fired some flares, identified a very straight road running through the fields and landed safely. He braked as hard as possible and then, suddenly, wham! He was groggy for a few seconds, but once he had come to his senses, he got out of his plane, the front of which was badly damaged. The other two members of the team were unhurt. Around them, lots of people in suits and a distraught bride in a beautiful white wedding dress! The track on which he had landed led to a farm. The nose of the plane had passed through the gateway, but the wings had been stopped dead by the walls. There was a party in full swing at the farm, because the bride was the daughter of the farmer. The next morning, one of the two motors, which had come away from wing, turned up in the slurry pit. The story did the tour of the aviation fields!

These episodes ended well for Phil and helped to make him optimistic and to ignore the dangers linked to his job as a pilot.

3

MEKNES, MOROCCO, OCTOBER 1943

Phil commands the Aquitaine group of bombers, which, since the Allied landings in North Africa, has rapidly become involved in the Tunisian campaign.

The airplanes they use are a bit outdated, Leo 45s, which don't fly high or fast and are easily shot down by German fighters. It's a lot of work when there are missions to prepare and, once again, he relies on Maggy to take care of his two children.

At the Meknes airbase, Maggy meets the wives of the other airmen and makes a number of friends. She starts sending out dinner invitations without consulting her son, who finds himself at home with airmen under his orders and with whom he has no real desire to mix business and pleasure. Maggy turns a deaf ear to his complaints and carries on as she chooses.

Phil is starting to feel lonely. He's been a widower now for more than six years, and he doesn't really have much of a private life anymore, with the war, his children to bring up and the chaos around him.

But Squadron Leader Philippe Destivel is a man in the prime of life and not a saint. He feels it's high time to start looking around him for some female company, even if the memory of his wife Anne still haunts him.

He notices the single women at the base: four young secretaries, three nurses, and several teachers. A few of them have a certain charm, including, in particular, one young lady he meets whilst picking up his children from the school that has been set up especially for the children of the airmen.

He arrives a bit early, in uniform, one Friday night at the school and starts talking to a woman who teaches the language of Shakespeare to the secondary school children. Phil knows that now they are under Allied command it's very likely that he will have to speak English at some point. Unfortunately, he chose to learn German as his principal foreign language at school. Still, it could come in useful now, if ever he is taken prisoner! He can write English correctly, but he speaks it badly, having never really had the chance to practice.

This rather reserved woman is called Gabrielle. She's pretty and must be in her late twenties. They have been talking for about five minutes when an idea comes into his head. Maybe she could give him English conversation lessons?

"I really must learn to speak English better" he begins. "Would you give me a few lessons? I'm not completely hopeless at written English, but I really can't speak very well. I'd pay you of course."

He realizes that Gabrielle is blushing, and that makes him smile.

"I don't have any adult pupils" she explains. "I never have had. You're a squadron leader aren't you? That would be a bit weird. I might feel intimidated. Will you let me think about it? I'm very busy you know. There aren't very many of us and my days are very full."

He doesn't want to pressure her, but he is pretty sure that she isn't quite as busy as she says. He has no telephone in the little house assigned to him on the outskirts of town, not far from the military airfield, and so he gives her his number at the base and asks her to phone him if she decides to help. He hopes that she will accept his offer. She doesn't have a telephone either, but they do have one at the school and she could use that. However, they do exchange addresses before going their separate ways. Phil hasn't told her that he is a widower, or that he has a dragon of a mother at home.

When she gets home, Gabrielle is in turmoil. It's the first time that an adult has asked her for lessons. This squadron leader seems nice, but she doesn't want to get involved. She's happy in Meknes.

Two years before, she was living in Paris and teaching at a private school. She was living in a small apartment, just below Montmartre. A young German officer had spoken to her while she was drinking a lemonade in the café below her apartment after work. Stupidly, she had told him where she lived. Things started to get complicated when the German officer returned the next day to court her. The problem was that he was charming. She didn't know what to do. She was clear in her mind that she really didn't want to have an affair with a German, but her heart and body had other ideas. She repulsed his advances firmly but gently, but he came back the next three days to try to see her.

Fortunately, a friend had told her that the Ministry of the Air was looking for language teachers to teach at the French airbases in Morocco. And that is how she rapidly found herself teaching English at Colombes school in Meknes. She'd had a lucky escape, but she'd been very careful about who she allowed to get close to her ever since.

Her concerns at Meknes at the moment are of a different type. She thinks that Phil is married, because he hasn't told her that he is a widower. She's worried that the squadron leader is only interested in seducing her. But she eventually comes to the conclusion that she's almost certainly worrying about nothing. Phil does need to improve his English and he's offering to pay her. Why not accept? In any case, she decides not to phone him, but to see if he makes contact with her, or whether it was just a passing whim on his part to become more fluent.

Three days pass. Phil decides to phone Gabrielle on Tuesday, towards five o'clock, when she should have finished teaching. She's still at the school and agrees to talk to him. She stops hesitating when he repeats his request and she agrees, without prevaricating, to give him English conversation lessons. They agree to meet for a first lesson the following Saturday, at the start of the afternoon, 2 o'clock, at the school.

For the next four days, Phil finds a bit of time in the evening, after dinner, to work on his English. He doesn't want to appear too incompetent and he revises everyday vocabulary, using the only manual he can find.

Before the lesson, he fusses over his clothes like a teenager going to a Saturday dance somewhere out in the sticks. Maggy is looking after the children. He didn't want to explain, so he told her that he was going to the base to prepare a mission for next week. It's a big lie, but what does it matter! He's wary of his mother, who knows how to ask awkward questions.

They both arrive on time, a little embarrassed. Phil has the impression that she has made an effort too. She's wearing a white blouse, fitted just enough to reveal her curves. The top three buttons are undone and the hint of her breasts attracts the attention of her pupil. He nevertheless manages to concentrate. They agree on the nature of the lessons. The contemporary English of everyday life. A life in which you get up, get dressed, eat, do your shopping and have fun by going to the cinema or theater occasionally, or spending time with friends. The hour of the lesson passes very quickly.

Phil manages reasonably well. She tells him so and encourages him. They say goodbye and arrange to meet up again the next week. Phil is very busy during the next seven days and the time flies past. They are pleased to meet up again for the second lesson and chat away in English as if they were friends. They each talk about where they come from, their parents and their childhood.

Phil explains that he is a widower and that his mother looks after his children. At the end of the lesson, he asks her to dinner at his house on Tuesday evening, if she is available. Gabrielle agrees straight away, without hesitation.

He's going to have to explain to Maggy that he has found an English teacher of the weaker sex and that she is going to have to cook her a good meal. He broaches the subject that Saturday nigh:

"Mom, I've been taking English classes once a week with a teacher from the kids' school. I need to get better at conversation. I have to speak English with the Allies and I'm not good enough. I can talk about technical stuff to do with bombers and flying, but I'm pretty weak at the rest. She's a young woman, and very nice, my teacher. She's called Gabrielle. I've invited her to dinner on Tuesday evening and I need you to cook her a nice meal."

Maggy's expression gradually hardens.

"OK, so you're taking English lessons. That's fine! But why with a woman? Why not with a male teacher? And why have you invited her to diner. I'm really busy on Tuesday. I'll never find time to do the shopping."

"You'll have time. I'm fed up with spending all my time with other officers or with couples. We get on well. I want to invite her here for dinner. I think she's a bit bored. It will make a change from the usual crowd" he says, adding, just to wind her up, "You'll see, she's really pretty too, and charming. I like her. So you'll cook her dinner. Understood?"

Maggy frowns and deep wrinkles appear on her forehead. She leaves the room in a dark mood.

Tuesday soon arrives. Gabrielle comes by bike and arrives for dinner at half past seven. Phil introduces her to his children, who are delighted to see a new face at the house. About a quarter of an hour later, Maggy comes out of the kitchen with a dirty apron tied round her waist. Her hair is a mess and she looks like she got dressed in the dark. After the briefest of nods in greeting to Gabrielle she tells everyone that it's time to eat.

Maggy has managed to get hold of a chicken and some potatoes. She doesn't say anything during the meal, and the atmosphere rapidly becomes very uncomfortable. The chicken is almost inedible, much too salty. Maggy sulks. At one point, Phil can hardly believe his ears: Maggy belches! After the dinner, which they polish off in three quarters of an hour, Gabrielle doesn't hang around, rapidly taking her leave and going go home. Phil is furious; he had imagined something completely different. Maggy is evasive. She pretends to have indigestion so that she can go to bed straight away.

On Friday, Gabrielle phones Phil to tell him that she doesn't want to teach him anymore. She explains that Maggy came to bawl her out at school, accusing her of trying to get her claws into her son. She doesn't want any trouble and would rather leave it at that. Phil is angry. When he gets home, he wants to have it out with his mother, but she is preparing the dinner. Once the kids have gone to bed, they find themselves alone.

"Gabrielle phoned me to say that she didn't want to give me language lessons anymore and that you had criticized her at school. What was all that about?"

"Yes, I'm sure you've going nowhere with that girl. She's far too young for you, she doesn't have any children and she has no experience of life. There's a war on. You need to concentrate on your family, your career as an officer and your future. You've got a lot of responsibilities. Aren't you happy with us?"

"That's got nothing to do with anything. I don't really know her very well, but I think she's nice. I've been a widower for years. I need conversation lessons in English and, frankly, I'd rather have a nice young teacher than an old harridan. Can't you understand that? You've no right to interfere in my private life like that. It's absolutely ridiculous!"

"You're my son. I know what's best for you. You should listen to me."

Phil can sense that it will not be possible to have a calm discussion. He is wound up, totally exasperated even!

"Mom, I've had enough. We'll have to find another solution. I'll see if I can find a way to get you back to France and I'll look for a governess here to look after the children."

Maggy throws a black look at her son.

"No, you're not going to do that to me!"

She walks out, shuts herself in her room and refuses to come out. The next day, Phil is still of the same mind, but he goes to knock on her door anyway. No response. Concerned, Phil forces the door open with his shoulder, to reveal his mother with a rope in her hand. There is a letter on her bedside table.

"What on earth are you doing? What's that rope for?"

Maggy doesn't answer, but starts sobbing. Phil realizes that she has decided to end her life, to hang herself. He feels obliged to back down.

"Mom, you're crazy! I was wound up. I don't want you to go

back to France. Don't worry about it. You can stay with us. But you must stop interfering in my private life."

Maggy has won and she knows it. She rapidly calms down. Phil will never know if she really intended to take her own life.

Two days pass. Phil doesn't want things to end like that with Gabrielle and he decides to go and talk to her. He turns up at the school at quarter to four after Maggy has already picked up the children. It's his lucky day, because Gabrielle is still teaching and he catches a glimpse of her mid-lesson. He waits until the last pupil leaves and then enters the classroom just as Gabrielle is packing up her things. She is a bit taken aback. Phil hasn't really prepared what he is going to say.

"Hi Gabrielle, I'm so glad I ran into you," he begins cheerfully, "It's not very easy talking over the phone, it's much better face-to-face! I need your lessons. My mother's a bit weird, you know, especially as far as I'm concerned. I should never have invited you round for dinner with her. She gets ideas."

"She's so unpleasant, your mother!"

"If you'd be willing to give me a few lessons, I won't tell her. She won't be any the wiser. We could meet up somewhere other than the school. I know a few out-of-the-way places in Meknes where we could meet up without being recognized. Would you be willing to do that? You know, I've been a widower for a while now and I'm a grown man who can do what he likes and think what he likes, even if he does have kids to raise!'

The ambiguity of Phil's question troubles Gabrielle. She hesitates and doesn't know what to say. She wants to know more.

"Where could we meet up for these conversation lessons? I really don't want to run into you mother. She scares me!"

"Does that mean that the answer is yes? Let me think about it a bit. We could meet somewhere different each time. That would make it more exciting. Let's get together at three o'clock next Saturday. There is a large rug shop at the entrance of the souk. It's called *les Perles du Maroc*. I know the owner and I'm sure he would lend us a small room for our lesson."

"Yes, OK" replies Gabrielle shyly. Phil is over the moon, and he blows her a kiss with his right hand on leaving. He is finding her increasingly captivating.

Phil asks Nassim, the shopkeeper, if he can use his back room for an hour for an English lesson. Nassim looks at him and laughs. "No problem" he says. At the appointed time on Saturday, Phil is in the shop. He soon finds himself in a small room full of different colored rugs. Gabrielle arrives ten minutes late. They have to sit on two pouffes, in front of a coffee table. Their subject of conversation is the war, and what is likely to happen in the near future: the retaking of territory. Gabrielle has tied her hair up in a bun, which makes her look a bit older. She is wearing a light blue blouse, a straight white skirt with a large belt and sandals. She is dressed simply, but Phil finds it charming. Her voice is soft. She's slim without being skinny and has long, fine hands. A real woman!

Gabrielle is troubled. She likes Phil's voice, with its intonations like a caress. He's in civil dress and is wearing a linen shirt. He has very light blue eyes and short light brown hair. He could almost be a German! He often looks directly into her eyes, smiling. He's concentrating to make sure that his accent isn't too French!

The hour flies by. They even run over a little bit. Gabrielle realizes and says that it is time to leave. Phil kisses her on the cheek when they part. Surprised, she blushes, but doesn't take offense, and she offers to meet up the next week, at the same place if possible. They leave together and then go their separate ways.

He really is attracted to this Gabrielle. Through the next week, he has several bombing runs to prepare and carry out on Rommel's troops in Tunisia. One of his crew members is killed. As always, it's a traumatic experience losing one of his own men.

One evening, just before dinner, Maggy asks him straight out "Swear to me that you won't see that girl that you brought home, that Gabrielle, again!"

That really is the last straw and he rapidly becomes exasperated, but he stands up for himself.

"Mom, that's enough. My private life is none of your business. Let me get on with my life. I've already told you."

Maggy still has gotten used to such direct responses to her interrogations. She doesn't say anything, but sulks in silence for two days. Phil has murderous thoughts towards his mother and there is rebellion in the air. Unfortunately, he can't see any real solution, because he hasn't dared suggest that she return to France since he found out about her suicidal ideas. He needs his mother to look after the children, but he knows that she will never change. What can he do? There doesn't seem to be a satisfactory answer.

The next day, Phil arrives early at the airbase. He is immediately summoned by Colonel de Frenoy, the commander of the station. They know each other well and are on first-name terms in private.

"Phil, I've got news for you. You'll never guess!"

He holds out an envelope containing a typed letter. Phil reads it and can't believe his eyes. He and his group are being sent to England.

"You and the rest of the Aquitaine group are going to be incorporated into the Royal Air Force" explains the Colonel. "You will leave soon by boat. You will form a French base, but you will be under British command. You'll have to leave Mers el Kébir behind, old man!"

Two other similar French groups had already left the month before to set up a bomber base in Yorkshire. They will have to do the same.

Phil is happy to be able to continue the fight against the Nazis and is curious to see the reputedly exemplary aerial logistics of the British. It will also provide him with his first opportunity to pilot a heavy bomber, with four engines, a type of plane that the French air force simply does not have.

"I should also tell you that you've just been promoted to lieutenant colonel" adds the Colonel. "Not bad at 39! But you thoroughly deserve it. You've shown yourself to be a good organizer, an excellent leader and you don't hesitate to expose yourself to the worst of dangers. You've proved that throughout the Tunisian campaign. Congratulations!"

Phil is flattered by this promotion that he wasn't expecting, but his thoughts turn immediately to his family.

"Will my mother and children be on the same boat?"

"I'm sorry Lieutenant Colonel, but the families are staying in Morocco. No special favors."

Unbelievable, unhoped-for news! Phil immediately realizes that this is an unmissable opportunity to escape from his dragon of a mother, at least for a few months! He had dreamt of it and God has organized it for him! He will miss his children terribly, but they seem to be able to cope with life with their grandmother, whereas he can't!

That night, Maggy greets Phil in a very bad mood.

"I'm not happy. Someone told me that you've been seeing

that Gabrielle again. We're going to have to talk about this."

Phil flashes her a huge smile and says "Mom, I've got two big pieces of news. The first is that I've just be promoted to lieutenant colonel and the second is that I'm being sent to England with the rest of the Aquitaine group. We're leaving by boat in a few days."

Maggy is delighted about the promotion of her son, even though she knows nothing about military grades. She also wants to know more about his departure for England.

"Well done! I'm proud to have a lieutenant colonel who's leaving for England as my son. It'll be an interesting experience! I've never been on a boat and the children haven't either. I can't wait."

"No, Mom, the families can't come with us. But it won't be for long, just a few months!"

Furious, Maggy changes from livid white to carmine red. She becomes enraged. She does not want to be left on her own with the children in Morocco. She wants to go to England too. It really would be too much to bear to be left here isolated in the middle of nowhere! Phil tells her that he will see what he can do, but he already knows that none of the families can go. Maggy will just have to get used to it. He is only too contented with this chance of freedom. It's just a shame that he will have to leave his children and Gabrielle behind.

They see each other the next Saturday, as planned. It's their last meeting. She knows about his departure. The English lesson is a bit sad. It's clear that both of them would have liked to take their relationship further. But it's the war. Phil pays for his lessons, says goodbye, and this time kisses her on both cheeks. He notices a small tear in her eyes and it moves him. It's a good thing that they didn't get the chance to go any further! So much easier to end a relationship that hasn't yet begun! But Phil has become aware of his loneliness, which has become a burden to him.

4

ON BOARD THE SAMARIA, IN THE MEDITERRANEAN AND ATLANTIC, NOVEMBER 1943

They are in almost complete darkness. The only light comes from the lightning bolts that illuminate the wings of the plane for a few brief instants. Phil, the pilot, can't see much and he's anxious. He wants to continue to climb, as he is hindered by the lack of visibility. Almost 10,000 feet! He needs to climb some more, whatever it takes, to escape from this peasouper that is threatening to bring him down. Eyes fixed on the altimeter, rigid as a broomstick, the plane about to stall. Almost 15,000 feet and still as much cumulus. The light refuses to show itself and the sun is still hidden. Phil is sweating despite the coldness of the cockpit. He's out of breath and afraid that he won't make it. He has never seen such thick cloud cover. Twenty-three thousand feet. The lightning bolts are becoming increasingly frequent and the cockpit is frosting up. That will make the plane heavier, and it will nosedive and break up. Thirty-three thousand feet! He can't believe it. Why haven't they hit blue skies yet? The pilot prefers to close his eyes, first for one minute, then for two. His last instants are approaching and he thinks about his children.

The plane is finally out of the cloud and is now flying about 300 feet above a very welcoming white carpet. The sky is a rich blue and the sun is still visible, low on the horizon. Phil relaxes, moved by the sober beauty of the sky. He can't really hear the motors any more, just a gentle purring on the edge of his perception. Phil has cheated death.

He opens his eyes. For a few seconds, he doesn't know where he is. He can still hear the sound of a motor, but the scenery has changed. His dream, almost a nightmare, is over. He isn't flying and, indeed, he isn't even on an airplane. Instead, he finds himself in a bed, in a cabin, on board a ship. It's all coming back to him. It is November 1943 and yesterday he boarded a luxurious Dutch cruise ship that is now being used to transport troops. He's on his way to England, but he doesn't know exactly where.

In his cabin, he is finally free! No more having to be home at a certain time, no more protests. It's been years since he has felt so unburdened. A new page is being written in his new life. He has left the old one behind at Meknes, in Morocco, at least for a few months. He had really needed that breath of fresh air! Everything had sorted itself out in the end.

It's still nighttime, but Phil isn't sleepy anymore. He gets up, pulls some clothes on in a hurry and goes out onto the upper deck, which is empty, and lets his mind roam. He thinks about the children he has left behind, Paul and Claire.

Paul is fourteen now and is starting to be a bit difficult. Hardly surprising now that he has hit puberty. Fortunately, he is very sporty and plays football with the scouts. An outlet for his hormonal tensions.

Claire is still very much a daddy's girl. She cried when he had to leave, sad and worried about what might happen to him. It was hard to leave them and he wonders when he will see them again.

Phil looks at his watch and goes back to his cabin to put on his uniform. He and his deputy, Captain Jopet, must start to interview all the airmen in their group, one-by-one. There are almost 70 of them and it's going to be tight, very difficult.

Their first interview is with Lieutenant Borne, a dashing pilot who wants to fight the Boche. Phil explains the situation. The lieutenant is appalled, red-faced with anger and has difficulty controlling himself.

"Sir, are you telling me that you want me to become a navigator? I'm a pilot, and only a pilot. I decided to go into aviation to become a pilot. I don't want that taken away from me. That's completely unacceptable!"

"For the moment, Lieutenant, I'm just telling you how things are. Do not forget that you are a military man and must obey orders. I can see that you're not too keen to change jobs. We'll let you know what we decide once we've seen everyone. That will be all for now. Please send in Warrant Officer Revel."

Borne is appalled. At the age of 25, he is considered to be one of the best pilots in the air force and they've dared suggest to him that there are too many pilots and that some of them will have to change roles in the bombing missions they are to carry out.

Phil is obliged to be firm, even though he understands only too well the lieutenant's fury. He has a lot on his plate in the next few days. He has to form 24 seven-man crews. His group contains 40 pilots and that is too many! He needs 24 pilots and no more than that. Some of the pilots will have to learn another job, bomber or navigator, for example, and they are not going to like it. They find it degrading, even though their rank as officers allows them to retain the status as captain of the plane, meaning that they are in charge and must decide what to do if there is a problem during the flight. But flying is their life, their reason for existence in their work. They embraced this career because they love flying and now they might have to give it up. It's unthinkable, impossible! None of them will agree. Phil will have to call on their patriotic fiber to make them more flexible.

Warrant Officer Revel comes into the cabin that Phil and his deputy use as an office. At 33, he is older than the officer that preceded him. They explain to him that they have too many pilots and ask him if there is another role that he might like to take on. They are giving priority to the younger pilots, with their faster reflexes. Revel is less stubborn.

"I get it. I'd like to be a navigator if you want me to change roles Sir".

Ah, if only they were all like him, thinks Phil.

They continue to interview the other members of the group for the rest of the morning. The pilots who have understood that their role is going to change look downcast when they leave. Towards noon, Phil decides to take a break for half an hour. He is going to stretch his legs on the upper deck.

Whenever Phil looks straight ahead or behind, he glimpses other ships and hears the regular murmur of their engines. To disguise their movements, they were headed due east when they left Algiers. Not really the right direction for England! Then, as night fell, they turned around and sailed due west. This maneuver was designed to enable them to escape the gaze of the German spies who monitored ship movements during the day.

The size of the convoy is reassuring. A real armada! No less than 18 ships, with two cruisers to escort them, four destroyers and two aircraft carriers to protect them from enemy fighters and bombers. Even in these conditions, the voyage could be eventful. There are still German submarines in the Atlantic, but the French high command is optimistic. Another similar convoy had made the journey without confrontation two weeks ago.

Phil feels good. The early days should be both peaceful and interesting. They will spend the first few months receiving specific training in the north of Scotland.

At first, Phil hadn't really understood why this learning phase was scheduled to take so long. But they had explained it to him. Missions to attack enemy targets will no longer involve five or 10 planes, but hundreds of bombers simultaneously departing from airbases spread all over the southern half of England. The planes must meet up at a fixed time to form a continuous fleet of machines that will then fly together to the target, to drop their bombs with the greatest precision, without any temporal drift.

A whole set of logistics. They will need to know how to maneuver these large heavy bombers, with their four engines and seven-man crews. They will need to learn how to fly in the night, in total darkness, with no lights on, to make sure that they are not picked up by flak. All this in the middle of a huge fleet of similar planes that they mustn't hit. They will need to master the art of navigation, be familiar with the maneuvers to be carried out if they arrive a little early or late at the rendezvous points, know how to drop their bombs at the right moment, and have the strategies required to avoid enemy fighters that have them in their sights. They won't be able to just "wing" it. They need proper, methodical, in-depth training.

Bombing missions over Germany might be dangerous, but they must be more glorious than the mission of November 8 1942, which Phil will never forget. That day, he was ordered to bomb the American allies landing at Fédala in Morocco! Bombing Hitler's enemies! He was appalled, but his command and some of his crews remained loyal to Marshal Pétain and considered the landings to be an act of aggression against France. Fortunately, he was saved by the bad weather over the beaches. He was relieved to be able to give his group the signal to drop their bombs elsewhere. They exploded in the open sea, a thousand feet or so from their targets. Not a single Allied soldier or ship was hit.

Phil runs over these last few years in his head like a film on fast-forward. When war broke out, Phil's hours had become very irregular, even though hardly any shots were fired for a year, during the "Phony War". Luckily, his mother had been around to look after Paul and Claire. After France had capitulated, Phil had been promoted to major and transferred to Vichy, with the rest of the French military, or at least what remained of it after the Armistice. He wanted to join De Gaulle in England, but material considerations had made that impossible. If he left, no more salary, no more accommodation. How would his mother and his children survive? He could find no answer to this question. So he reluctantly stayed at Vichy. All four of them had lived in hotel rooms that the military had attributed to them. A strange period in a strange war!

Phil didn't have much to do, but he had to be there. They didn't always have enough to eat each week. Every weekend, he had to deal with logistics. He and his two children would go out on bikes. Their outings were highly enjoyable. They stopped at farms along the way to try to buy food, poultry, vegetables, fruit. This officer and his children had quite an effect on the farmers. They were easily moved and sold them whatever they had, at prices that were not too prohibitive.

On Sunday evenings, Maggy was there, waiting for her troops, to assess their offerings. There were compliments, but criticism too. "What a lovely lettuce! But the potatoes, they don't look very edible! And that chicken, he looks like he's run a few races!" Phil had the impression that his mother took a certain delight in criticizing the yields of their bike trips. Claire was the apple of her father's eye and Maggy also liked to give her a good telling off. That was bound to annoy him!

They spent an often difficult year at Vichy, until Phil was sent to North Africa, to Meknes in Morocco.

5

BUCKINGHAMSHIRE, UNITED KINGDOM, NOVEMBER 1943

John Luxley is sad. He has met so many that never returned. Guys that he played cards with, or chess, in the officers' mess. Time went by quietly until they had to prepare for a new mission. The designated crews eventually took off. For some targets in Germany, the round trip was long, more than 10 hours in total. They weren't expected back until the next morning.

They were relieved when they saw the planes come back. When one or several bombers were missing, they tried to find out what had happened to them. There was still hope. Some could have had mechanical problems or damage due to German flak. When that happened, the planes tried to land at the airfields in the far south of England, very close to the North Sea, which had been specially designed for planes in distress. It would then take the crews up to a couple of days to make it back to their bases in military coaches. Others might have been obliged to eject from planes on fire. There wasn't always time for all the crew members to jump out of the plane with their parachutes. The pilot often remained at the controls to keep the bomber flying. The plane could break up or crash before he had a chance to get out.

For some, these evacuations happened over Germany. Most

were taken prisoner, but some were machine-gunned down before they hit the ground or were subsequently lynched by hateful civilians exasperated by the bombing of their towns. Finally, some planes crashed before anyone could get out. In such cases, none of the seven members of the crew would ever come back.

John is English. He is a lieutenant and a bomber pilot in the Royal Air Force. He has just completed his tour of operations. In other words, he has carried out the total number of missions generally assigned to a crew. Thirty times he has left with fear in his heart, telling himself that he would almost certainly never come back. At 27, he feels that he is too young to die.

His last mission, which aimed to destroy the factories at which the Germans assembled their armored vehicles, near Leipzig, had been the most trying. Exploding shells! The rear gunner and the flight engineer killed instantly. Two engines on fire. He had been sure that the plane was going to break up. There was considerable damage. Miraculously, he had managed to get his plane back to England. But it had become unflyable. John had given the order to evacuate. The mid-upper gunner had been the first to parachute out of the plane, followed by the bombardier and the wireless operator. John can't really remember what happened after that. He lost consciousness and when he came round, he found himself attached to his parachute. He made it to the ground with no problem. For unknown reasons, the carbonized body of the navigator was found in the remains of the plane, which crashed a few seconds after he had given the order to evacuate.

John had faced a long interrogation on what had happened during the last few minutes of the flight, up until the moment the plane crashed, but he couldn't remember anything. Total amnesia for that period of a few minutes! The inquiry had concluded that the navigator's parachute must have remained attached to the plane when he had jumped. Three deaths in this accident.

John had wept for his friends. They had been only 22, 25 and 27 years old. They had died during their last mission over Germany. How ironic!

John likes flying. In 1941, he had volunteered for the Royal Air Force. He wanted to be a fighter pilot, but had instead been trained as a bomber pilot. What John would most like now is to go back to his research, because he is really a mathematician! John is a specialist in probability. He has a PhD from Oxford and was about to start teaching when war broke out.

He has a meeting in an hour with the commander of the base, who should be able to tell him more about his fate. Today, November 10 1943, he will learn what is to become of him.

He returns to his room to prepare himself and to brush his uniform, which has been somewhat neglected recently. He rides his bicycle to the meeting with his superior officer, who receives him warmly, taking several minutes to congratulate him for having successfully completed these dangerous missions. He then tells him about what the air force is cooking up for him. They propose to demobilize him. He will go back to civilian life, but he will take up a scientific post at Bomber Command in Buckinghamshire. They need mathematicians specializing in probability. That's his domain and, as an added extra, he knows all about the art of bombing. Dual competence. He can't tell John anything more, because he doesn't know any more. John has two days to respond to the offer.

It doesn't take John long to decide. This mathematician's post intrigues him. He asks himself what they could possibly want a probability specialist for at Bomber Command. It must be more fun to work as a scientist, and much more useful for winning the war, than to become an instructor of new recruits, from whom he would have to conceal some of the horror of these missions. He accepts this offer the very next day and takes up his new post three days later.

John travels by train to his appointment, in Buckinghamshire, about 40 miles north-west of London. Bomber Command is camouflaged in a very dense forest, sheltered from German bombers. John must first make a stop at Richmart, a small town in the Wycombe area about five miles away from Bomber Command HQ. He is going to stay with a family there, and he will be given a bike for his journeys to and from work.

He is surprised to find that the address he has been given is that of the local vicar. When he rings the doorbell, it is Edith, the vicar's wife, who opens the door. She knows he is coming. She and her husband have volunteered to provide lodgings for a young Bomber Command employee. But not just anyone! They have already refused two young people whose CVs they didn't like. John Luxley's CV, on the other hand, had attracted their attention. John is himself the son of a vicar and that, for them, is sufficient guarantee of good behavior.

Edith shows him around the house. It was built in the 19th century. It has 11 rooms, but the vicar's family only occupy four of them. John is going to have a quiet time of it. His room is vast and isolated in a wing of the building that he will have all to himself. He has a double bed, a desk, a large Victorian wardrobe for his things and a bathroom. His window looks out onto some hundred-year-old oaks.

Just like the good Englishwoman she is, Edith prepares him some tea and biscuits. It's five o'clock and John is hungry. He didn't eat much for lunch and he appreciates this little snack. He uses the opportunity to study his hostess more closely. She must be about 45. She is tall, red-haired and looks shapely, but she is austere and not very friendly. Her strict manner of dress is in keeping with her social position as the vicar's wife.

For Edith, it's an opportunity to get to know her new lodger. She is not sorry to find herself alone with John, because she wants to know more about him.

"They told us you were a mathematician, that you have a PhD from Oxford and that your father is a vicar. That gave us several good reasons to take you. Robert, my husband, will be here tonight. He has a great deal of respect for mathematicians. He likes their rigor and the logic of their reasoning. Second, Oxford has an excellent reputation around the world and they don't take just anybody. Robert knows that well because he was there himself for two years, during his theology studies. Finally, we are only too happy to welcome the son of a vicar to our home. It's a guarantee of morality. But, tell me, I must ask you something as the information we were given about you was very sketchy. I don't want to be indiscreet, but what have you been doing since the beginning of the war?"

John realizes that she doesn't know about his years with the RAF. But her questions are too direct. John doesn't like her inquisitive tone. He doesn't want to answer, doesn't want to satisfy her curiosity.

"That's a long story. I'll tell you another time."

Edith doesn't appreciate his reticence, becomes tight-lipped and shuts up. It's John who takes up the conversation.

"Do you live on your own with the vicar in this big house? Doesn't it get you down?"

"We have a daughter, Margaret. She's at school at the moment but she will be home soon. You'll meet her at dinner."

John wonders what the child living in this austere house with a mother who doesn't seem to be much fun and a clerical father could possibly look like.

Edith gives him the key to the house and then shows him the bicycle that Bomber Command left for him. This bicycle will be his means of transport to work. Dinner will be at 7 p.m. John thanks her warmly, settles in, puts away his things and then goes for a ride on his bike. He discovers a small town. Five thousand inhabitants, apparently. A history, a past, of which he knows absolutely nothing. It's been there since the Middle Ages and a previous prime minister lived there. It's a nice place, but very hilly, making cycling a bit tiring. There are several pubs, which will provide a valuable resource for his down time.

John decides to have a drink at the Angel Inn. The place is almost empty. John takes him time over a pale ale on tap. It's his favorite beer and he tastes it like a wine. He begins by admiring its beautiful amber color and its foam and then enjoys its bitterness, which is penetrating and remains on his palate for a long time. This beer rapidly lifts his mood. His new life is exciting and he is keen to join Bomber Command. One more night to wait. For now, he will content himself with getting to know his host family better.

John arrives at his lodgings a quarter of an hour before dinner. He can get to his room by entering the house through a back door. This leaves him with a certain amount of autonomy in his comings and goings.

At seven o'clock on the dot, John appears in the dining room, where he meets the vicar, a welcoming man, about 50 years old, who welcomes him and serves him with a glass of sherry to mark the occasion. Edith joins them and says that Margaret will come and eat with them after the aperitif. She's dolled herself up. She's wearing a pearl necklace that she didn't have on earlier, together with a gold bracelet that she must have inherited from her family, because John can't imagine the vicar having enough money to offer her jewelry like that.

The conversation rapidly turns to the war, which, at the end of 1943, is a major preoccupation for everyone. It's clear that the Germans can no longer hold their positions. The Allies have landed in Italy and are regaining territory. Everyone wants the hostilities to end soon. The fighting has already been going on for almost four years. The English haven't been spared. London and other towns have been bombed and a lot of civilians have died. Robert, like Edith before him, rapidly starts to question his lodger.

"How about you John? What have you been up to since the start of the war?"

John doesn't want to talk about it, not now. He was traumatized by all those months of bombing, with anxiety before and during each mission. He is very vague in his response because it isn't a subject he wants to talk about.

"It's been difficult for me too" he says.

The vicar wants to know more, but he doesn't want to pry. He tries to rephrase his question, but finally gives up. John is relieved. Maybe he'll talk about it eventually, but later.

It's at this moment that Margaret shows up. John was expecting a schoolgirl. He's surprised to find that Margaret is a beautiful young woman with blond hair, a large straight nose and well formed pink lips. She already has the figure of a woman, not a teenager. She is wearing a green uniform, consisting of a blazer bearing the school badge and a straight skirt. She has a chain around her neck. John is delighted with her company, or at least her appearance. Margaret shakes his hand warmly.

"Hello Mister Luxley, welcome to Richmart. You know it's a bit dead around here. There aren't any big towns near. I hope you'll liven this house up and make us all laugh. We need that with this war that everyone goes on about all the time. My parents said that you're a mathematician. That's brilliant. You'll be able to help me with my homework. I'm more arty really. Maths brings me out in a rash!"

"Margaret, don't fool around with the lodger. You're giving

him a very strange impression of yourself," interrupts the vicar. "Take no notice John, Margaret's a bit direct. You need to know how to put her back in her place."

The prospect of teaching Margaret is not an unpleasant one to John. Cheekily, he says "If you're not too useless, and your case is not completely hopeless, if you promise to try hard, then I accept to try to win you over to a new passion."

It's a bit ambiguous and rather daring. John realizes this and explains.

He launches into a diatribe on the beauties of mathematics, describing the development of geometry by the Ancient Greeks and that of algebra, facilitated by the invention of Arabic numerals, which are actually really more Indian in origin!

The vicar listens with interest and can see that his lodger is passionate about his subject. Edith lightens up a bit. John discovers that the vicar also knows about the history of mathematics. When they get to talking about probability, John's specialty, he realizes that Robert is entirely comfortable with the concepts of median, variance and mode. The same is true for the laws of Poisson and Gauss!

"You seem to know about these things Robert. Do you like probability too?"

"Yes, very much. I did a degree in mathematics before studying theology and thinking about becoming a vicar. I was at Oxford, like you."

The conversation continues agreeably during dinner. Before going to bed, John thanks Edith and Robert warmly for agreeing to house him for a few months. When he says goodnight to Margaret, she looks into his eyes and holds his hand in hers for slightly longer than expected. John smiles and returns to his room somewhat moved.

Decidedly, life has taken a turn for the better! Even Edith found favor in his eyes that evening! He's staying with a nice family. The daughter of the house is pretty, undoubtedly hopeless at mathematics, and will need his help. What good luck!

He goes to bed tired. His appointment at Bomber Command HQ is at 10 o'clock the next morning. He leaves plenty of time to get there, an hour by bicycle. That's much longer than the three miles or so should take. But if he gets a flat tire, he'll need a bit of time to repair it. He can't possibly arrive late on his first day!

He falls asleep straight away. But, towards 2 a.m., he has a nightmare. His plane is on fire. The others have jumped with their parachutes. He is looking around desperately for his own. The plane is burning and will soon crash. At the moment the flames reach him he wakes up, sweating and breathless, full of dread. John feels how deeply traumatized his missions have left him. Almost every night, his sleep is interrupted by these bad dreams. It takes him an hour to get back to sleep.

He wakes early and prepares his own breakfast. His journey to work takes him through Richmart, and then along the edge of the woods. The road then penetrates the forest for about a mile and a half before it reaches HQ. The forest is dense at this point. The buildings mustn't be visible from the sky. John feels like he is arriving somewhere sacred. This is where the daily bombing missions are prepared. The logistics must be complicated some nights, when several hundred bombers are sent to their targets.

When he arrives at HQ, his papers are examined thoroughly. He is then taken to a brick building a bit larger than those around it. He is told that he will be seen by the Commander-in-Chief himself, Air Chief Marshal Hudson. The Marshal comes into the waiting room after a few minutes, to call the new recruit into his office. John is impressed. He knows what it means to organize these mass bombings over Germany that are designed to destroy the war machine. The Marshal asks him to sit in a lounge area incorporated into his office. They sit on two brown club armchairs on either side of a coffee table. A young woman in uniform comes in and serves them tea. Hudson starts by congratulating John on having completed his 30 missions.

"Well done for being so courageous. I know it's very hard and risky, but we have no choice. Lots of crews are lost and we have to replace them. It's not easy. You now have experience in the heavy bombing of Germany. You understand perfectly how we work. It's here at HQ that the objectives are selected. We base our decisions on information provided by our spies on German soil and in France. They manage to tell us where the principal installations responsible for the construction of planes, boats and weapons are located. The Germans also have factories producing synthetic petrol. They have depots for arms and ammunition. We're trying to destroy all that. Once we have chosen the objectives, we have to decide how many bombers will be needed to complete the job. Finally, to make sure we get all the planes required, we have to ask each airbase to commit a certain number of planes. For each mission, RAF personnel must also go to tens of bases to brief the pilots, navigators and other crew members. It's all very complicated. Do you understand?"

"Yes" says John, "I understand entirely. I experienced all that from the other side, that of a pilot, for two years. I was wondering why you need mathematicians like me to improve this tactic, which already seems to be well developed?"

John can't see what his role is to be until the Air Chief Marshal explains that this command center also includes a research center, the Operational Research Section or ORS. This is the research center that makes use of mathematicians.

"I'll explain what we want from you. The system we use to analyze operations after the missions have taken place is imperfect. We want to know if the losses are similar at all the different bases.

Several factors are involved. Geographically, some of the bases are further north or west than others, making the missions longer. Some bases have Lancaster bombers, others have Halifaxes. The nationalities of the crews are different. A lot of them are British, but some are Canadian, Australian, New Zealanders, South African or Polish. We're even going to have some French crews in the RAF soon. They want to take up the fight again after three years of collaboration with the Nazis. Even if all the crew members undergo sophisticated, standardized training with us, they don't all have the same experience or the same military culture. We have the impression that there may be large differences in results between the different airbases, but we're not sure. So, in a nutshell, I expect you to develop an effective system for analyzing our losses after missions so that we can take corrective action if required. Is that clear?"

"I see, Sir. In any case, I now understand why you need probability specialists."

John observes the Marshal closely. He finds him a bit vulgar with his very British but frankly ridiculous moustache. He would look so much better without it! He looks like he's been stuffed into his uniform, even though he isn't really fat. He doesn't look like a bundle of laughs. John hasn't seen so much as a glimmer of a smile since their conversation began. And to think that this is the man who decides which German soldiers and civilians will live or die!

Hudson then explains the organization of the ORS, which has three divisions. John is being assigned to the division responsible for analyzing the losses of aircraft during bombing runs, to try to improve things.

There are about 30 people, all civilian researchers, at the ORS, and almost the same number of WAAFs. These young women are members of the Women's Auxiliary Air Force and they must submit to military discipline just like the men. They are a precious help. They carry out many tasks, including visual analyses of the photos taken by the crews to assess the efficacy of the bombs, and the many calculations required to analyze these results. But they also serve the tea and provide a bit of conviviality in this command center, which is otherwise very austere.

After half an hour, Hudson has transmitted all the information he wanted to. He has Malcolm Bowen brought in. Bowen is the head of the division of the ORS to which John has been assigned. He will show John the building in which he will work and his desk, and will introduce him to his principal colleagues. John leaves Hudson's office with a request to provide a first report on his reflections after 10 days or so.

"You've met the big boss," begins Malcolm, "Not everyone gets that honor. He's a bit dry, completely focused on his mission, and he spends all his time working. He lives here full-time, doesn't sleep much and only leaves the site to go and talk to important politicians like Churchill. He's a funny old bird our Hudson! He plays such a key role in the war effort but no-one knows it."

John visits the center, part of which is underground. He is impressed by the operations room, where the missions are prepared. It's teeming with people. One vast room with a very high ceiling, with multiple possibilities for displaying the geography of countries at war. A large map of Germany just over 16 feet tall and 26 feet wide immediately catches the eye of anyone entering this room.

The offices of the ORS are located in a small dedicated brick building surrounded by majestic oaks, which make it rather dark but help to protect the occupants from any undesirable elements that might like to fly over them and take them for a target. John shares an office with another mathematician, an Australian by the name of Joseph Anderson. He puts John at his ease by telling him how glad he is that he has arrived, because he has had enough of being all on his own in a 25-foot square room, thinking all day.

At the ORS, the day ends at 5 p.m. At this time of year, it's almost dark when John leaves on his bike. It's a bit chilly in November but, fortunately, climbing the hills soon warms him up. At 5.30 p.m., John reaches the village, Richmart. A good beer will undoubtedly make him feel better, and he stops at the Angel Inn, the pub he discovered the day before.

Over a pale ale, John contemplates his working day. The people he met at the ORS seem nice enough. Malcolm Bowen has explained to him in detail what they expect from his work and has given him a confidential report describing all of the data recorded during each operation. He has 10 days to prepare a report concerning the various research objectives he has been given, indicating the methods he plans to use to achieve each objective. This will include the collection of new types of data and the methods of interpretation he proposes. He has access to the ORS library, where he can consult the key works published over the last 10 years on the calculation of probabilities and statistics. He has already recognized the names of famous statisticians, like Fisher and Pearson, whose work he had learnt about at Oxford.

John's thoughts then lead him to more private considerations. He appreciates his freedom but doesn't always find it easy to live alone. At 27, it's clearly time for him to find a girlfriend. Until now, he has been happy to be single. These last few years have been very busy. At Oxford, during his PhD, he had a fling with a young librarian called Mary. Over a period of four months, they saw each other often. But John knew he wasn't really in love. He had preferred to break up before the situation got too complicated.

More recently, during his bomber pilot training in Scotland, Ann, a 37-year-old WAAF that he met at a dance at the airbase, had initiated him in the ways of love. With her, he had discovered many pleasures. Tender, affectionate and imaginative, she had known how to take the initiative in ways that had delighted him. For him, she had been a marvelous teacher. They had separated when John had had to leave Scotland at the end of his training. He had written to her several times, but his letters had gone unanswered. Another young apprentice pilot had no doubt replaced him! His heart wasn't broken, but he missed her bed and her welcoming arms for some time.

John continues to let his thoughts wander. He thinks again about his recurrent nightmares, his nocturnal terrors, linked to his horrible experiences as a pilot during these last few months. There was a certain paradox to those missions over France and Germany. The scenery was often superb. Those seas of sunlit clouds that they discovered after leaving the airbase in the rain were so beautiful. Even with the prospect of very difficult moments ahead, John was sensitive to the poetry and serenity of these spaces reserved for aviators. But the first contact with German flak brought him and the rest of the crew back to earth and the hard reality facing them. An atmosphere of death prevailed. Luckily, as the pilot, John had to concentrate on the job in hand, stopping him from thinking too much about the worst that could happen. But no mission was anodyne and he was filled with dread when the time to leave approached. It was when they came back and were flying over England again that the tension decreased and they could once again make the most of these seas of tranquility.

Six in the evening. John finishes his beer, telling himself that he must get back in time for dinner. He leaves the pub, gets back on his bike and steers himself, in the twilight, towards the house, with the happy prospect of seeing Margaret and her parents again. As he starts to climb the final hill on the way to the house, he notices a small crowd of people and an ambulance. Forced to stop, he asks someone what's going on.

"Ah, it's a worry. It's our vicar. I saw him pedaling rapidly up the hill on his way home. He was going fast and he had a funny turn. He was in a lot of pain and he was clutching his chest, on the left, where the heart is. He was pulling terrible faces with the pain! We called an ambulance to take him to the hospital. Poor man. I hope he's going to be alright."

6

SCOTLAND, UNITED KINGDOM, DECEMBER 1943-MARCH 1944

Phil has been savouring the pleasures of the north of Scotland for two months now. He and his crew members are training at the RAF base at Lossiemouth, a fishing port with a large beach and rows of pretty houses. It's far enough north to be out of the reach of German bombers and fighters. The airmen rapidly find it too cold, especially with the ever-present dampness that accentuates the feeling of cold on days of wind and fog. But the French who have come to fight with the RAF receive a warm welcome. They mix with other airmen in training, many from England, but others from Canada and New Zealand.

Phil finds it very neat and tidy. The wooden buildings are laid out in regular rows. The officers are privileged, as always in the military, with individual or double rooms. The younger airmen are housed in dormitories, waiting for rooms to be vacated when other groups leave the base at the end of their training. The British and French flags fly on the flagpole. The base's motto "train to win", which sums up the general mood of the place, is displayed at the entrance. The training must be meticulous, organized and intensive. It's unequivocally a matter of beating the enemy, whatever it takes.

After their arrival in England, they followed an initial period of specialist training. As a pilot, Phil spent more than a month at Long Newton near Gloucester, in the South-West of England, close to Wales. He enjoyed his training missions over Oxford, in one of the school's two-engine planes, particularly suitable for instrument flight rules and flying at night, his specialty before the war broke out.

Phil isn't disconcerted by the damp weather in Scotland, or by the short days and biting cold of the season. They are just over 550 miles from the Arctic Circle. The sun comes up at 10 in the morning and goes down at about half past four in the afternoon. Despite the glacial aspect of the place, the atmosphere is excellent. The teams get on well and they are all happy to be flying together, frequently and for long periods. They are getting ready to celebrate Christmas away from their families.

Phil is taking great delight in his freedom. A ball has been organized on December 24, before midnight mass. The commissioned and non-commissioned officers and the female staff get together to dance. The alcohol is flowing freely and many of them are very unsteady on their feet after an hour. As a result, the dancefloor is sparsely populated. Phil can ask all the ladies he likes to dance with him without worrying about what Maggy thinks! Some of the WAAFs are young and attractive. The uniform doesn't make them look any less feminine. They are flattered to be asked to dance by a French colonel with a certain charm. They are not averse to Scotch either, which rapidly makes them giggly and languorous. Phil likes dancing, particularly when he can feel an attractive body ready to snuggle up against him. But he has a certain rank to respect, unlike some of the others, who are already completely drunk. Not wishing to upset anyone, he asks all the most highly ranked WAAFs to dance, including some who are officers. At half past eleven, the music stops, and those who are still standing make their way to the chapel for midnight mass.

Phil is a bit distracted during mass. He thinks about his

family. Letters take almost a month to get to him from Morocco. His children are well and their school marks are good. Paul has joined the scouts and has made lots of friends. Claire is taking dancing classes. His mother is the same as ever, giving lots of advice and asking about who he spends his time with in Britain! Maggy is clearly unaware that the British, to boost their war effort, have recruited many women to carry out diverse tasks, from cooking to aircraft engine maintenance, not forgetting pilot guidance. If only she knew! Some of these young ladies knock on his door in the morning to bring him his breakfast!

The next day, December 25, the WAAFs organize a party to which the entire group is invited. Presents are distributed and there is to be a dance in the evening. Phil has instructed his men to remain sober for at least two hours and to brush their uniforms before coming. The WAAFs have done a good job. Most of them are Scottish and they invite the airmen to join them in local dances. They have hired a band with two bagpipe players in traditional dress. They start with "Dashing White Sergeant", followed by "Stripping the Willow". The dancers have to form circles of six, which come together and then break up again. And when the dancers dance alone, they mustn't be as stiff as a rod. They have to move with grace and style.

These dances are like the balls of the time of Louis XIV in the 18th century. Everyone has a great time, especially Phil. The WAAFs seem to be very fond of these charming, gay little French men trying their best to speak English. No-one feels like they're at war tonight, because, this far north, the geography of Scotland provides sound protection, keeping the Germans at bay.

Training starts up again during the next few days, and continues right up to December 31, when the next ball is held, this time in the officers' mess.

January 15, and another ball. These are good times for Phil. He wishes he was 25 again, rather than 39. It's not that he feels old, but he's the oldest of the group and, added to that, he is also the boss, which means he has to behave himself during these parties. However, that doesn't stop him from wanting to woo some of these women.

He and his crews are now at the start of an enthralling period of training in bombers, in Vickers Wellingtons to be precise. It was in airplanes like these that the English dared venture as far as Berlin in 1940, to taunt the Nazis and drop a few bombs. And Cologne had its fair share in 1942, when more than 500 airplanes of this type arrived to smash up the entire town, sparing only the cathedral. This two-engine airplane is heavy and not very maneuverable. Thirteen tons when fully laden, six crew members when in operation, but it can still climb to almost 23,000 feet.

The instructors start by insisting that Phil and the other pilots perform an unimaginable number of take-offs and landings, to get them used to this unruly great beast. Next come outings with an entire crew, often lasting almost five hours, that see them flying all over England and the surrounding seas. The flight plans, which must be scrupulously respected, resemble those of their future missions, the ones they will accomplish after the completion of their training. Flying with little or no visibility, rendezvousing with the other airplanes at a given location and a precise time, flying in formation, simulating the dropping of bombs over a target, taking photographs after the bombing to evaluate its impact. Phil loves these training runs, and he's not alone. The crews end up baptizing them "cross-country".

Time passes rapidly until mid-March, when Phil is due his first leave. Ten days of freedom to go wherever he wants. For him, it's a first. Never before has he found himself in a situation like this, being his own master, 24 hours a day, with no constraints, without having to ask anyone else's opinion, with no children to look after and no mother on his back! Incredible!

But, what should he do with this short vacation? It's the war. France is still occupied and Morocco is too far away. Even London isn't all that close and is regularly bombed. It's the perfect opportunity for him to get to know Scotland better. The days are getting longer, nightfall is later, at about seven or eight o'clock, depending on the cloud cover. The first signs of spring are starting to appear.

Phil wants to go somewhere on his own, to find himself and to isolate himself a bit. Being part of a crew is great but, on an airbase, everyone eats all their meals together in the officers' mess and you spend a lot of time with your colleagues. It all gets a bit boring after a while.

Loch Ness isn't far away, about 40 miles. Phil is very skeptical about the existence of "Nessy", the famous sea monster, but he's heard a lot about it in France over the last 10 years. He decides to start by spending a few days in this region and then, if he has enough time, he will go and discover Edinburgh, the capital of Scotland.

On March 20, 1944, the first day of his leave, he takes a coach to Inverness, where he asks about the hotels and guest houses close to the lake and its monster. They tell him to go to Foyers on Loch Ness, a nice little town with a big waterfall that flows into the lake, and some hotels. It's not far, about 20 miles.

Phil enjoys fishing when he has time. He buys a fishing rod and starts by walking around the town of Inverness, which is dominated by its red brick castle and rather pretty, crossed by a river. He walks for about two hours, has a quick lunch in the pub, where he sips a pint of bitter and tries some smoked trout and boiled potatoes. He then takes the bus, arriving at Foyers in the middle of the afternoon.

It's a solemn site, looking down the lake and surrounded by forest-covered mountains. He rapidly finds a hotel that suits him,

Loch Ness House, less than a hundred yards from the lake and located in a vast Victorian residence with several outbuildings. There aren't many tourists in wartime Britain and most of the rooms are free. He meets the manager of the hotel, a Mr. Doyle, a former soldier injured at Dunkirk in 1940, who returned to civilian life once he was well enough. Mr. Doyle seems to like French pilots and offers him a large room with a lake view.

Phil dumps his things in the room and walks towards the banks of the lake. An old fisherman that he has trouble talking to because of his strong Scottish accent offers to take him out in his boat. Phil finds himself in the middle of the lake, charmed by his surroundings. On the other side of the lake he can see a ruined castle, the keep of which is still standing. In some places, the forest continues down the hill, right to the water's edge.

Phil then returns to the hotel. It's not yet time for dinner, and he whiles away the time writing a letter that he has been meaning to write for a few weeks. But he needs peace and quiet to do it, because he needs to find the right words. He had known Captain Dumaine, a bomber pilot like himself, at Blida in Algeria. Dumaine had stayed in Algeria, but, two months ago, his plane, a Leo 45 had suffered a technical problem and crashed just after take-off, at the start of a mission in Tunisia. Dumaine had died instantly. His wife had had their third child 10 days before the accident. A few months previously, this officer had introduced Phil to his wife, Françoise. Phil had been struck by her beauty, with her very dark eyes, and her intense spirituality. He had made her laugh a lot during that evening, but it wasn't all light-hearted. He had sensed in her a great force of conviction and strong character when, inevitably, the conversation had turned to the war, the Germans that they needed to drive out and the Allied landings of November 8 1942, in which Dumaine had participated, helping the Allies to progress despite the opposition of the partisans of the Vichy regime.

And now this woman finds herself a widow at the age of 29, isolated in Algeria and unable to return to France, which is still occupied. It cannot possibly be easy for her and he is determined to express his compassion. He writes:

Dear Mrs Dumaine,

I have recently been made aware of your terrible bereavement. I was very fond of your husband. You now find yourself alone in Algeria, with three children, the youngest of whom is still a baby. This situation must be very difficult for you, both emotionally and practically. I hope that you have good friends around you in Blida who can help you. My thoughts are with you and I hope to see you again one day, in a free France....

He carefully puts away this letter, having managed to avoid the conventional platitudes of condolence. Phil is struck by the fate of this woman, to whom he feels a certain closeness. He also has children to look after and he knows that it isn't easy. He will post this letter when he returns to Lossiemouth.

In the meantime, he will eat his dinner in the hotel dining room. There is already one couple seated in the dining room. A man in his fifties with a wife who is clearly much younger. Phil is curious to know why this man is taking his holidays at the moment in a country at war. He tastes the food he is served. The dishes are of excellent quality. A brown trout from the river Foyers, which flows into the lake, served with a butter sauce and vegetables, including excellent potatoes and carrots, followed by sheep's milk cheese and a dessert consisting of a very agreeable sort of chocolate eclair. Much better than the usual English fare that is spoken of so badly in France. But then he's in Scotland, not England.

After dinner, Phil goes to the room that serves as a bar and asks for a single malt whisky. The couple from the dining room join him there and engage him in conversation. Mr. Watson, the man, is the director of a large factory near Glasgow, the Singer factory, which makes sewing machines. The atmosphere among the workers has been poor for a month and, like the miners, they have been preparing to strike, despite the war. He has been obliged to give in to some of the demands of the unions and an agreement has just been signed. Times have been tough for him recently. He's taken four days of vacation in the calm of the Highlands to forget what has just happened. Phil isn't entirely sure that the woman with him is his wife, but he knows how to be discreet and enjoys talking to this man who has traveled a lot. Mr. Watson, in turn, is interested in Phil and is astonished to find that French airmen are now under British command in the RAF, even though the centuries-old antagonism between France and England is far from resolved.

The next day, Phil feels like walking. The hotel staff indicate several possible hikes, showing him the route on a map of the area. He feels like climbing and getting a panoramic view over Loch Ness. He begins his voyage of discovery by going west, towards the higher mountains. He is carrying a picnic prepared for him by the hotel and is guided essentially by his own sense of direction. Phil walks like that for about three hours. It's cool. The sun is out and it lights up the mountains. He passes through deserted forests, in which well maintained paths lead him towards higher ground. After a certain period of climbing, the trees become sparser and are replaced by large green meadows.

He walks along the banks of Loch Mhor, another smaller lake, and stops on the heath to eat his lunch at the edge of a mountain stream. He appreciates its pure, cold water. He makes himself comfortable by pulling up some clumps of grass and sitting on them. He eats the goat's cheese sandwich that he was given by the hotel and loses himself in his thoughts.

A few minutes pass. He hears a herd of sheep bleating, with each bleat louder than the last. When he sees them, the animals are a couple of hundred yards below him and have arrived at the stream to drink. A shepherd, in the middle of the herd, is with them, but against the light, all Phil can see is a frail silhouette. A large dog barks occasionally and forces the sheep to get back into line when they separate from the rest of the herd after drinking. The sheep must be very thirsty, because they jostle against each other forcefully when they sense that the water is near.

Phil sees the shepherd fall over backwards, knocked over by a ram. Three minutes later, the shepherd is still on the ground and has not moved. Phil decides to go and see if he is alright. As he approaches, the large dog comes towards him threateningly. During his childhood, Phil spent the long summer holidays in the country in the Beauce, and his grandfather had taught him not to be afraid of dogs and to speak to them warmly, but firmly. Phil asks the dog to come to him so that he can stroke it. The dog, trustingly, comes towards him, full of affection.

"Is your master OK?", Phil asks him. "Come on, let's go and see if he's hurt himself."

He clears a path through the sheep and prepares to greet the shepherd, who hasn't heard his approach and is still lying on the ground. He is astonished, because he soon realizes that the shepherd is actually a shepherdess. He can see a few light hairs poking out of her headscarf. She is wearing a long skirt, a white blouse and a tartan scarf predominantly blue in color. Phil asks her if all is well. He can see a little blood on her right temple and he talks a bit louder as he is not sure she has heard him. The shepherdess begins to open her eyes, scared and a little disorientated. He asks her, in English, what happened. She doesn't answer at first, but she soon comes to her senses and explains that she tripped after being pushed by a large sheep and that she hit her head on a rock. She has a strong Scottish accent that he has difficulty understanding.

Phil tries to reassure her by explaining who he is.

"I'm staying at Foyers for a few days, at the hotel. I'm a French officer, airman, bomber pilot. Boom boom over the Germans. Do you understand? My name is Phil, short for Philippe, and I'm a lieutenant colonel. What's your name, your Christian name I mean?"

Phil's onomatopoeia makes her smile and she seems less wary.

"My name's Lily. My parents keep sheep and I'm supposed to be helping them. My two brothers had to leave the farm to join the army, because of the war, and my dad isn't very well."

"Where is your parents' farm? Is it far from here?"

She hesitates a bit before replying, "It's not very far, about a mile from here. A small farm that we use when we stay with the sheep on the hills. The grass is very good for them here."

Lily tries to stand up, but she is dizzy and she stays sitting down on the ground. Phil is a little worried, concerned that she might have a problem due to the blow to her head. He offers to help.

"Looks like you're having trouble walking. Wouldn't you like to return to the farm you were talking about for a rest? I can come with you if you want."

After a pause, Lily asks "Are you sure you have the time? Would you really not mind? I would like you to help me get the animals back to the farm. I'm not sure I could run after my sheep if any of them start to stray from the herd."

Lily gets up, and this time manages to remain standing. Her cheeks are flushed. Phil takes a clean handkerchief out of his pocket and wets it in the stream.

"You've cut yourself, near the temple. May I clean you up?"

Very gently, he removes the blood, which has begun to coagulate. The wound is small, in all likelihood not serious. There isn't much to see after he has cleaned it up. She thanks him with a large smile, which makes Phil realize that she is very pretty. Blue eyes, little dimples when she smiles, thick blond hair with a few red highlights.

"I'll make you some tea when we get there, provided you don't let any of the sheep get away!"

"I'll do my best. I want to see how you make tea!"

They set off on their way. Lily points out all the sheep that are starting to stray from the herd. She laughs a lot when she sees him run after them each time she asks. She exaggerates a bit.

"Faster, the sheep's getting away. Watch out! There's another one to your left."

He is out of breath but amused by this game. Fortunately for him, they reach a place where the grass is less interesting to the sheep, which stay close together without trying to get away.

After a 20-minute walk along a winding path, they arrive at the farm Lily had told him about. There are two buildings. One to house the sheep overnight and another for the humans.

"Introduce me to your parents before making me tea" Phil says, "I'd like to meet them."

"But I've been looking after the sheep on my own for the last few days. My parents have stayed down the mountain, close to the loch. My dad isn't very well. He has heart problems. The doctor said he needs to rest."

He can't believe that Lily lives all on her own in the hills, where there is no-one. What a strange life for a young woman who must be in her twenties!

"Aren't you afraid all by yourself?"

"Yes! A little, at night, when there are strange noises, but it's OK during the day. The region is deserted. I have a dog and I know how to defend myself if someone comes looking for trouble!"

After she has got all the sheep safely into their barn, she shows Phil round the farm. There is a large kitchen that also serves as both a dining room and a living room. There are two bedrooms, each with two beds. The walls have been whitewashed. The floor is tiled. There is nothing hanging on the walls. The decoration is a bit austere, but the rooms are very clean.

Lily prepares some tea for Phil and herself. They drink it together. She also offers him some biscuits. He wants to know more about her life as a shepherdess.

"Lily, what do you do when you can get away from the sheep?"

"I love fishing in a lake not far from here. It's full of fish. Do you like fishing?"

"Yes, I go fishing sometimes, in France. I even bought a fishing rod in Inverness so that I can fish in Loch Ness. It's in my hotel room."

They chat about everything and nothing. She's very jolly, likes smiling and Phil likes her jokes. But the time passes quickly and Phil looks at his watch. It will take him at least three hours to get back to Foyers, and that's if he doesn't get lost.

"Lily, I'm sorry but I will have to go. If I don't come back they'll worry about me at the hotel. I was very pleased to meet you. Look after yourself."

"It's a shame that you have to go. If you come back to see me tomorrow, I'll make you a nice lunch. Would you like that?"

Phil doesn't have anything special planned for the next day and Lily is charming. He accepts the invitation. She kisses him on the cheek when he leaves.

"I'll bring you some beer if I can find some" he says.

Phil heads off in the direction of Foyers. On his way back, he pays particular attention to his surroundings, because he wants to be able to find his way the next day. As expected, it takes him almost three hours to get back to the hotel.

That night, in his bed, Phil thinks about his shepherdess. What an unlikely situation! He was walking in a deserted area and he found a very pretty young lady, as bright as a button, who has invited him to lunch at her farm in the middle of the pastures, far from civilization. How romantic! Phil goes to sleep early. He's had a long walk and he needs to recover.

He's in great shape when he gets up the next day, gets ready and applies some eau de Cologne so that he smells nice. He warns the hotel manager that he might be late back, because he doesn't want to be a slave to the clock. He leaves at 10 a.m., with two bottles of Scottish beer that he bought at the hotel. The path is not difficult to find.

He finds Lily very happy to see him again, in the process of cooking a fish on a wood-burning stove. There is no gas or electricity in this isolated farm. Just a water tank and a pump to provide water. She is dressed a bit differently and has a different scarf around her neck today. Another tartan, but this time violet. She has made herself a sort of floral crown, with the pink flowers of the season. Her low-cut blue blouse reveals a hint of attractive cleavage. She's really very attractive, this young girl! Phil kisses her on the cheek as he arrives. It's as if they've known each other for ages.

She has laid the table for two in the large kitchen. She doesn't have a tablecloth, but she has decorated the table with some white pebbles, wild flowers, and a few leaves and small branches. It works very well. Lily explains that she got up early to take the sheep to the lake, three quarters of an hour away. She had enough time to do a little fishing and was lucky enough to bag a decent-sized salmon, which she intends to serve with a few potatoes.

They devour the juicy pink flesh of the salmon with pleasure. Phil is surprised by Lily's table manners. She is very natural, carefully licking her fingers after having removed the bones from her fish. It's all simple and delicious! Lily, curious, tries to find out if Phil is married and has children. He tells her that he is a widower and that his two children are in Morocco with his mother. She doesn't ask about the death of his wife. Mischievously, she asks if he has a girlfriend. Her cheekiness makes him smile and he replies that he doesn't, but that his work keeps him very busy. Phil asks her if she has a boyfriend. She bursts out laughing and says that there are few young men in the region and those that there were have left to join the army. She blushes as she adds that she doesn't like old men. Phil serves her another glass of beer. She finds that this beverage goes very well with the salmon, but says that she doesn't often drink alcohol. He finds it disturbing when she announces joyfully, under her breath, as if it were top secret, that "her heart is there for the taking"! Phil smiles but doesn't want to show his emotion. The meal continues agreeably, the glasses of beer decreasing their inhibitions and lubricating their exchanges.

Phil has never passed such a precious moment, away from prying eyes, with such a young, pretty woman. He asks himself what Lily must think of him. He asks her how old she is. Twenty-one years old. Only just an adult! He is 18 years older than she is!

Phil is attracted to Lily and senses that she is happy to have him there. They are both footloose and fancy-free. He really wants to show her that he likes her, but he doesn't want to spoil the charm of the day.

Lily asks him to help her with the washing up. She teases him because she finds him a bit awkward, as he doesn't know where to put things. After the washing up, she suggests that they go for a walk. She wants to show him one of her favorite places. They walk for a good quarter of an hour to a mountain stream. They follow it upstream together. The vegetation gets increasingly dense. They find themselves under a green vault that lets a few sparse rays of sunlight through. A little further up, they arrive at a small lake, the banks of which are carpeted in moss and tall grass, surrounded by steep slopes. They can see a waterfall a bit higher up. Lily says that she finds this place romantic and mysterious, as if inhabited by magical creatures that watch over her and those she loves. She's delighted to share it with Phil.

She sits on the moss, soft as velvet, and then lies down. Phil cuts some grass to make two pillows, one for her and one for him. They lie close to each other. Birdsong brightens up the scenery. Lily and Phil stay silent for a few minutes, listening to the birds. Phil's thoughts are in turmoil. He really likes Lily, but he also wants to protect her. He mustn't let her down. He takes Lily's hand in his, and Lily squeezes it. They stop there. He will have to leave her soon, in an hour or two. They face each other, gazing at each other tenderly. They doze for a while, hand in hand. Lily wakes up first and stands up. She asks Phil if he likes "her place". He thanks her for showing it to him. He will never forget it. She says that she will never forget Colonel Phil coming to pay her such a sweet visit.

They return downhill together to the farm and Lily offers to accompany him on the way back with her sheep. He stays with her for another hour, but then it is time to leave. Phil prepares to say goodbye. Lily comes towards him, smiling, sure of herself, and offers him her lips. Phil is charmed and his lips briefly brush hers. They gaze at each other for a long time, damp-eyed. Phil turns and leaves. They wave at each other several times.

Phil continues his descent, lighthearted and happy with these moments spent with Lily. Her pretty, laughing face is imprinted in his memory and stays with him. A beautiful souvenir for the rest of his life. Phil is a romantic. He is proud to have resisted the desire that invaded him. This pretty young, woman, who is funny and isolated, did not deserve to be seduced and then abandoned two hours later!

The next day, Phil leaves Foyers and catches a bus from Inverness to Edinburgh, where he stays three days at the George Hotel to finish his leave. He has never stayed in such a luxurious establishment before and he learns to like this town with two faces. He walks for a long time in the mediaeval quarters close to the castle, soothed by the memory of little Lily.

7

BUCKINGHAMSHIRE, UNITED KINGDOM, MAY 1944

Since his arrival at the ORS five months ago, John Luxley has been working hard. Air Chief Marshal Hudson in person has asked him to use his talents as a probability specialist to try to understand why human losses differ markedly between airbases. A simple effect of chance, or is there another explanation?

John started by analyzing the process. He rapidly realized that the problem he had been asked to solve was far from simple. There are several reasons for this complexity. The RAF bomber bases are numerous; there are several tens of them around the country. The crews are of different nationalities. Many are British, but others come from various Commonwealth countries, such as Canada, New Zealand and South Africa. All the crews have received the same training in Britain, but their experiences in their countries of origin have been very different. They don't all use the same planes. Some are flying Lancasters, others Halifaxes, but there are also lighter bombers, like the Wellington. And they haven't all been in action for the same amount of time. Some began in 1940, others later, and a number of them only a few months ago. The airbases are not all located in the same place and some of the planes have to travel much further to bomb Germany or France. By chance, several groups have been involved principally in long-distance missions, whereas others have mostly been given objectives nearer to home.

John quickly realizes that he is faced with a real conundrum. But he quite likes that. It's more stimulating for him to resolve a difficult problem than to solve a puzzle that would be child's play. However, he must, absolutely, come up with results rapidly. Hudson had got him working a fortnight after his arrival. At that stage, John could only really explain to him why the problem was complex and he was well aware that the big boss wasn't enthusiastic about what he heard.

John had then focused on the data that he could obtain without too much difficulty. He started to create files for each airbase. He excluded those also involved in the transport of troops and material when necessary. This task had demanded time and energy. It was a huge effort just bringing together all the information, recording it and archiving it correctly!

Fortunately, John has a good understanding of bombing from the air, an activity in which he has been heavily involved for more than two years. He already understands what can influence the vulnerability of the plane and its crew. The experience of the pilot is linked to his age and is a variable that must be taken into account. The planes are not all equivalent. The Lancaster is reputed to be easier to fly than the Halifax. Some planes have undergone full maintenance recently, whereas others have been damaged and repaired, which might make them behave differently.

John's reasoning also takes into account well known causes of planes failing to return from their missions. Flak, for starters, which can create a veritable wall of fire when the fleet of planes, or stream, approaches its target. Then, the German fighters. There is also the tragic problem of planes hitting each other. It's difficult, when a thousand planes are flying without lights during the night, to fly so close together without a risk of touching and crashing. Mechanical problems are not rare. The engines of these planes are powerful, but not entirely reliable, even with the loving care bestowed on them by the ground staff of mechanics responsible for their maintenance.

After three days, John has come up with what he hopes is the definitive data set for his analysis. Hudson feels that progress is slow, but John has the unfailing support of Malcolm Bowen, his direct superior at the ORS. He knows only too well how important it is to define the data on which you are going to work if you want to obtain results that are of any use.

John gets on well with Malcolm. They have weekly meetings, during which John tells Malcolm about his progress and asks his advice for the most difficult aspects. Malcolm is always very receptive, which reassures John.

His proposal is finally accepted. John's analysis will focus on the last six months of bombing missions. He thinks it will take him a month to get hold of the latest data. He will be assisted by another mathematician, William, a recent arrival at the ORS, younger than John and working under his supervision. John has managed to convince his superiors that the calculations should be carried out in duplicate and compared, to eliminate the risk of human error.

During this period, John has found himself in an unusual situation. Antony, the vicar in whose house he is living, has effectively had a heart attack. He is being treated at Buckingham Hospital, about 30 miles away from Richmart. His wife, Edith, is exemplary, taking the bus to visit him every day. When she can, Margaret accompanies her. At dinner, John finds himself alone with the two women. Since the vicar's heart attack, the conversation is a bit dull. It's obvious that the two women are sad, worn down by what has happened to their husband and father. They are concerned, because Antony has an irregular heartbeat and the doctors are cautious about his prognosis. He might have another heart attack, and this time it might kill him.

When the vicar fell ill, John wondered whether it was a good idea for him, a young single man, to carry on staying with two women, one of whom, Margaret, was very young. He didn't really want to move, but he didn't want Edith to be uneasy about his presence. Two days after the vicar's heart attack, when Margaret had left the living room to go to bed, John broached the subject.

"Edith, I feel very sorry for you at the moment. You're in a very difficult situation. I know how worried you are. Maybe you don't want a stranger living in your house at the moment. I would understand entirely if you wanted to be on your own with your daughter. I'm sure it would be more suitable. I can talk to my bosses and see if they can find me another family to live with."

To his great surprise, Edith responded directly, without digressing.

"No, you're not in the way at all. On the contrary, it's nice to have you here. You cheer up the house a bit, and we need that at the moment. I often talk about you with the people from the village and none of them seem at all judgmental. Everyone knows that you're not on holiday here and that you're working hard for Bomber Command."

He appreciates her response because he has noticed that Edith has been warmer towards him recently. She had seemed a bit crabby at first.

He decides to take a few precautions nevertheless. Edith sometimes gets back late from the hospital, when the bus is not on time. He tries to stay in his room and doesn't go to see Margaret while she is reading or doing her homework in the living room. Margaret sometimes knocks on his door. John has the impression that she comes to ask him questions for every math problem that she has to solve. Afterwards, she likes to stay and chat with him, asking him questions about his childhood, his family, and amusing herself by comparing the upbringing of a son and a daughter of vicars. John's upbringing seems to have been stricter than her own. She says that her father eventually forgives her all her whims and transgressions.

Tonight, Edith has come back from the hospital more relaxed. She has been able to have a long conversation with the head doctor, who has explained that the irregularities of her husband's heart rate are disappearing and that his prognosis is therefore improving. Of course, the vicar will need to rest before going back to work. The best solution now is for him to spend a month in a nursing home. Then he can come home and take up his ministry again, so long as he is careful not to overdo it.

This good news bucks up the spirits of his two companions, who become more cheerful. Edith even goes to get a bottle of port to celebrate the occasion. During dinner, Margaret expresses an interest in John's activities at Bomber Command, asking "John, what exactly do you do at the ORS. What do you work on all day?"

"Unfortunately, it's a bit difficult to say exactly, because my work is secret. But, without going into detail, I can say that I have been asked to compare losses of human life and bombers between different airbases, to try to determine why certain disparities exist. Is it just chance or is there some reason, something that we could change to make things better. Do you see? Does any of that make sense or am I being completely opaque?"

"I understand. But what do you know about bombing? You've had your nose in your books and your mathematics research until now."

John is stung by this reflection of Margaret's and cannot help but reveal his past.

"That's where you are wrong. I didn't want to talk about it before, because it's a period that I found very difficult. I don't like going over it, but for two years, I was the pilot of a heavy bomber, in charge of a crew of seven men. I carried out 30 missions, 20 of them at night, over Germany. I was even awarded a medal. I recently received the Distinguished Flying Cross, one of the highest accolades an airman can receive, and I'm proud of it, even though I'm not sure I deserve it. It was that experience, together with my training in mathematics, that led Air Marshal Hudson, the head of Bomber Command, to offer me this job. I was demobilized before coming here to take up this post as a civilian researcher."

Edith is struck by what she has just heard.

"Oh John, congratulations, I underestimated you! You should have told us earlier. What modesty! You've waited months to tell us that you're a war hero. So you were an officer in the Royal Air Force?"

"Yes, I was a lieutenant. I'm a civilian again now, but in a few months, I will no doubt return to my job as a bomber pilot, once my research mission at the ORS is over, if we haven't got the Nazis by the throat before then. After a certain number of missions, we call it a tour of operation, we're put out to grass for a few months because it becomes impossible to take any more. It's extremely difficult to bear. Generally, after a tour of operation, pilots go on to become instructors. There are losses, about three per cent, at each mission, so we need to train new crews all the time. Some missions mobilize more than a thousand bombers, leading to the loss of about thirty planes. With a crew of seven in each plane, that makes more than two hundred dead or injured airmen that we have to replace. There aren't enough British airmen. Our Commonwealth allies participate a lot. They are admirable because their countries are not directly at war with Germany and their capital cities haven't been bombed like London has."

"I'm really very impressed. You must have amazing memories from that period?"

"Amazing isn't the word! That period was horrible. I saw too many of my comrades go out on missions and not come back. But let's talk about something else. I'm glad the vicar's health is improving. Can he really come home soon?"

"He'll have to spend a month in a nursing home first. Then, if all is well, he can come home and take up his ministry again."

Despite the sadness of the situation and the worries it generates, a harmonious balance is established between Edith, Margaret, and John. Both the women have rapidly come to appreciate having this young, rather handsome and very kind man to themselves, even if he is a bit taciturn.

All three of them are aware that they have another month in which to share this intimacy, but that the atmosphere might be different afterwards.

After dinner, John is not feeling very pleased with himself. He didn't want to talk about his time in the air force as a pilot. In general, he prefers to remain silent on that subject, so as not to have to answer questions about it. Every time he talks about it, he is sure to have nightmares during the following night and to be filled with dread during the day. Margaret had caught him off guard with her implications, which were not very flattering.

John rapidly returns to his room. He tries to think about something else, by throwing himself into the complicated calculations that he had begun during the day, working almost until midnight. The Sandman finally catches up with him and he falls asleep quickly.

At three o'clock in the morning, John's sleep is disturbed by dreams of the war. He is in his plane, returning from a mission. A German fighter has surprised them and has just fired on them. The cockpit has been hit and is three-quarters destroyed. The pilot and navigator are hanging out of the plane. The navigator is being carried away by the wind. He clings to John. Even though he is holding on, he can feel that he is going to let go. The big leap into the dark is imminent, at 13,000 feet. How many seconds until he crashes into the ground? John senses a presence at his side and hears someone say "It's alright, John. I'm with you. Relax".

John starts to emerge from his nightmare. Edith is next to him, sat on his bed.

"You had a nightmare, John. You called out very loudly and I came to see what was going on."

John opens his eyes. He is still distressed by the dream and he looks at Edith in her nightshirt. There isn't much light in the room, just the light filtering in from the stairs, where she had switched the light on to come up to his room. Maternally, she tries to comfort him by patting his shoulder. He feels a need to be comforted and he turns towards her, places his head on her chest and wraps his arms around her like a small child.

"It was nice of you to come up to see me," he murmurs. "I needed that. The nightmare was horrible. I often have dreams like that."

Without thinking, John places his hand on Edith's breast. He finds the sensation calming, through the fine material of her nightshirt. He begins to stroke her breast repeatedly, very delicately, and he feels a strong desire growing in him. It's been more than a year since he last caressed the body of a woman! For a fraction of a second he tells himself that he is making a big mistake, but his desire gets the better of his judgment. She isn't reticent and she holds him tighter. In the half-light, John explores the unctuous body of his landlady. She has a generous bust, a bit on the heavy side, but so agreeable to fondle in the palm of his hand. Edith adores these unexpected caresses and does not remain inactive herself, excitedly playing with the manhood of her partner. Their tongues explore each other slowly and she opens her legs slightly when John's hand descends to her pubic hair and he uses his middle finger to caress her lower down, in the warm, wet zones. Panting rapidly, she makes no protest when he wants to penetrate her and has trouble stifling her cries, bearing witness to a pleasure that she may never have experienced before. They don't say anything.

Edith, still dazed by their love-making, which was as daring and exciting as it was unexpected, leaves John without saying a word. He goes back to sleep and doesn't wake up until seven o'clock. She prepares him a good breakfast and welcomes him with a warm smile. John thinks that Edith is a strange vicar's wife. He's not early, so he doesn't hang around. He eats his breakfast quickly and leaves on his bike for work.

During the morning, John has some work to finish with his young colleague William that he will then discuss with Malcolm. He needs to concentrate on this task. But, during the afternoon, he can't help but think of Edith. His questions return. Neither of them had planned what had happened between them. The emotion of the moment had been strong. But what should he do now? What should he say to her? Should he leave the house or stay but go back to how things were before? Maybe he could continue to have a very sensual affair with Edith for a month, until the return of the vicar? Would that be risky with Margaret in the house? What is to become of their three-way dinners? Will Margaret suspect something? And what will the atmosphere be like when the vicar returns?

John can't answer these questions. Edith must be asking herself the same things. Only together can they find the answers. John will need to have a long chat with her. He isn't sure about how he feels. Everything had happened so fast, so spontaneously. He'd never even considered the possibility that something could happen between them. With Margaret, the thought had crossed his mind, but with her mother, the vicar's wife, it had been a real surprise. On top of everything else, a woman whose husband, a cleric, was in hospital!

John is a bit anxious when he goes home in the evening. When he gets there, Edith hasn't yet arrived, because she has gone to the hospital to see her husband, as she often does. Margaret is studying in the living room. She calls John when she hears him come in. John is ill at ease. Margaret asks him to help her with a geometry exercise. He solves the problem in half a minute, but doesn't hang around afterwards, leaving her to finish her homework.

Edith arrives and tells Margaret how her father is getting on. He's doing well and his transfer to the nursing home is imminent. Edith seems to be in a very good mood and prepares dinner enthusiastically. The mood is lively during the meal and Edith is behaving naturally. It's her turn tonight to ask John some questions about his work. She asks about the buildings he works in, the people involved and is very surprised when John explains that they work with a large number of women, not all of whom are subordinates. Could Edith be worried about this close contact with these young women?

John rapidly goes up to his room and reads before falling asleep. After sleeping for an hour, he wakes up and starts thinking about Edith again. He had made the first move. But she hadn't minded, and that was how it had all started. Nevertheless, John regrets what happened. Even if Edith's putting a brave face on it, she must be feeling terribly awkward all the same! Cheating on her husband, who is in hospital with a serious heart problem, with a much younger man, while her daughter is in the house. How very audacious!

John is convinced that he should talk to Edith. He will explain that he was still half-asleep after his nightmare and that he wasn't thinking straight. He will apologize and promise her that it won't happen again. He hopes that she won't throw him out or complain to his superiors.

John is in the process of asking himself how to raise the subject when he hears a little noise from behind the door. He gets up, opens the door carefully and sees Edith, with her index finger pressed against her lips, indicating that he should keep quiet. She comes in. John tells himself that he will be able to apologize. He whispers "It's good that you've come to see me. I wanted to apologize for last night. I lost my head. Honestly, I'd just had a nightmare and…"

She interrupts him by placing a finger on his mouth, and deftly lets her nightshirt drop to the floor, the only clothing covering her nudity. John is stupefied, but cannot help admiring Edith's body. He hadn't had the opportunity the night before, because they had remained wrapped in the sheets. She isn't skinny. She has generous breasts and her thighs are shapely, without being fat. She presses herself against him, undoes the cord tying up his pajama bottoms, which fall to the floor, unbuttons his pajama top and caresses his torso.

John was not expecting that. He tries to talk to her anyway.

"I'm not sure that what we're doing is right…"

But Edith doesn't let him finish. She presses her lips against his whilst stroking his manhood, which rapidly swells, conquering his doubts.

John will explain another time. They don't talk but pleasure each other immensely. Edith then goes back downstairs, in the half light, to her room. John is surprised by her ardor and her initiatives. This time there is no doubt, it was premeditated on her part.

John is increasingly perplexed. He doesn't love Edith and he has the disagreeable impression that he is no more than a sex object subject to the authority of a beautiful woman more than 15 years his senior! He had never imagined that such a thing might happen to him. It's all because of the war! This infernal conflict is at the root of this entirely unexpected situation. John wonders how things will evolve. Should he do something to make things go back to how they were? Or should he simply shut up for the moment and take things as they come?

When he arrives at the ORS, he learns from his superior that the big boss wants an update from him at the end of the afternoon and that a meeting has been organized for that very day. John is not given any precise agenda. He is intrigued and a little anxious, because he would have liked a few days more to complete his statistical analyses correctly, now that he has most of the data he needs. So as not to look stupid, he spends the day writing a summary of the data collection, the methodology he is using for the analysis and the preliminary results he has obtained, which are all negative. He has found no significant difference between the losses at the different bases, a finding that amazes him.

He is shown in to the Air Chief Marshal's office at 5 p.m., and he is asked how things are going with his work. The Air Chief Marshal appears anxious and is only half-listening to the start of John's presentation, the details of which appear on ten pages of carefully written text that John has already given him. He very soon interrupts.

"John, we have a serious problem. Our losses are far from negligible. At the end of June, 20 of the 200 planes involved in the bombing of Blainville were taken down. That's a loss of 10%, when the predicted rate is only 3%! Do you realize how bad that is?"

"But Sir, surely there are missions with very low loss rates that compensate for the losses you are talking about?"

"John, I receive letters from the commanding officers at our bomber bases telling me that we are not replacing the airmen we lose quickly enough. We're not managing to train enough new airmen. The number of crews available for missions is decreasing. We will soon have to decrease the number of bombers sent on each mission and that just isn't acceptable! When we examine the aerial photographs taken after our operations, we often realize that the objectives are only damaged, not completely destroyed. We need to increase the number of planes, not decrease it. And that's without counting the worrying messages our spies are sending us that the Germans are developing new highly performant fighter planes. You know how we work in terms of the number of missions any given crew is asked to perform?"

"Yes Sir. It's not long since I completed my own tour of operations."

"Oh yes, of course. I was forgetting that you were a pilot yourself. Our crews are currently asked to undertake 30 missions. I know that these bombing runs are a source of great anxiety for the crews, and that we can't ask too much from them. But maybe we could develop a different way of counting missions and deciding which teams to rest. Do you get my drift?"

"Sir, could you start by explaining how this magic figure of 30 missions was chosen in the first place?"

The Air Marshal looks slightly uncomfortable for a moment, but then replies "It wasn't easy. We based our reasoning on the fact that, given the observed losses, all airmen, whatever their function, pilot, bombardier or gunner for example, had about a fifty-fifty chance of still being alive at the end of the 30 missions. A one-in-two chance. It's rough, very rough, but we're at war. I'm not sure that the current system is entirely fair. I know that some airmen finish their tour of operations with much more than a fifty-fifty chance of survival!"

It rapidly comes home to John that the military hierarchy, in its great cynicism, was fully aware of the implications when it set this figure of 30 missions. It wasn't based on criteria of physical or mental endurance. They gave the crews only a one-in-two chance of getting out alive. That isn't much.

"I would like to ask you now to think up a better way of defining the number of missions to be completed by each airman", the Air Chief Marshal continues, "Maybe you already have some ideas? I'd like you to interrupt your current work and focus on this new problem. It's very important. We'll see how you are getting on in a week."

John leaves the Air Chief Marshal's office a little disappointed. For one thing, he doesn't really want to stop the work he is doing at precisely the moment at which he is likely to start getting answers to the series of questions he has been posed. On top of that, this new problem is a bit vague and concerns individuals rather than airbases. But he doesn't have a choice. He will think about it, even if he is already dreading working on this subject.

John doesn't lose any time. The new problem has already sent his brain cells into overdrive. He returns home highly focused on his work and wanting to find answers to this new question rapidly.

He dines agreeably with his two companions. Edith is very jovial and Margaret, a little surprised, puts this good humor down to the improvement in her father's health. After dinner, John is concerned that Edith might come up to his room in the middle of the night and ask him to perform! He carefully locks the door to his room. He falls asleep towards one o'clock in the morning and wakes up well rested, a little later than usual. He did not hear Edith at his door during the night. He realizes that she has already left and has prepared him a breakfast, leaving two slices of bread waiting to be toasted.

At the ORS, John focuses on his new task. He immediately sees the way forward. He realizes that the problem isn't really all that complicated. In fact, it's quite trivial. Indeed, after each mission,

Bomber Command works out its losses. After a few days, they know how many pilots, navigators, bombardiers, flight engineers and gunners have died. This makes it possible to work out the probability of losses for each mission and for each individual airman taking part in a given operation. John immediately realizes that he needs to do separate calculations for each type of airman because, whenever there is a problem resulting in a need to evacuate the aircraft in mid-flight, it's the navigator and the pilot who jump last. This means that the risks are not the same for each category of airman. That's a hypothesis that he needs to check! To work out the risk run by each airman after n missions, all he needs to do is to multiply all the probabilities of remaining alive after each mission. Simple!

John tells himself that he needs to obtain individual data for each airman, the missions he has carried out and, for each mission, the percentage of each category of airman killed. Easy peasy!

Once he has all these data and has done his calculations, John will present his results to Marshal Hudson.

With this system, an airman should be put out to grass when he reaches the magic threshold of a probability of 0.5 of still being alive. Not before and certainly not after! A one-in-two chance of dying! John is persuaded that this method will lead to shorter tours of operation for many airmen. They will have him to thank for having done some simple probability calculations for them.

8

GAITFORD, CAMBRIDGESHIRE, UNITED KINGDOM, MAY-JUNE 1944

The members of the 24 crews of the Aquitaine group (now squadron 502)arrive at the Gaitford airbase, from Scotland, on May 4. A second group of French bombers, the Mayenne group, should join them in the next two weeks. The base is under the command of Colonel Maillard, who coordinates the crews in the air and on the ground and liaises with British High Command. The pilots have had a month to get to grips with the Halifax bombers assigned to them. Huge monsters, with a wingspan of almost 100 feet, and a range of over a thousand miles. They can fly at altitudes of about 23,000 feet and reach cruising speeds of about 250 miles per hour. They are equipped with four Bristol Hercules 1600 horse-power engines, each with 14 cylinders. One hell of a fire-breathing dragon! Not very easy to fly, but reliable at least.

All the crews at the base are housed in corrugated metal huts. But on their arrival, many were disappointed to find that there were no female auxiliary staff. Only men. The distractions lie elsewhere. The reputed prowess of the French lover no doubt led the High Command to entrust the administrative and logistic tasks at this base only to men.

They are each given a bicycle, because the living

accommodation is about a mile from the mess where they will eat, the recreation rooms in which they will relax and the aircraft hangars. These bikes will give them a bit of freedom, providing them with the means to go as far as Peterborough, a large town less than four miles away. The base also has its own chaplain and a doctor.

Phil has written to his children and his mother once a month since leaving Morocco. He says as little as possible about the war, so as not to worry them, and finds more amusing things to talk about.

Letter from Philippe Destivel, sent from Gaitford airbase to his daughter Claire and his son Paul on May 13 1944:

Dear Claire,

Well done for your progress in dance. The waltz is very difficult, but I'm sure you manage it perfectly. I have just moved into this base at Gaitford, where I hope to stay for a while. I'm a bit spoilt, thanks to my grade and my post. I have a corrugated metal hut all to myself. It's barrel-shaped and split into two rooms (a bedroom and a living room), with a bath, a sink, and running hot and cold water. It's a bit basic, but it isn't cold here anymore and we're in the middle of fields, in the open air. So, I've unpacked all my bags, which have increased by two large suitcases since I've been in Britain, for the first time. The other officers are a bit more cramped. They have to make do with a quarter of a barrel for the captains and a half barrel for the squadron leaders. But everyone is making it as much like home as possible. I'm glad we've finished moving around all the time. I must stop now and write to Paul.

Love from Dad.

Dear Paul,

As you're a man now, I can tell you that I flew over France for the first time in almost four years on May 10. It's a shame we were met with gunfire, but let's hope that we will soon be met with flowers, when we finally manage to rout the bloody Boche...

Today, June 1 1944, Lieutenant-Colonel Philippe Destivel is particularly busy. His group of bombers, the Aquitaine group, is going to participate in its first real mission outside of Britain. The training period is over. The objective is a telecommunications station close to Cherbourg. He has been asked to ready twelve aircraft, each carrying about five tons of bombs. Phil is astonished by the target that has been chosen. Why Normandy when there are so many military and industrial targets to destroy in Germany, particularly in the Ruhr valley? Phil doesn't really get it.

He was very keen to participate in this mission himself, but as group leader, he must stay put during the first bombing mission, to check that everything goes to plan. It's a sort of trial run of the precise and effective organization established by Bomber Command. He was asked to select twelve crews and put them on standby. Pilots, navigators, bombardiers and other airmen have attended a one-hour briefing session, with each specialty in a different room.

Phil is in the control tower. He arrived half an hour before the planned departure time of the planes. He is thinking about the time he has spent in Britain so far. It's been a real vacation up to now! A vacation with fun flying activities, organized by the British, spiced up by evenings with the WAAFs and a trip to Loch Ness that he isn't ready to forget.

As he has changed location several times over the last six months, he hasn't been able to find a female companion. That's a shame, even a little sad. He's been a widower now for seven years! It's a difficult life, but he tries to stay positive. He has escaped from his dragon of a mother. The letters he receives from his children suggest, fortunately, that they like living with their grandmother in Meknes.

This is the start of a new era that will be different. There are serious hopes of seeing the fall of Nazi Germany, Hitler and all the others! It's no longer a case of training, but of fighting a war, which is considerably more dangerous. There's a rumor doing the rounds that, on average, 3% of the bombers don't come back after each mission over Germany. Three percent isn't very much. No reason to feel terrorized.

They are now only a few seconds away from departure. He sees the first Halifaxes coming into view. Rapidly, the order is given to take off. The pilot gives a thumbs-up from the cockpit, indicating that everything is fine. His four engines begin to turn over, at the right speed. They make a deafening noise. Phil is moved. It was six months ago that they began their intensive training. Today is the big day. The serious stuff starts here. The plane makes its way down the runway and can be seen leaving the ground 40 seconds later. Another plane follows it, a minute later. In less than a quarter of an hour, all 12 bombers have taken off. Phil prays that they will all return to the base safely tonight.

Five hours later and Phil is like a father waiting for his kids to come home. He sees the first bomber come back, rapidly followed by the other eleven. They are all there. None of them seem to have been damaged. Phil goes to one of the briefing rooms. Each captain gives a precise report of his mission on his return. They bring the photographs they took just after releasing their bombs, so that the damage on the ground can be evaluated.

The pilots are rather enthusiastic. No fighters came to attack them. Just flak, but not very dense, and they managed to hit their target. They seem to have caused a lot of damage. They were guided by the colored flares or "skymarkers" that the English pilots had released to indicate the precise spot at which the bombs should fall. This technique, introduced during the war, makes it possible to carry out infinitely more precise mass bombing missions. But there is a downside. Signaling the targets is very dangerous and a number of the so-called "pathfinder" planes responsible for releasing these flares were brought down by enemy fighters.

Phil selects himself for a bombing mission a few days later.

Excerpts from the diary of Philippe Destivel

5-6 June 1944
My first real war mission since my arrival in Great Britain! During the night, nine planes from my group took part in the bombing of a battery at Isigny that protects the bay of Grand Vey. In total, a hundred or so planes dropped about 600 tons of bombs, in an attempt to destroy the German bunker and its six canons. We were participating in the preparation of the ALLIED LANDINGS, which began a few hours later! I can see now why we were asked to bomb the telecommunications station near Cherbourg. At last, the Allies have landed in Normandy! How wonderful! How long until Paris is liberated?

25-26 June 1944
I was writing to Paul when I was interrupted by a phone call from Air Commodore Walton asking me for four Halifaxes to go and bomb Montorgueil the next day. The target is the warehouses and the launch platform for the pilotless aircraft that bomb London, the famous V1s. I took part in this bombing, with two other crews. Above the target, I saw an English bomber explode, apparently hit by a bomb from another RAF plane flying above it. Being killed by your own side, what a strange fate! I didn't see any fighters. There was no flak either.

28 June 1944
Bombing of Blainville near Lunéville, with five planes from our group. All those from Gaitford came back safe and sound, even though there were 200 planes in the stream. Twenty bombers from other bases were brought down, including five from Pocklington and one from Full Sutton (10% losses. That's much too high!). Twenty planes brought down means almost 140 airmen killed. For the moment,

our group has been lucky. No losses. Let's hope it lasts!

6 July 1944

I took part in the bombing of Marquise (Pas de Calais). Another launch platform for flying bombs. The ceiling was low on our return to Gaitford and I was sent to Driffield. I landed with a bomb that we hadn't managed to release over the sea despite our best efforts. This bomb, unloaded by British workers, was left just under the bomb launcher. When I started up the engines to leave, as I was trying the fourth engine, I saw two ground mechanics running as fast as they could towards a shelter about 200 yards away. One made it to the shelter while the other one made a few desperate signals with his hands and then followed his colleague. I gave the order to cut the motors and evacuate the plane immediately. When I got out, I saw my crew standing around the bomb, the tail fin of which had been carried away by the wind generated by the propellers when I was testing the engines. Our two English mechanics had figured that the bomb was about to explode!

Throughout the month of July, Phil is very occupied. He carries out several missions himself, essentially to assist the progression of the Allied troops by destroying marshalling yards and V1 sites. He also takes part in the bombing of Stuttgart, which requires more than nine hours in the air.

When he isn't actually flying, he is involved in the preparation of missions for his crews, organizing the replacement of sick staff and trying to manage the organization of plane repairs as best he can with the mechanics. He also often greets the crews on their return and is present during certain debriefings.

On July 18, during a bombing of German armored vehicles at Falaise, near Caen, the Aquitaine group loses its first plane, brought down by flak. None of the crew managed to parachute out of the plane. Seven men lost. The pilot, Captain Guillonnet, was a good friend of Phil. This really brings it home to Phil that the training period is well and truly over. They have moved on to more serious business, and that leaves Phil pensive. If something happened to him, what would become of Paul and Claire, his children? He dare not think about it too much and tries to reassure himself a bit by reminding himself what he has been told, that there is only a 3% chance of dying in any particular mission. But Phil really needs to think about something else. Too much tension over the last six weeks. Too much stress, too much responsibility. Four of the seven members of the team that was lost were married and had children. Six children had lost their fathers in a single incident!

Fortunately, he has two days of leave at the end of the week and, on Saturday 22 July, Phil can take it easy because he isn't working. He even has a lie-in, lounging around in bed despite the constant humming of planes taking off. He even manages to drift back off to sleep and dream of Lily and her sheep. In his dream, she invites him to lunch again and prepares an enormous pike. But a low-flying plane wakes him up once and for all. It's eleven in the morning and Phil asks himself what he is going to do all day. He decides to go and have lunch in town, in Peterborough. He has heard about a hotel-restaurant next to the cathedral where the cooking is apparently good despite the rationing and where the French airmen from the Gaitford base are particularly well appreciated.

Phil takes his time to get washed and puts on a casual civilian outfit. He's not unhappy to be out of military uniform and the responsibilities that go with it for a couple of days. When he is on leave, his deputy, Captain Jopet, replaces him. Captain Jopet is highly competent and Phil knows that he can pass him the reins for a while without worrying about what might happen.

He takes his bike to cover the miles between the base and the town. He pedals at a leisurely rhythm, breathing in the summer air that smells so good now that the wheat has just been harvested. Clouds of sparrows are looking for lost grain. As in France, there are poppies, little spots of red that remain intact, in the fields. It's a winding road and he has to make some effort to get over the hills that surround the town.

It's one o'clock when he arrives at the Lion Hotel. It wasn't hard to find, because it's right next to the cathedral, a landmark visible from the edge of the town. He meets his counterpart from another group of bombers from the base, Squadron Leader Vigard. They are friends and they decide to eat together, with the proviso that they will not talk about the Gaitford airbase.

They are not far from the sea, which represents a reservoir of choice morsels of food for the English, whereas the lack of labor has made meat a rarity. They order a fish that they think is the English equivalent of what they would call *"lieu"* as they aren't very sure about the translation. They also order a bottle of Muscadet *sur lie*. Phil is a bit concerned because the wine was bottled in 1937 and is almost seven years old. But the precious liquid has perfectly survived the years and hasn't oxidized at all.

They talk about what they plan to do after the war, when the Germans have left their country for good. Optimistic, at least on the surface, they don't even contemplate the possibility that they might be killed before the final victory. Vigard doesn't want to remain in the air force and would like to set up an airline. He hopes to be able to borrow enough money to buy two or three planes. He is looking for potential partners and asks if Phil would like to join him. Phil doesn't refuse and says that he will think about it. They will stay in touch when they return to France.

When they get to the dessert, a small band arrives to liven up the atmosphere. The bandleader starts by introducing the five musicians and then moves on to the progression of the Allies in the face of strong German resistance in Normandy, a subject about which he speaks with emotion and respect. Finally, he tells all the gentlemen present, the customers of the restaurant, to feel free to ask the ladies to dance. They're waiting for nothing but that!

Phil turns round to observe the different tables, asking himself who they could ask to dance. Vigard says that he is a hopeless dancer and he doesn't want to make an idiot of himself, but he encourages Phil to ask the lady of his choice to dance. At the next table, there is a woman in her fifties, with a man of about the same age and a young woman of about 22, slightly plump and with red hair, undoubtedly their daughter. Phil gets up and approaches their table.

"May I have the honor of asking the young lady to dance?" he inquires of all three of them. "My name is Philippe and I'm a pilot from the Gaitford airbase."

It's the mother who replies, saying "My daughter Anna is very flattered and will gladly accept your invitation. Show Philippe how well you dance, Anna."

The girl in question blushes and doesn't look particularly happy, but she gets up, visibly constrained by the rapid acceptance from her mother, who replied in her place. No hint of a smile on her face!

The band strikes up a waltz. Philippe knows how to dance a waltz, but Anna only knows the basics! Phil gives the impression of someone driving a large, uncontrollable truck. He spots his colleague, who is watching them with an amused look on his face and is visibly finding it hard to suppress the attack of the giggles that has begun to afflict him. On turning his partner around, Phil notices a woman finishing her dessert, in a dark corner of the restaurant. She is alone at her table and doesn't seem to be either old or ugly. He can't see her very well, but tells himself that he will ask her to dance next time, as his experience with Anna was less than convincing!

At the end of this magnificent waltz, Phil goes and sits down for a moment. Vigard congratulates him on his performance, still doubled up with laughter. From his seat, Phil can no longer see the lone woman at her table; she is no longer in his field of view. It's a shame because he would like to get a closer look at her. He waits until a second waltz has finished and then rapidly stands up to go and ask her to dance.

He walks towards her, cheerfully. She is smoking a cigarette, and her face is rather dark. There is a book on the table that she has been reading during her lunch.

"May I ask you to dance with me Miss?" he asks. "I'm an officer, a pilot at the Gaitford airbase a few miles away."

The young lady raises her head from the book, an English translation of *"Rouge et Noir"* by Stendhal.

"Thank you for asking, but I'm afraid I can't accept."

She then returns to her book, without offering any other explanation. Phil is disappointed, because he finds her attractive. She looks about 30 or so, a bit older than Phil had guessed from a distance.

Phil is respectful and doesn't push his luck, but he wonders what she meant. Why couldn't she accept? Several possibilities present themselves in the face of this response. She doesn't want to because she doesn't want to dance or because she finds it difficult to walk or maybe because she is waiting for someone. Phil tells himself that he will never know and tries his luck at another table, where three young women are lunching together. He deftly avoids vexing anyone by asking "Ladies, would one of you be kind enough to dance with a poor French pilot from the Gaitford airbase called Philippe, who likes dancing and has just been refused by a very attractive lady, which has made him doubt his own charm?"

All three smile and discuss in hushed voices, before one of them replies, smiling "Yes, willingly, provided you dance with each of us in turn. Is it a deal?"

"Of course, a single request and three acceptances, I'd be delighted? Who wants to go first?"

Again, they discuss in hushed tones for a few seconds. There are two brunettes and a blonde, and it's the blonde who gets up. They must be in their twenties. Phil finds them a bit difficult to understand because they have a rural accent rather than received pronunciation. It's the blonde's birthday and they have come to celebrate at the restaurant. Phil has a nice time dancing with them. After these three dances, he leaves the dancefloor and notices that Vigard has gone, but that he has left a note: *"Bye bye Phil. I'm off on a bike ride. I've paid the bill. You can pay next time, after you've given me a few dance lessons!!!"* Phil likes this colleague and tells himself that they should stay in contact when they get back to France. Maybe they could set up a company together. An airline; that would be brilliant!

He leaves the restaurant and goes for a bike ride, wandering around the English countryside, which is full of flowers in this month of July. Everywhere he looks he sees rosebushes with red, yellow or pink flowers. There are lots of zinnias in the gardens, adding other tints to the palate of colors. Phil returns to his "home sweet home" at the base at the end of the afternoon and writes his letters.

The next day, Sunday, after a lie-in, he feels like going fishing. He hasn't used the fishing rod he bought in Scotland since his arrival at Gaitford. He has been told how to get to a river located about a mile and a half from the base, in the surrounding countryside. He gets the staff of the officers' mess to prepare him a picnic, puts some water into a flask and takes a canvas bag for any fish he manages to catch. He puts everything into a rucksack, ties his fishing rod onto his bike and leaves towards noon. He heads towards the Deune, a tributary of the river Iles.

Phil pedals along narrow roads. He is surprised to see a group of gypsies with their Romany caravans and horses in a field. The women are wearing long colored skirts. Their skin is dark. Phil had never imagined that these populations had crossed the sea to settle on an island like Britain. Maybe they were circus people? What else would they be doing here in a country at war? What nationality were they? Could they possibly be British? How odd!

He rapidly finds the river, exactly where he was told it would be, flowing under a dilapidated old bridge over which the little road he is happily pedaling along passes. There is a footpath next to the river. He dismounts and decides, at random, to follow the river upstream rather than downstream. It's a pretty place. Lots of white wild flowers. Dragonflies and clear water. After a couple of hundred yards, the river bends and heads off to the right. He walks, pushing his bike, to this bend, as he doesn't want to be seen from the road and is looking for somewhere a bit off the beaten track for some peace and quiet. The surroundings in which he finds himself suit his needs well. Several trees have been planted close to the banks of the river and have spread their branches over the water. The leaves of a weeping willow stroke the surface of the river.

He lays his bike on the ground and sets up his fishing equipment at a site at which the watercourse is wider. His fishing rod is very simple, without a reel. He has brought some bread with him to use as bait.

The place is deserted. Phil can concentrate on the float at the end of his line, scrutinizing its movements whilst waiting for it to sink, brought down by a fish caught on the hook. After ten minutes, he still hasn't seen the float begin to tremble, but he isn't too concerned. Fishing relaxes him and takes him away from his everyday routine. He thinks about those close to him, his two children and his mother, who is best off where she is in Meknes, leaving him some respite since he has been in England. He thinks about his life too, his dead wife, but also the future that he needs to build, which currently seems very fuzzy, with all the uncertainties linked to the war.

Phil is still daydreaming when he hears a noise. He can't see anything at first, because of the bend in the river. Then, looking into the sun, he glimpses a silhouette on a bicycle. Someone who isn't afraid of getting a flat tire on this little path following the river. He realizes that it's a woman pedaling very carefully. She has a fisherman's hat on her head and she soon arrives at his position. He greets her by asking "You're not afraid that this path will give you a flat tire?"

"No, they're solid tires. You can't get a flat. Not very comfortable, but very convenient. Have you caught anything, any fish? I've never seen you here before. I often come to fish here. There are loads of fish, but I don't think you're in the best place."

"No, I haven't caught anything, but it doesn't matter. It relaxes me to fish and I need that at the moment."

Phil is slightly troubled because he has a vague impression that he knows this lady. He rapidly figures out who she is.

"Hey, you're the lady I saw having lunch at the Lion Hotel in Peterborough yesterday. I recognize you. I asked you to dance and you refused. You were reading an English translation of Stendhal's *"Le Rouge et le Noir"*. You're a bit more friendly today! I didn't recognize you at first in your fisherman's outfit. Trousers, fishing hat, boots. You looked different yesterday, much more feminine!"

"I recognized you straight away. You're a pilot at the airbase near here aren't you? From your accent, I would say you are French. I didn't know there were any French pilots in the RAF. You can trust the military. That's why I'm talking you more freely today than yesterday. I couldn't yesterday. Maybe I'll explain why."

Phil is amused by the change in this woman's appearance. He likes the soft timbre of her voice. She is tall. He had only seen her sitting down the day before. She is almost as tall as he is. Her fishing hat makes her seem even taller. The stray hairs escaping from it are blond. She must be about 35 years old.

"My name is Philippe," he explains, "But my friends call me Phil. Philippe Destivel. Before I came to England I was stationed in Morocco. The climate was different, but the summer is pretty good here this year. In France, we think that it rains all the time in your country. I can see that that's not necessarily true."

"I'm Victoria, Victoria Miller. I live about a mile from here, on the edge of the village of Gaitford. I fish to find myself something more interesting to eat. If you like, I could show you some better places to catch fish not far from here."

Phil is not displeased to have a fishing companion. He gathers up his things and the two of them push their bikes along the path running alongside the water. Victoria points out that there are many birds, just as there are in marshes. She seems to know a lot about ornithology. She uses English names for these animals that Phil doesn't know and doesn't know how to translate. They walk like this for about three hundred yards, along the banks of the river, which winds back and forth at this point.

"Let's stop here. There are lots of fish, you'll see.'

Victoria prepares her fishing stuff. She uses earthworms that she found in her garden as bait. Phil knows that fishermen need peace and quiet.

"I won't bother you. I'll go a bit further down the river."

"But you're not bothering me. I don't often get the chance to talk to pilots. Tell me what you're doing here."

Phil explains the current strategy, supporting the Allied troops that have landed in Normandy to be met by fanatical German resistance, and destroying the V1 bases along the French coast facing England. Victoria listens carefully and asks how the crews feel about the dangers they face.

"You know, there are losses of about 3% for each mission. So, fortunately, the risks are not high. We all want to go back to France. When we leave on missions, we are always thinking that the fall of Germany will come soon. We don't feel much danger, although there are some who are completely terrorized. I'm naturally calm and I've always been lucky. I've had a few problems, but I've always come through them unscathed. We call it *"baraka"* in Morocco."

Phil looks closely at Victoria. She has white skin and high, well defined cheekbones. Maybe she comes from a family of Slavic origin? She has a few freckles on her face. She is charming, beautiful even. Her large green eyes suggest she is enthralled by Phil's stories of the war and her gaze is intense. Phil doesn't want to talk for long about what he does. Their conversion is interrupted by the fish. Victoria has a bite and she gradually reels in her line. A fair-sized gudgeon has got itself caught on her hook. She seems to know what she is doing and easily brings it in to the bank.

"You see. We've only been here ten minutes. I'm sure you won't be disappointed."

Phil hasn't set up his line yet. He sets to work. Victoria gives him a worm, praising its merits as a much better bait than bits of bread.

She's watching Phil too. He is quite tall, like she is. She finds him handsome. She likes his blue eyes. He smiles a lot and has a calm, but firm gaze. She finds him reassuring. The kind of man you just can't help trusting. He has a strong French accent when he speaks English, indicating his origins, and she likes listening to him.

"You speak my language very well" she tells him.

It's a compliment that he appreciates. He's been living in this country for more than six months. He has indeed made considerable progress and no longer needs to think through his sentences before opening his mouth. Almost every day, he has long, highly technical phone conversation with the air force general responsible for all the British airbases, including Gaitford. This has obliged him to make progress.

Phil is less lucky than his Sunday-afternoon companion. In the next half an hour, he doesn't catch anything, whereas she pulls another two fish out of the river. She bursts into laughter, and asks cheekily "What are you waiting for? Are the fish scared of you?"

He starts to laugh too, not even remotely vexed and happy to have amused her. Phil tells himself that he knows next to nothing about this beautiful woman, other than the fact that she fishes and lives at Gaitford. But he doesn't want to ask her questions, preferring instead to discover her character and her tastes gradually. They talk about everyday things, commenting on the heat, the smells of the countryside, the birds and the noises they hear. She doesn't ask him anything about himself, his past, his social position, his rank, his education or his family. They both feel that they have connived to hold back information about themselves during this first meeting.

Phil has brought a snack with him. Not much, just some biscuits, a bit of marmalade, a bottle of water and two bars of chocolate. It really isn't much, but oh so much in wartime, when you can't find anything anymore! He asks Victoria to share it with him and she willingly accepts. She has brought a piece of cake that she made with her own fair hands. They share everything.

Phil would like to see Victoria again. He tells her so and she smiles at him. He doesn't have much free time, but he thinks that he should be able to get away for a few hours the following Saturday. Victoria doesn't know if she will be free. She never knows very far in advance when she will be free, but she will do what she can to come to the same place, at about three o'clock next Saturday, to fish. She is the first to glance at her watch and leaves first, hastily, simply waving gracefully once she has mounted her bicycle. Phil finds her departure a little too sudden. He would have liked to say something a bit ambiguous and charming to direct their relationship towards the more personal, but Victoria didn't give him the time. He wishes it were next Saturday already.

9

BUCKINGHAMSHIRE, UNITED KINGDOM, JUNE 1944

John isn't doing well. His nights are increasingly filled with nightmares and he has daily anxiety attacks. He gets up tired. At this start of the summer in 1944, John should be making the most of the nature blooming around him, the sun warming the atmosphere and the sweet perfume of roses emanating from gardens. But he feels guilty and is not really sure why. Antony, the vicar, has returned from the convalescence home to take his rightful place in the family and his parish.

But it's not John's relations with Edith that are tormenting him. Fortunately, he was able to resist when she returned to pay him a nocturnal visit after five days of abstinence undoubtedly due to physiological conditions making life a bit uncomfortable for his partner. He had managed to find the words, not too violent, but firm, to explain to her with diplomacy, and without hurting her, that making love to such a beautiful woman had been a source of great pleasure but that the situation was too difficult. They would have to stop seeing each other at night. Margaret might find out and, after his illness, the vicar did not deserve to find an adulterous wife who had abandoned her self-control while he was getting better and a lodger who had regularly pleasured his wife better than he had ever known how.

At the start, Edith took it badly and bossily insisted. Although it wasn't true, John had explained that it was sad for him too, but he found the situation disturbing and felt too bad about her husband. Edith finally came round and accepted his decision.

What is bothering John at the moment is his own mental balance. He can feel that things are getting worse, whereas he should be forgetting these difficult final moments of the war and his accident, when he and his crew had had to leave a plane on fire and in the process of breaking up. But people had died, and as captain of the plane, he felt partly responsible, even if he thought that he had behaved appropriately.

At the ORS, John has made good progress on the task he has been given. He had some difficulty obtaining the data he needed to quantify the risk to the life of each airman. But his results are interesting, and show differences between the different categories of airmen. He has to go and talk to Marshal Hudson today. The Marshal's only concern is the potential impact of the risk score developed by John on the availability of air crews. Will it result in fewer or more crews being available for missions?

The meeting takes place at four o'clock. John is surprised when the Marshal asks him to come to his office on his own to present his findings. He had thought that he would have a larger audience.

John explains that he has worked on the data for 100 crews that have completed their 30 missions, selected at random. In other words, he has information for 700 airmen of all categories, from pilots to gunners. The Marshal interrupts him rather feverishly.

"John, did you identify airmen who completed their tour of operation with a score of more than 0.5? Any with a score of 0.6, for example, which would mean a six in 10 chance of surviving if I have understood correctly?"

"Yes, some. It would be easy enough to count them, if you want the exact number. Overall, the risk scores lie between 0.3 and 0.65. You see, we have found quite a few disparities. Some airmen complete their missions with a 65% chance of still being alive, whereas others have run a much greater risk of dying, with only a 30% chance of surviving."

The Marshal listens carefully to John. He seems to be happy with the approach developed and with the results obtained.

"Your results are very interesting. Well done! I now need to think about what we can do with them. It's a bit of a delicate matter. I need you to provide me with a table of the risk scores for each airman, in alphabetical order. How quickly can you come up with such a table? In the next 48 hours?"

"Yes Sir. I think that should be possible."

"Back to work then. Don't waste any time. Oh, and by the way, before you go, I have a comment to make! You haven't shaved in at least three days. Go and shave! You may not be a military man at the moment, but you are working on a military site and your appearance must be correct!"

The Marshal shakes his hand and says "I'll see you again in two days, at the same time, here in my office."

The very next day, John begins to organize his results and to create the table that Hudson requested. He has to work for some of the night, because he needs to check the calculations, organize them and present them correctly, with the posts and details of the 700 airmen, the missions they carried out, the risks of each mission and the details of the calculation of risk score for each of them. John sleeps at the ORS, after letting the family know that he isn't coming home. He is ready in time for his next meeting with Hudson.

Hudson doesn't make him wait. He gets John to describe the way in which the results are presented. He's a quick thinker and he doesn't need long explanations to understand. John has carried out a few additional statistical tests, which he now explains.

"I also carried out several analyses comparing the risk scores of pilots with those of gunners, in particular. I came to the conclusion that, on average, the pilots complete their tour of operations with a risk score markedly higher than that for the gunners. Some pilots finish their tour of operations with a 20% higher chance of dying than the gunners. Lots of pilots shouldn't have carried out more than 25 missions, whereas the gunners could have continued for longer."

These comments cause the Marshal to frown. He does not comment on this aspect of the work but looks sideways at John.

"John, you really are starting to look like a tramp. I asked you to shave."

"Yes Sir, but I had to work all night in my office. I stayed overnight at the ORS without my razor."

"OK. But don't forget tonight!"

John is amazed that Air Chief Marshal is so interested in his facial hair. He has other things to worry about, but there you go! If it entertains him to focus on the appearance of the ORS scientists, why not? It must be the obsession of a career military man. But, OK, John tells himself that he will shave tonight.

John is tired but cheerful when he arrives at the vicar's house at the end of the evening after stopping at the pub and ingesting two pints of beer. His head is spinning a bit, but the alcohol has calmed his anxiety and he feels better.

During dinner, he explains that he has developed a system

that will make it possible for certain airmen who have already done too much to be rested sooner. His hosts are impressed and congratulate him. They didn't realize that mathematicians could influence the lives of men so directly. He omits to tell them about those who might have to carry out a larger number of missions.

After dinner, John goes straight to bed, as he hasn't really slept for 36 hours. He is tired but agitated, and cannot get to sleep, asking himself what he has got himself into. With hindsight, he regrets having proposed a system likely to prolong the tour of operation for some airmen. Being asked to carry out a few additional missions will be like a death sentence for some of them.

His alarm clock rings just as he is drifting off into deep sleep. He gets ready rapidly. When he arrives at the ORS, he finds a message from Hudson on his desk, asking him to set up the systematic calculation of risk scores for all the airmen under the orders of Bomber Command, to be updated every fortnight. He will have two assistants, two WAAFs, for this task. But there is no information about how the High Command has decided to make use of his work.

This annoys John, who goes to see the big boss' personal secretary and asks to see Hudson. But the Marshal will be in London for high-level meetings for two days. Undoubtedly he has decisions to take with Churchill about the bombing of German cities or other current targets. She offers him an appointment at the end of the evening in three days' time. John isn't happy about it, but he has no choice.

John spends these three days redoing all his calculations several times over. He is really scared that he might have made a mistake and want to be sure that there are no errors. He has stopped filing his papers away and his desk has become a total mess. He sleeps little and badly, waking up in a cold sweat several times each night. In his nightmares, the crews leave on their last mission. Their planes are blasted into smithereens by the German flak. John attends their funerals, powerless. Each time, seven coffins are lined up. The widows are present, with their children, and they harass him, blaming him for their misfortunes.

Despite this lack of sleep, John gets up early to go to work. He drinks coffee after coffee to stay awake. His hands begin to tremble slightly.

When the time of his appointment arrives, the secretary is aghast at his appearance and dress.

"You can't possibly see the general like that. What on earth has happened to you? You're all hairy. You still haven't shaved. Your shirt is hanging out of your trousers. Look at your hands. They're covered in grease!"

Effectively, the day before, John had had a problem with his bike. The chain had come off. He had gotten dirty mending it and hadn't had time to wash his hands.

"No, I must see the Marshal! It's very important."

The secretary makes him wait, worried because John takes documents from her desk, looking at them feverishly and passing from one page to the next as if he were looking for something in particular. He is finally ushered into Hudson's office. Hudson comes towards him to greet him but stops short about a yard in front of him, with a grave, questioning look on his face.

"What are you doing here in that state? Get out! Have you gone completely mad?"

John stays where he is and begins to deliver a monologue. He speaks rapidly, talking about the method used and the limits to its validity, the calculations that he has repeated three times or more over the last few days, the nights he hasn't slept, the deaths for which he will be responsible. He castigates his superior officer, demanding that he explain right now how his method will be used, screaming that he refuses to do any further work on this subject until he knows whether it will shorten the missions of pilots reaching the fateful threshold of a "one-in-two" chance of dying.

At first, Hudson is ready to request assistance to haul John physically out of his office. But he reflects a little and says, very amicably, "Don't get yourself worked up. Everything will be fine. We haven't yet decided how to use your risk score. I'll let you know when we have. Don't work on this subject anymore. Go back to what you were doing before, the work I stopped you doing. You seem worn out to me, on edge. Have a rest. You should go and see a doctor. Go and see the doctor at our center this evening. If you're having trouble sleeping, he will help you. Take a few days leave if you need to."

The Marshal asks his secretary to contact Dr. Blake, the ORS general practitioner, to organize a consultation for his overworked mathematician. A quarter of an hour later and John is in a consultation room at the infirmary, sitting opposite this doctor, who examines him, takes his blood pressure, listens to his heart with a stethoscope and then talks calmly to him.

He gets his patient to talk, for almost an hour, about the war, his current work, his anxieties, and his insomnia. At the end of the consultation, the doctor suggests a course of treatment.

"The first important thing you must do is sleep. I'm not really in favor of using hypnotic drugs, but I think, in your case, that it is important that you manage to sleep at least three nights in a row. I'll give you a few tablets. After that, I want you to go and see a military neurologist who looks after airmen like you that have lived through some difficult moments. He has developed some effective therapeutic techniques. I know him very well. I will contact this colleague of mine, who works at a hospital not far from here. The change of air will do you good. Are you willing to give it a go?"

John leaves the ORS quite late and the family have already started their dinner when he arrives home. The vicar and Edith are a bit disconcerted by his unusual appearance. He realizes and explains.

"Please excuse my appearance! I've had an enormous amount of work to do over the last few days and I've been working day and night. I'll have a shave tomorrow morning. I have three days off and if I don't get some sleep I will crack up."

John doesn't hang around after dinner. He takes one of the pills he has been given and goes to bed without getting undressed. His discussion with the doctor has done him good. He falls asleep almost instantly and sleeps through for 12 hours. Three days to relax, to walk in the woods around Richmart and recuperate.

The sleeping tablets work wonders and he sleeps deeply. No dreams, so no nightmares. Of course, he's a bit out of it the next morning, up until lunchtime, but then he's pretty much in great form. After a cycle ride in the woods he does a tour of the local pubs, where his beer consumption largely exceeds that indicated in such circumstances. John avoids talking about his past. In the evening, he throws himself with delight into reading a statistics thesis that one of his colleagues from Oxford has sent him. He also writes to his parents, telling them about his first few months at the ORS, and the nature of his research. He knows that his parents are relieved that he is not flying any more, even though they were very proud when they learned that he had received a prestigious decoration.

After four days off, John goes back to see Dr. Blake, who has organized for him to be admitted to Princess Mary's Hospital at Halton in Buckinghamshire, not far from the ORS. It's an RAF medical center, and he will be followed by Dr. Peterson.

"At the weekend, you can go and wander around London, if the Nazis don't send too many flying bombs to the capital!" jokes Dr. Blake. He then explains the planned treatment.

"You will see Dr. Peterson. He uses hypnosis. He gets his patients to talk a lot and he's a good listener. I know several airmen whose lives have been turned around in the space of two or three weeks, allowing them to find their peace of mind again. You can trust him. He's very human. I know that he always gets good results."

John is intrigued. He has never really taken hypnosis very seriously. People falling asleep just because someone says "Sleep". He doesn't really believe it, not at all in fact. But, on the other hand, they don't go in for any old nonsense in the RAF hospitals. He respects and admires the military doctors who are very dedicated in this time of war, and not motivated by money.

Two days later, in the morning, John takes a bus that transports him all the way to Halton. The hospital is vast and very clean. He has an individual room, small and spartan, but with an unimpeded view of the neighboring field. He has an appointment with Dr. Peterson for the next day.

After another agitated night, John prepares himself for his interview with the neurologist. What will he say about John's current state? John doesn't really know whether he should make things sound worse than they really are or try to minimize the intensity and repercussions of his anxieties.

Dr. Peterson is a small man with a large moustache. He offers John a cup of tea before beginning the consultation.

"No thank you, Doctor. It's very nice of you, but I had one 10 minutes ago."

"Very well. We'll get to know each other straight away. I'm a good friend of Dr. Blake, who often sends me patients. He's told me about your problems, but I'd rather act as if I know nothing about them. Can you tell me about yourself, what you've done, what you're doing at the moment, your childhood and any current or recent suffering? I'll begin by just listening to you."

John tells him about his mathematics studies, his PhD at Oxford, the war, his training as a bomber pilot and then his 30 missions, including the last one that has given him nightmares, and about his new job with the ORS at Bomber Command.

John talks for a long time. Dr. Peterson is very attentive and takes notes, displaying no desire to interrupt his patient. At the end, John indicates that he has recounted the essential details, but the doctor wants to know more about his problems.

"Can you tell me more about your current problems?"

"Yes Doctor, that's easy enough. Everything to do with the war upsets me. I avoid talking about it. I have terrible anxiety attacks and I often have nightmares that seem to be linked to my last mission, during which several members of my crew died. At the end of these painful dreams, I see the widows, who reproach me, and I find that hard to stand. I feel guilty for something, but I don't really know what. I'm also finding it hard to do my job at ORS. I feel guilty. I have the horrible impression that young airmen are being sent to their deaths because of me. I've been feeling agitated lately. I've had lots of work and I've had to work into the night. I'm tired, but I can't get to sleep. That's how things are at the moment. What do you think?"

"I prefer to avoid jumping to conclusions, John. But if it's any consolation, you're not the first pilot to be a bit disturbed at the end of his missions. We'll leave it there for today. We'll continue tomorrow morning. Go out into the countryside this afternoon. Don't hesitate to tire yourself out physically. Walk for a long time, go for a bike ride and pedal fast. We'll find you a bike. I'll see you at the same time tomorrow."

The next day soon arrives. This time, Dr. Peterson makes John lie down on a couch and sits in an armchair next to him.

"I'd like you to tell me again about this last mission that was visibly very difficult for you to bear, as the captain of the plane. Tell me about it again, but in more detail. Take your time."

John hates having to think about that last mission again. He generally avoids talking about it. But he has no choice. He must be as precise as possibly. He recounts feverishly "It was in '42, no '43, at the end of October. A mission to Leipzig. Destruction of synthetic petrol factories. A long time in the air to get there. It was a long way away. Six hundred bombers involved! We were packed together really tightly. The lights were on at first, but we switched them off once we had left England. A very dark night. Sinister glows when two planes hit each other. It was awful. Dense flak. I was really scared. We got caught in the glow of a projector. But I managed to get us out. What bastards! We arrived at the target on time. Colored markings, highly visible. We dropped two tons of bombs. Photos taken 20 seconds later to check on the damage and then back to England. Everything was fine until Belgium. But some bugger of a Luftwaffe fighter, a Junkers, managed to infiltrate the stream. Invisible. No-one saw anything. The fighter shot several times. He took us out. The flight engineer and the rear gunner were injured, screaming, and then it went quiet. Dead! Holes everywhere in the plane, but I managed to keep flying. I tried to get us back to England. No way were we going to parachute into enemy territory! They were shooting at us like dogs. We reached England, but the plane was starting to nose-dive, uncontrollable. Emergency evacuation ordered. The mid-upper gunner, the radio-operator and the bombardier jumped. That left just the navigator and me. I passed out. I came round attached to my parachute a few seconds before I hit the ground. I was told that the plane had rapidly broken up into three pieces. There's a gap in my memory. I don't remember the moment I jumped out of the plane. It's a complete blank!"

"So, two people died then?"

"No, three. We found the body of the navigator in the debris of the plane, completely carbonized. His parachute must have got caught when he jumped. He was carried away by one of the bits of the plane. It's horrible. I feel terrible when I think about it again. It was atrocious!"

John is effectively pallid and sweating, anguished by the evocation of these memories.

"What did the commission of inquiry conclude? They always hold one don't they?"

"Yes, there was one. It was the commission that rapidly came to the conclusion that the navigator's parachute must have got caught on part of the plane, dragging him to the ground. Like I said, I don't remember anything."

"Thank you John. That was a very full description. I understand. I think I now know enough about your case to offer you an original treatment with which I have already obtained good results. I hypnotize airmen who have suffered mental traumas. I worked on hypnosis techniques for a year in France, in Paris, before the war. I get very good results. I imagine you would like to know what will happen?"

"Yes of course! But I must confess that I'm not sure I believe in hypnosis."

"It's very simple. You lie down. I talk to you softly and ask you to relax and to empty your mind. I try to take you to a state of consciousness somewhere between sleep and your normal state of alertness. When you are in this state, if you manage it, you lose all sense of time. I ask you questions about your recent and more distant past. This helps me to understand better what is going on in my patients' heads, and talking rather than bottling things up helps my patients. Most of the time, they don't remember what they told me. Are you willing to give it a go? You can always stop if you don't like it or if it frightens you. If you agree, we'll start tomorrow. Is it a deal,

John?”

        “Yes, OK. I would love to see if you can hypnotize me, but I still don’t really believe it.”

10

GAITFORD, CAMBRIDGESHIRE, UNITED KINGDOM, JULY 1944

The British have had enough of seeing London, their beautiful capital, cruelly pounded by the hundreds of flying bombs killing innocent victims every day, and the devastating destruction they leave in their wake. The Allies have been informed by their spies that a large new V1 base close to Calais will soon become operational. Phil takes part in the armada of bombers that try, at the end of July, to put this new launch pad out of action.

July 28 1944 Excerpt from the diary of Philippe Destivel I bombed a flying bomb launch center next to Hazebrouck, between Lille and Calais overnight. All the planes in our group got back safe and sound. On the way back, the spectacle of the English defenses stopping the robots from crossing the coast was like something out of a fairy tale. Very dense flak lit up the night. Once we were over the English coast, we switched our lights back on and were more relaxed. I couldn't stop thinking about Victoria. I hope to see her again tomorrow.

Phil goes to bed late after returning from his mission. He sleeps well and wakes up happy on Saturday morning. He is free to do as he likes and he can go and relax a little before the appointed time for fishing. His deputy will replace him until the next day.

July 29 1944 Excerpt from the diary of Philippe Destivel
I wrote to mom and the kids this morning. She doesn't realize that the Germans
are still in France, even though the Allies have landed in Normandy. In her last
letter, she asked me to tell her when I will be coming back to Meknes. Soon, I
hope, she wrote, because the Allies have regained France…

Phil doesn't have a very full wardrobe, but he dresses casually. A sky blue shirt, a beige sweater in light cotton and some pale canvas pants. Towards midday, he takes his fishing rod and leaves on his bike, with a picnic in his rucksack, a notebook and a pencil to write, if he feels like it, and *"Vol de nuit"*, a book by Saint Exupéry that he has never had time to finish. Phil doesn't hurry. He first cycles to Peterborough, as he wants to spend some time in the cathedral, which has a particularly beautiful facade. He stays there for half an hour, seated in one of the pews.

Phil was raised as a catholic, by his parents, who practiced the religion without asking many metaphysical questions. He doesn't consider himself to be a believer, even though he finds the existence of the world, and his own existence, astounding. He doesn't understand and he knows that he never will understand what exactly he is and why he is there. But it doesn't really matter. He can live like that. He doesn't have a choice anyway.

But today he can't resist the temptation to pray for his children and to ask the divine powers to watch over them to make sure that nothing bad happens to them in these troubled times. They are so far away, his kids! He always worries about those who are close to him, but thinks little about his own death. It's as if the war can't get its hands on him!

He has no trouble finding the place where he fished the week before. An hour to wait before seeing the Victoria he encountered last week! He sits on the grass, eats his picnic and then lets his mind wander while the sun warms him, reminding him that summer has well and truly arrived.

He asks himself if he wants things to continue as they have begun with Victoria. Their exchanges haven't allowed them to learn who they really are. Over the last six days, he has often asked himself questions about this woman. Is she married? Does she have children, a job? But on the other hand, he is worried that her responses will disappoint him. For the moment, he knows nothing about her private life and everything is possible between them; she appears to be entirely free. While waiting, Phil plays with a coin. Heads she's married! And the coin falls heads up. Drat! But it's only a game! Heads she has children, and it's heads again. Drat and double drat, she has children!

He takes out his notebook, because he feels like writing a poem, an ode to Victoria. He doesn't see himself as a great writer, but he likes writing simple poems that bring a smile to the face of those for whom he writes. Phil is inspired, and this little trifle trips from his pencil onto the page:

> *Bonjour Madame la reine de la pêche*
> *dont j'ai envie de revoir les jolies mèches,*
> *les yeux au regard intense et les lèvres rieuses.*
> *Grâce à vous ma semaine a été bien heureuse.*
> *J'ai peur d'être déçu si je ne vous vois pas venir,*
> *alors que mon corps à votre vue est prêt à frémir.[2]*

Phil reads his poem out loud. He thinks it is awful and laughs about it. He then takes up his book, *"Vol de nuit"*.

---

[2] Good day to you, the fishing queen
Whose pretty hair I long to see,
With intense eyes and laughing lips.
Thanks to you I've had a happy week.
If you don't come, I'll be disappointed I fear,
Whereas my body is ready to tremble as you near.

When Phil looks at his military watch, it's half past three. Victoria is still not there. Thirty minutes after the appointed time! She hasn't been able to get away, or she didn't want to. What a huge disappointment! A female presence is no small thing in this place, where he spends all his time with men. He wants to know more about this Victoria. He occupies himself with his book. The author talks about what he felt when he was flying alone at night, in the darkness, or the half-light. It was the same for him during his training at Lossiemouth. They didn't have the same risks of collision that they now faced and that sent shivers down the spine, obliging the pilot to concentrate to an extreme degree.

"Well, you're not going to catch any fish like that, are you?"

Phil lifts his head and sees a smiling Victoria a few yards away. He hadn't noticed her approach.

"I was worried you weren't coming. I was disappointed. You know I'm more interested in you than the fish! I was reading a book written by a French airman, Saint Exupéry. I don't know whether his reputation was good enough for his work to make it across the Channel. Have you heard of him?"

"Yes, but not in the domain of aviation. I've got a copy of an English translation of a book that he published in New York last year *"le Petit Prince"* it must be called in French. It contains some pretty watercolors painted by the author."

"You're one ahead of me there. I've been lucky enough to meet the writer, but I haven't read *"le Petit Prince"*. What's it about?"

"It's the story of a child who discovers the world through his child's eyes, astonished by what adults think and say. Very moving. He discovers that love can be very prickly! I can bring it along if you like. An American airman gave it to me a few months ago. You can read it while I fish. That reminds me, I should set up my line. Aren't you going to?"

"No, I think I'll just sit next to you if you don't mind. I like it when we chat quietly so as not to scare off the sharks willing to throw themselves on your hook."

"Yes, OK, you can sit next to me. I'll give you a fishing lesson. Tell me what you've been up to this week."

"This week? Oh! Bombing missions to stop Nazi flying bombs falling on London. They are launched from the north of France. It's not a bad job, is it? The spectacle when we returned was fabulous. As beautiful as fireworks, but ten times bigger. English flak firing on these flying robots. The noise, the crackle. Some of the flying bombs explode in the sky. Others catch fire and dive towards the ground before reaching their targets. It's bizarre. It's a war, but I manage to find a form of beauty in some of the things I see. Does that shock you? Even over Germany, at night, the towns on fire, the flak, planes burning, the powerful projector beams. It's beautiful! The trouble is that they can bring us down. It gets a bit tricky when we reach the target. There are German fighters everywhere. We have to keep concentrating."

"But aren't you terrified by these blazing infernos?"

"Not really. I'm a bit apprehensive sometimes, but I have to concentrate, as the pilot. There's no room for fear. Fortunately, we haven't had many losses yet. We've been lucky. When the Allies landed, we thought that the Germans would retreat, we would pursue them and destroy them within the German borders, but we're not there yet, far from it. They are putting up strong resistance. It's likely to take much longer than I thought. It's the end of July. We hope that they will leave France by October. We'll see. It would be so good if they do! You don't know what it's like to have your country invaded. Imagine Peterborough with a *Kommandantur*, swastikas everywhere and a British prime minister collaborating with the Third Reich. You'd find that strange, wouldn't you?"

"Yes, I can't even imagine it. We're very insular here, protected by our geography. Your Emperor Napoleon managed to conquer much of Europe, but he didn't even try to invade us, even though I'm sure he really wanted to."

It's hot now, at the end of July. Phil takes his sweater off and remains in shirtsleeves. Victoria still has her fishing hat on, but the rest of her outfit is much more feminine: a floral dress and leather sandals, rather than the boots she was wearing the week before. She has discreetly made up her eyes and her lips are highlighted in vivid red. The last time, Phil had guessed that she was beautiful. Today, her beauty is self-evident to anyone who looks at her, and Phil doesn't deny himself the pleasure. She talks to him as if they have been friends for a long time, and that disturbs him.

Victoria continues to fish. They talk about London, which has been bombed again, Churchill, and the great English and French writers Trollope and Balzac, evoking the works of these authors that they most appreciate.

Victoria catches a bleak, too small to keep, and then hooks a trout that ends up getting away from her, which makes her laugh.

"You frightened it off, Phil. It preferred to go back into the water!"

"If it's only the fish I'm frightening, then all's well!"

It's a bit of a leading phrase, but Victoria makes no comment. They continue to talk like that for more than an hour. Phil becomes a bit dreamy at one point and says, smiling, "It's funny. We talk about anything and everything, without trying to find out more about each other. Do you think we do it on purpose?"

"Undoubtedly. It's not an accident. It's very rare, I believe. People who don't know each other and start talking rapidly ask each other questions about their lives, their families, their jobs. We've chosen another way. All I know is that you are French and a pilot at Gaitford, and you, what do you know about me?"

"That you know a fair amount about fishing, that you can look like a country girl or like a more sophisticated city woman and I'm in no doubt that you like literature."

"If we don't ask each other questions, it's because we're afraid of the answers we might receive. Don't you think? Or maybe we're worried that some responses will lead to new questions that we don't necessarily want to answer. At least not yet!"

Now she's being ambiguous! He asks "Do you really have things to hide Victoria? Bad things that would make me want to run for the hills?"

"Who knows? But I certainly wouldn't want to make you run away. It's a rare thing, having a handsome French airman in our kingdom from time to time."

The way that Victoria says this suggests that it was meant as a joke, but she looks at Phil tenderly all the same.

"You know, Phil, I can't stay any longer today. But before I go, I would like to suggest that we play a game. We will each allow ourselves the right to ask the other a question, but only one. We will write the question on a piece of paper, if you've got one, and then we'll draw lots to see who has to answer first. How does that sound?"

"What an odd game! But OK. I'll tear two pages out of the notebook I brought with me and we'll take five minutes to think about the questions we want to ask."

Victoria rapidly puts her fishing stuff away and straps it onto her bike. They both start thinking, looking at each other and smiling from time to time. Phil thinks, of course, that he would like to know whether Victoria is free or married, but he's too afraid of the answer to ask the question. He knows that that would break the charm of their fishing sessions. What he would really like to know is whether Victoria likes him. He doesn't ask much for the moment, he just wants to know how much interest he has excited in Victoria's head.

They draw lots. It's Victoria's turn to pose her question first.

"Here's what I wrote. It's simple and short. My question is: Phil, do you like painting? You have to answer."

Phil is amused. He wasn't expecting that. He thinks for a few seconds before answering.

"I don't know much about painting. However, I think it's an art that can be understood without a great deal of culture. When I was a child, my introduction to drawing was restricted to the lessons I had at high school. My parents didn't know anything and taught me nothing about art. Later, when I was a student, I went to the Louvre several times. I liked it. Let's say that I am not impervious to painting. But, why do you ask me that?"

"Phil, it's one question each, and only one answer. We'll see about the rest later. Now for your question. It's your turn."

"My question is, do you have something against military men?"

Victoria also seems to be amused. She answers rapidly.

"I've nothing against the military. I've met a lot of them, from different forces. I found them very different. The infantrymen from the army seem to me to be steeped in their traditions. Naval men have a fascination for the sea, exoticism. Airmen are different. They're a new species that only came into being about thirty years ago. They don't have any traditions yet, very few references to the past. They have to invent themselves. What I like in military men is their disinterestedness, a certain ideal, and what I don't like is when they're too keen on hierarchy, order and obedience. You see, I have mixed feelings."

Phil can't help adding "It's very true what you say. But have your really met so many?"

"We said one question each. I have to go now. Do you have any free time in the next few days? There's something I'd like to show you."

Phil is intrigued.

"Next Saturday, about 2 o'clock. I think I can get someone to replace me at the base. On the riverbank again? You've got a new fishing rod and you want to show me how it works?"

"No, I want to show you something else. Come to my house. I live with a sick elderly lady in an isolated house on the northern edge of Gaitford. It's on the Yale road, three hundred yards outside the village. There's a house and a small outbuilding that looks out onto a dirt track to the right of the main entrance. Take your bicycle through the entrance discreetly and knock gently on the door of the outbuilding. OK?"

Just as she had the week before, Victoria rapidly mounts her bicycle. She blows him a kiss with her left hand and Phil is over the moon, like an infatuated teenager.

Over the next few days, Lieutenant Colonel Destivel takes part in several missions.

August 3 1944. Excerpt from the diary of Philippe Destivel I bombed the wood at Cassan, near Isle Adam. A munitions dump, spare parts for flying bombs and a V1 storage site. There were more than a thousand planes. This forest has now been obliterated. It's sad. I often went there to collect lily of the valley 25 years ago. On the way back, I got a good view of the Rouen region. I got back tired. Lots of German flak. Desportes was hit and his plane crashed.

Some of the crew got out. We were followed by an aggressive fighter, who pushed us back the way we had come. Our rear gunner was hit. Received a letter dated July 5, from Meknes.

On August 4, Phil hears of the death of Saint Exupéry. He had had a long meeting with him in Tunis in May 1943, when the town was retaken. Saint Exupéry was already known as a writer in many countries. His reputation extended well beyond the borders of France. As a pilot, he was no longer young and could have sat out the rest of the war, continuing to write his books. But Saint Exupéry had come back from the US to participate in combat missions, with the premonition that he would lose his life that way.

In *"Pilotes de guerre"*, two years earlier, he had written "I have committed my flesh to this adventure. All my flesh. And I know I will lose." It had been said that he had needed to use the influence of people in high places to obtain authorization to participate in war missions, because of his great age, as he was in his forties. What a fate! And now he was dead. He hadn't returned from an observation mission over France. No-one knew what had happened. Engine failure or had a skillful German fighter brought him down?

All the airmen knew who Saint Exupéry was, but not all of them liked him. His literary glory placed him more in the camp of writers than in that of pilots. People like to recognize talents in one domain only, not in several. Some, a little narrow-minded or jealous, think that you have to take sides. Saint Exupéry was a very courageous pilot, not afraid of risk, but he was also a bit absent-minded, capable of forgetting to lower the landing gear when trying to land!

11

MEKNES, MOROCCO, JULY 1944

Maggy needs to spend the morning at Meknes airbase because she has financial matters to sort out. If she is to be able to use her son's bank account, money needs to be paid into it, and it hasn't been! Phil's salary hasn't been paid for two months and Maggy is starting to be a bit strapped for cash. It's undoubtedly an administrative problem, but she needs to find a solution rapidly. Before leaving for England, Phil had given her power of attorney over his bank account, to allow her to manage day-to-day with the children. He is paid a small part of his salary in pounds, which he receives directly at Gaitford, but the rest is paid into his account in Morocco.

Maggy has phoned Warrant Officer Fieschi, who takes care of problems of this type, and an army jeep is coming to pick her up at ten o'clock. Maggy has dolled herself up a bit. At 70, she still doesn't have white hair, just silver streaks. She has put on some lipstick and outlined her eyes with some kohl, which is easy to find at the Berber market. As the mother of a lieutenant colonel, she wants to look the part.

The jeep is on time and Maggy proudly gets in next to the driver. It's the first time she has ever found herself in a military vehicle with a driver all to herself. She can't help smiling with pleasure when she feels the wind caress her face. Fortunately, she had thought ahead and tied a headscarf around her head so as not to arrive disheveled. It's hot in July at Meknes, almost 95°F in the shade at three in the afternoon. A little wind is welcome, even if she can bear these temperatures with no difficulty.

It's a short distance in the car. But some of the streets are completely blocked by an odd, dense crowd, consisting of humans, mostly dressed in *djellaba*, and a large number of sheep. They arrive after 20 minutes and the jeep passes through the barrier at the entrance to the airbase. The base is no longer very busy, because most of the airmen have left for England, to bolster the ranks of the Royal Air Force. There have been no more military operations in Tunisia since the defeat of Rommel a few months earlier. The base now serves as a training center for new airmen still wishing to go to England.

Warrant Officer Fieschi's office is a wooden shack and it's particularly hot. A secretary takes Maggy to a waiting room containing three chairs, identical to those usually found in high-school classrooms, for visitors to sit on. There is already another woman there. Quite a young woman, and not unattractive, with her hair tied up in a bun on top of her head. She is slim, like many women in this period of war in which it's not easy to find food every day. Maggy rapidly strikes up a conversation, as she always does when she spends more than three minutes in the presence of someone she doesn't know.

"I have an appointment with Warrant Officer Fieschi to sort out some administrative problems. How about you?"

"Yes. I've already been kept waiting for almost an hour. I was told that he was coming back. He was here, but he was called away by the colonel who runs this base. I'm starting to get a bit fed up. It's really hot in here. Maybe we could open the window to get a bit more air in here. Would you mind?"

The lady is very polite, which pleases Maggy, who doesn't like people looking down their noses at her.

"Yes, that's a very good idea. Let's open the window. It's like an oven in this waiting room."

Maggy is curious to know who this person is and wants to know more about her. She is clearly pretty, very classy even! She has never met her before.

"I'm here to try to sort out some big money problems," she begins. "My son is in England. His salary hasn't been paid for two months. It's a complete shambles. Everything is chaotic at the moment thanks to the war! How about you?"

"I've come from Algiers. I live near Algiers with my sister and my children, who are being looked after for me while I'm here. I have money problems and I would like to return to France as soon as possible. I was told that the administrative offices for the airmen from North Africa were centralized at Meknes, so I flew here in a military plane yesterday. I'm going back to Algeria tomorrow. The military are paying for me to stay at a hotel, the *Hôtel de l'Oasis* near Medina. I don't know anyone here."

Maggy is intrigued by this woman, who seems a bit lost. There have been far fewer distractions since the airmen left. She decides straight away to ask her to dinner at her house that evening.

"That's really nice of you," the woman replies, "But I wouldn't want you to go to any trouble. Do you live far from here?"

"Not really. I'll ask a friend to come and pick you up in his car towards half past seven. He can't refuse me anything. My name is Marguerite, but everyone calls me Maggy. You can too. And you, what's your name?"

"Françoise."

At that moment, Warrant Officer Fieschi puts in an appearance and apologizes for having been delayed. He greets the ladies and calls Françoise into his office. Maggy has just enough time to say "The driver will call for you at the entrance to your hotel at 7.30 tonight. I'll see you later and I'll make sure to cook you some good grub!"

Françoise finds this last phrase of Maggy's rather unusual. "Good grub", what an odd expression! This woman, who is not particularly young, strikes her as a little strange. What is she doing in Meknes? Why is she dealing with her son's financial problems? Surely he is old enough to take care of them himself! Undoubtedly she will find out more tonight.

Warrant Officer Fieschi is very polite to Françoise, who seems to be overwhelmed by events. She wants to return to France as soon as it is liberated. Of course, she knows it's not possible yet. But she has had enough of being isolated in Algeria with her children. She also has financial problems. He understands her questions and can see that her life is, effectively, not very easy. He agrees to provide her with answers to her questions as soon as possible, by mail. Connections between Meknes and Algiers have been restored. Letters only take a week to arrive and in the next ten days, she will receive an official letter enabling her to receive an interim payment directly from the air force in Algeria whilst awaiting a definitive settlement and monthly payments. It's too soon to talk about going back to France. She will need to wait until Paris is liberated at least.

Françoise leaves the office reassured about the short term. She doesn't see Maggy again because she doesn't go through the waiting room. As far as her return to France is concerned, she knows that the request is absurd. The Allies only landed in Normandy three weeks ago and they are still fighting.

It's Maggy's turn next to enter the warrant officer's office and explain her problems. No salary for two months.

"I'm very sorry, but the financial management of the salaries of the officers who have gone to fight in England is a real nightmare because their families have remained here. The families need money and so do the officers. They have a number of expenses to meet in England, for their civilian clothes, their entertainment and travel when on leave, presents for their friends and so on. I can pay you an advance corresponding to one and a half months of salary. I'll settle up the rest next month. Is that an acceptable solution for you?"

He leaves the office for ten minutes and then returns with a large envelope full of bank notes. Maggy is delighted. She likes having cash and doesn't necessarily trust bankers. But she will have to find somewhere to hide this little nest egg.

She now needs to concentrate on the preparation of her dinner. She realizes that she knows her guest's first name, but that she forgot to ask her surname. She wonders if it would be a good idea for Paul and Claire to eat with them. No, they can stay for the drinks beforehand, but then she and Françoise will eat on their own! It will be easier to talk that way. She's a bit mysterious this Françoise!

After being driven home in the jeep, Maggy walks quickly to the little house of the road mender. This Moroccan fought in the trenches during the Great War and is a friend of Maggy. It is he who has a car in a serviceable state, or almost, a 1934 Renault Celtaquatre.

They first met when he was repairing the edge of the road opposite her house. They had a long discussion. She found him pleasant and helped him with the administrative formalities he had to go through to recuperate his inheritance from his grandfather. Effectively, Slimane can't refuse her and agrees to go and collect Françoise from the *Hôtel de l'Oasis* as agreed. They will go together. She may trust her Moroccan friend, but she still wants to make sure that Françoise is safe.

She then goes to the Berber market to do the shopping for

her dinner. Her friend Slimane has taught her how to make *couscous*, but she doesn't know if her guest would appreciate typical North African cooking.

Mutton and poultry are the only meats available on the market. The mutton, which is not necessarily very young, can have a very strong taste and not everyone likes it. It's less risky for her to buy a chicken, which she plans to use for a *poulet basquaise*. She finds all the ingredients she needs. Some bell peppers, a few tomatoes, some onions, garlic and chili. Oranges for dessert, which Slimane has taught her to prepare, perfumed with orange flower water. A rosé wine, a *vin gris* from Boulaoine, in case her new friend Françoise wants something alcoholic to drink. Maggy likes wine. Before she married, she had worked in a vineyard with her father, in the Orleans region.

Maggy and Slimane set off in the car at seven o'clock. Slimane knows where the hotel is and, at the appointed time, Maggy enters the lobby of the hotel, where Françoise is waiting for her, sitting on a sofa. Both have made an effort for the occasion. Maggy is wearing her best cotton dress, bought at Meknes. Françoise has made herself up very discreetly.

When they arrive home, Maggy begins by presenting her grandchildren to Françoise. She's as proud of them as if she were their mother.

"Françoise, this is Paul, the eldest, he's fifteen, and Claire, his little sister, who is nearly fourteen. Their father, my son that is, has left for England. He commands a group of RAF bombers at Gaitford. In the meantime, I'm looking after the kids. My son is a widower and we weren't allowed to go with him, unfortunately. I tried to insist, but the families weren't allowed to go. It's a real shame. I wonder how long we're going to stay here. But then again, we're not unhappy in North Africa, and we're better off than many. We've got food. Here, I can have a maid, a local woman, to help us.

It doesn't cost much. And you, Françoise, what are you doing near Algiers?"

"My husband was an air force officer. He stayed in Algeria when his colleagues left for England. Unfortunately, he had an accident in his Leo 45. He was killed instantly. I have been a widow for a year now, with three children, the youngest of whom was only a couple of weeks old when his father died. I also wonder how long I am to stay in Algeria. All I'm waiting for is the chance to go back to France. I know it's not possible at the moment. I can't wait for this horrible war to be over!"

"Your life can't be easy, on your own with three children. I suppose you have family in France who could help you? It's just occurred to me that we only know each other by our first names. We should introduce ourselves properly. My surname is Destivel and my son is a lieutenant colonel."

"But I know you son! Well, a little, anyway! My husband, Captain Dumaine, invited him to dinner once. I thought he was very nice. A man with lots of class. We passed an agreeable evening together. He wrote me a condolence letter from England when he heard what had happened. A very sensitive letter that I found very touching. I would be delighted to see him again."

"It's a small world! So, you know my son and he wrote to you from England. I'm just surprised that he never spoke to me about you and your husband. How secretive of him!"

This last comment makes Françoise smile. Her lieutenant colonel son can't have had much fun living in North Africa with a mother like Maggy, who clearly likes to rule the roost.

"What will you do when you get back to France?" Maggy continues.

"I don't really know to be honest. Both my parents are dead.

My journey began with the exodus from France. We were in my house in Burgundy in June 1940. When the Germans invaded France, my husband flew over our house in his plane and dropped a written message for me. We managed to pick it up. It was like something out of a novel! In the message, he told us to get into our Hotchkiss as quickly as we could, to flee the Germans, and to go to our cousins in Pau. That's what I did. How about you Maggy, did you leave France in a hurry like that?"

"No, I stayed in Paris until the armistice. I was looking after Paul and Claire. After the armistice, my son was based at Vichy, with the high command, for a year. I was able to go to him with the children. We lived in hotel rooms. Then Phil was sent to Morocco, to Meknes. But you said you had a house in Burgundy. Is it big enough for you, your sister and your children?"

"Yes, it's a beautiful old house with 10 bedrooms, close to the vineyards of Montrachet. It was grandfather de Belloy who bought it. It has a big garden, almost five acres. I hope to go back there, at least for a while, after the war. But I can't see myself spending my life there. That would really be cutting myself off from the rest of the world! It's great as a country house. But where should I go next? Maybe Paris? I'm still young. I can hope to remarry. I've never lived in Paris, but at least there's life in the big city."

Maggy is moved by Françoise, who describes her situation with the greatest realism, but without complaining. She can tell that they don't really belong to the same social class. She has noted from their conversation the existence of a vast country house, a grandfather with an aristocratic name and an expensive car. She tells herself that at least Françoise can't be short of money. But she wants to check anyway, so she asks "Have you got enough money to raise your children? Or do you have to work?"

"Fortunately, although I'm not rich, I have enough income to support myself, my sister and my children. That's all thanks to my inheritance from my father, who died in 1915. I have an attorney taking care of my money, but I haven't heard from him in four years. I imagine that I will also receive a war widow's pension after the war, at least while my children are still at home."

"And your brother, do you get on well with him? Couldn't he help you?"

"No, he's a priest. He's a very nice man, but not much fun. He's always checking that I practice my religion conscientiously, and that my children hear about God and say their prayers at bedtime. I'm a believer at heart, but you can go too far!"

Françoise admires Maggy, who, at her age, has come to the aid of her son who has gone off to fight the war in England, and has been looking after his children for the last few years. She thinks that if her mother had still been alive and in good physical health, her life would have been much simpler. Maggy must have humble roots. Her way of holding her knife and fork would not be acceptable in polite society! But that doesn't detract from her human warmth. It was really very kind of her to invite Françoise to dinner without really knowing her.

Françoise likes the *poulet à la basquaise* and compliments Maggy on her cooking skills. The dinner continues agreeably. Maggy, who is very curious, asks questions that make Françoise laugh, about her first loves before she married, and her life at Verdun, where there were probably some handsome young officers. Before Françoise leaves, Maggy asks her for the address of her house in Burgundy and gives her the address of her flat in Paris. Slimane, who has been sitting in his car throughout the dinner, takes Françoise back to her hotel at the end of the evening. The next day, Maggy cannot resist the temptation to write to her son to tell him about her meeting with Françoise Dumaine.

12

ST MARY'S HOSPITAL, BUCKINGHAMSHIRE, UNITED KINGDOM, JULY 1944

John wakes up intrigued by his first day of hypnosis. Today is the day when Dr. Peterson is supposed to make him fall asleep at his command, but he still doesn't believe it. How will this doctor manage to put him in a trance, just like that? John is a rational being. Studying mathematics has rendered him impervious to such practices, which he considers to be akin to magic. He is skeptical, but serene. It will be his therapist's fault and not his if the session is unsuccessful.

He arrives on time for his appointment. The doctor doesn't keep him waiting and asks him to enter a room containing only a comfortable armchair, behind which there is a chair. He makes his patient sit down and stands behind him.

"John, today I'm going to try, above all, to get you to relax. I don't think I am going to put you in a trance. Things will happen like this. We are going to talk for an hour, and you are going to try to be as relaxed as possible. I will ask you to perform several relaxation exercises. I need you to cooperate fully. Do you have any questions?"

John replies gaily "No Doctor, go ahead. I'm ready. The armchair I'm sitting in is really soft and I'm afraid I will fall asleep very quickly!"

"OK. Let's start. Don't close your eyes. Focus on the piece of paper on the wall in front of you. You see the circle with a dot in the center? Stare at it. Continue to contemplate this circle. Gradually relax all the muscles of your body. We'll start with your feet. Concentrate on your feet. Gradually relax all the muscles in your feet. Is it working?"

"Yes, no problem."

"Now concentrate on the muscles in your legs. Keep staring at the circle and relax your calves completely, then your thighs."

The neurologist continues, asking John to relax the muscles of his abdomen and back as much as possible. He then spends time on John's neck and face.

John is still awake, but he is effectively becoming increasingly relaxed. He feels almost numb. This exercise lasts almost half an hour. The doctor then continues in a clear, firm voice, "Continue to relax. We are going to talk about your first war mission. Do you remember your first mission John? Think about it again. You are entering the plane with your crew. Do you remember John?"

"Yes, I remember it well. An easy mission."

"Think about the take-off, the moment when you pulled on the joystick and your plane took off. Do you remember?"

"Yes, I watched the ground moving further away. Then we arrived above a splendid sea of clouds and I told myself 'Serious stuff today, I have to concentrate. I mustn't make any mistakes'".

"Were you afraid?"

"No, not at all. I was focused. My navigator gave me the coordinates to follow. I regulated my speed as best I could. The mission over Germany went very well. Not much flak. We arrived over the objective precisely on time. We dropped the bombs, took photographs and returned to base without a hitch."

"That's very good. Now close your eyes. Think about the end of this first mission. Rest for a few moments. Relax."

John closes his eyes and continues to think about his arrival on the ground. Descent through a layer of cloud. A long descent. John thinks about it for a long time. Enormous maybe. First mission successful. No problem. John is so relaxed that he falls asleep. Dr. Peterson is satisfied and lets John sleep for about ten minutes.

"That's very good, John," he says softly, "You're really relaxed now. I don't want to do any more today. Our first session is over."

John opens his eyes and, for a few seconds, he isn't entirely sure where he is.

"I was so relaxed that I nearly fell asleep!"

Dr. Peterson smiles and doesn't tell him that he was actually sleeping deeply for ten minutes.

"My aim today was to get you to relax. I think we succeeded. It's very important for the rest of your treatment that you manage to relax completely. We will continue tomorrow morning. Goodbye for today, John. Go and do some sport this afternoon. A long bike ride. Go tire yourself out."

"OK, doctor. I'll see you tomorrow then."

John gets up from the armchair, very sleepy, astonished to find that he feels like a nap. He yawns as he gets up, causing his doctor to smile again.

John follows the doctor's advice to the letter. That afternoon, he goes on a long bike ride, on a bicycle without gears, which forces him to make a considerable effort as he pedals uphill. One stop in a pub for a quick pint of bitter and he's off again. In the evening, he is exhausted from the 40 miles he has covered at quite a speed. He sleeps straight through until three in the morning, when his fears catch up with him. He wakes up covered in sweat, with cataclysmic images of a plane accident in his head. He manages to get back to sleep and doesn't wake again until 8 a.m. He goes to meet Dr. Peterson as planned, for his second hypnosis session in the same comfortable armchair as the day before.

"OK John, today we will begin by repeating the muscle relaxation exercise from yesterday. Don't forget to keep focusing on the circle on the wall in front of you. This time, you will start relaxing by concentrating on the muscles of your face, gradually descending to your legs, and ending with your feet. Start by concentrating on the muscles in your forehead. You look worried. Your forehead is lined. You have problems John. Your forehead should be smooth. Let it relax. Yes, very good!"

This muscle relaxation exercise takes less time than the day before. Once it's over, the doctor says "You're going to think about your last war mission. I want you to image that you are taking off again for this last mission. Were you relaxed that day?"

"Yes, all the crew members were happy to be finishing our tour of operations. It was our 30th mission. We had plans for the days of leave we had owing us before our transfer somewhere else without having to fly any more or be scared of being shot down."

"John, you are going to think again about what happened when the German fighter started to shoot at you on the way back. Do you remember the German fighter?"

"Yes, I remember it well. There were bursts of gunfire from behind. The rear gunner hadn't seen anything because it was so dark. He alerted me over the intercom. He shouted that he and the flight engineer had been hit when they went to check a valve at the back of the plane. He was shouting so loud that I had trouble understanding him. But his voice then rapidly faded away. He must have lost a lot of blood. When the navigator went to see how they were, he found them both dead. He told me what he saw. I couldn't go to see for myself, as I was flying the plane. The flight engineer must have died instantly; shrapnel in the head. He had a hole in his skull. The rear gunner was hit in the throat. He bled to death."

"What did you do then? Did you give the order to evacuate?"

"No, the plane was difficult to fly, but I managed to keep it in the air. I didn't want us to have to parachute out over enemy territory. I got the plane back to our coast, to land on one of our emergency landing strips. But the plane got more and more difficult to fly."

Dr. Peterson realizes that John's state of mind is changing. Until now, he has been calm. Ever since he started talking about the end of his mission, his arrival over England, John is no longer comfortable. He fidgets in the armchair and he is starting to sweat. His diction, which has been clear up until now, becomes increasingly difficult to understand. John isn't in a state of hypnosis. He is wide awake, but very agitated.

"You seem nervous" says the doctor, "Try to relax the muscles of your face. Look at the circle in front of you. Are you feeling anxious?"

"Yes doctor, I don't feel very well. I would like to stop there for now."

"OK John, but we will stop gradually."

The doctor again asks his patient to breathe deeply and to relax for a few minutes. John seems to have pulled himself together and is smiling again.

"That will be all for this morning, John. We will continue our discussion the next time. Try not to worry. So far, you are reacting like most of the traumatized patients I've treated. Nothing out of the ordinary. You're heading in the right direction. I'll see you again after lunch. Two sessions today. We need to move forward."

John returns straight after lunch. This time, the therapist sits in the chair behind the armchair, once John is comfortably installed.

"Relax gradually, just like you did during the first two sessions, except that this time you are going to close your eyes straight away. You will keep your eyes closed throughout the session."

Again, the doctor asks his patient to relax all the muscles of his body, progressively. After a quarter of an hour, John is peaceful, so peaceful that he looks like he is sleeping. The doctor asks him to move his right hand and then his right arm. John does as he is told. With a look of satisfaction on his face, the doctor says "We're going to talk about your last war mission, a mission over Leipzig. Your plane was hit, but you managed to bring it back to England. At one moment, you felt that it was becoming uncontrollable. You gave the order to evacuate. Do you remember?"

"Yes, I remember. It was a complete panic!"

"Who jumped first?"

"The upper-middle gunner, the radio operator and then the bombardier."

John, impassive, answers all the questions. No more signs of anxiety. Dr. Peterson continues, "Now it's the navigator's turn to jump. He jumps, John. Can you see him?"

"No, he doesn't jump. I remember. He hesitates. I don't know why. He doesn't jump even though I order him to. He's too scared to jump and he freezes like a statue."

"So, what did you do John?"

"I sensed that the plane was going to break up. I was terrified too. I wanted to get out of the plane straight away! I needed to jump as quickly as possible, but the navigator was blocking the passage leading to the escape hatch. So I shoved him, I pushed him. He fell down. I jumped. My parachute opened after a few seconds. I didn't see any other parachutes. The navigator didn't jump. The plane broke up into three pieces, which crashed into the ground."

Dr. Peterson has succeeded. He understands everything. John feels terribly guilty because he pushed his navigator out of the way and jumped before him. The pilot is supposed to jump last. At the end, John, in the panic of the situation, had even made him fall over. He finds this episode unbearable. His mind preferred to replace this sequence by a big blank, a period of amnesia. That's what's troubling John and generating his panic attacks and nightmares, even though he doesn't remember what happened any more.

"Now open your eyes," he says, "That's right, can you see me? Do you remember what you just told me, about the end of your last mission?"

"Yes, I remember everything now. I see what happened. It's horrible. I shoved the navigator out of the way. I left the plane before he did. I should have jumped last. I'm distressed. I didn't do what a pilot should do. What I did was really bad! I'm responsible for his death. I'm a killer!"

"No John. You panicked. Your navigator was also too distraught to jump. You have accomplished great things these last two years. During your final mission, your survival instinct overrode the rest. We're programmed like that. You can't do much about it. If your navigator had managed to jump out of the plane, you would have been the last to jump. Don't feel guilty about it! You can have regrets, but no more than that. John, all of this stays between us. You will probably feel better now, much better. I think that you will stop having panic attacks and nightmares. You can get up now. I would like to see you tomorrow morning, just to conclude your treatment. Today, I managed to hypnotize you and you got your memory back. The hypnosis sessions stop here, you don't need them anymore. You've managed to free yourself from the 'taboo' that was ruining your life."

John thanks Dr. Peterson and goes back to his room. He lies on his bed, feeling completely worn out. He is no longer anxious, but he is sad, because he now understands why he couldn't remember the end of his last mission. He falls asleep and doesn't wake up until lunchtime. He feels a need to tire himself out in the afternoon. He takes his bike and pedals rapidly, without stopping, for four hours. Tired, he doesn't even eat dinner, but he has a peaceful night, without waking.

John sees Dr. Peterson as planned. The doctor asks if he has had any more panic attacks. John explains that he simply feels tired and sad. The doctor confirms that the anxiety will not return. He must simply learn to deal appropriately with what he has learned about himself.

Dr. Peterson thinks that it would be better for him not to return to work at the ORS. He has spoken with the Air Chief Marshal over the phone. John will be offered a military post and will train bomber pilots until the end of the war. But first, he has the right to a few weeks of convalescence.

The next day, John leaves the hospital and finds a bus to take him back to Richmart and the vicar's family. The vicar is well and hasn't relapsed. Margaret tells him that it seems like he's been away for ages. Edith seems to be very happy that he is back. They are all delighted to see him again. John finds his reception very agreeable, even if he doesn't deserve it. He wants to be nice to everyone at the moment.

John sees Edith differently now. She used to annoy him with her bossiness. He watches her smiling at him during dinner. At the end of the meal, John finds himself alone with her for a moment in the kitchen, while they are helping to clear the table.

"I think I will be leaving tomorrow," he whispers. "I'm not sure I will be coming back. I would like to say goodbye properly. If you can, come and see me tonight. Come up to my room. I would like to talk to you."

Edith says nothing, but smiles.

John lies in his bed thinking again about what he has discovered about himself. He would like to apologize to his navigator, but he is not around to listen. What a terrible shame! A few seconds of panic and he had destroyed two years of courage and intrepidity. His doctor had advised him not to tell anyone what he had done. But right now he would like to take to someone who could forgive him, but he can't imagine who. What should he do?

If Edith comes to see him, as he asked, he will thank her for looking after him over the last few months, say goodbye and tell her that he feels lucky to have met her. No need for a repeat of their salacious behavior while the vicar was in hospital!

John ends up falling asleep, not in a particularly happy frame of mind, but his fears and nightmares have left him. He has left the door to his room ajar. He is asleep and doesn't hear Edith, who quietly steals up the stairs. He doesn't hear Edith take off her dressing gown and her nightshirt. Entirely naked, she slips into bed next to him, delicately, without brushing against him. John doesn't hear anything at first. But then he senses a presence and feels an affectionate hand caressing his chest. In the darkness of the room, he can't see the features of his hostess, who is disposed to listen to him this time.

"Edith, I wanted to say goodbye to you alone, and properly. I've got a long period of leave, at least until the end of the month. Then I'm to go and become an instructor at a training center for airmen. Tomorrow, I will leave to see my parents, close to London, for a few days. After that, I'll see. I wanted to thank you for welcoming me here and looking after me. Without you, my stay would not have been so happy."

John puts his arm around Edith's shoulder, and tries to kiss her gently on the right cheek, but Edith turns her head and their lips meet. He pulls her towards him to hold her body against his. His hands discover her nudity. He obtains great pleasure from running his hands over the softness of the relief that defines her femininity. Edith has a very soft body. He adores squeezing her breasts. She responds to his caresses and leaves John satisfied, after a quarter of an hour of pleasure. She hadn't counted on having any more such moments of love since he had convinced her that it would be wiser not to continue their relations once the vicar had returned.

13

GAITFORD, CAMBRIDGESHIRE, UNITED KINGDOM, AUGUST 1944

Phil has trouble getting time off on Saturday August 5, the day on which he is due to see Victoria at her home. He has to explain to the colonel, his direct superior, that he really needs some time off to recover. A plane was hit during the last mission. Some of the crew members hadn't been able to parachute out in time. Another four deaths. The other crew members are in Germany, at best prisoners of war. The colonel doesn't fly and doesn't understand the nervous tension and the fatigue that some of his men suffer due to the stress of these missions. He finally agrees and Phil's deputy, Captain Jopet, will take command of the group during his short absence.

This Saturday, despite the buzzing of the Halifaxes taking off, Phil has a lie-in and sleeps until 10 a.m. He wakes up peacefully, but intrigued by his date with Victoria, because he will finally find out a bit more about her, see her house, and discover a part of her world and her secret garden.

Phil finds his own existence strange because he is living two parallel lives. Firstly, that of a warrior with missions to accomplish. It is his job to fly from Gaitford, drop his cargo of bombs on a target in Germany or elsewhere and come back. Almost like a delivery man, who has to take things to an address, where he leaves them before returning to his starting point. Delivery men transport objects like furniture, food or clothes. In his case, it's bombs. He delivers bombs, and it's more dangerous. Those on the receiving end of his deliveries are enemies, not clients. If he gets back safe and sound after a few deliveries, he can have some time off and live his second life. He has lodgings and a bicycle. He can go for walks, sleep in a hotel, eat in restaurants, drink a beer in the pub, make friends, fish; in other words, lead a normal life. The important thing is to come back alive from these deliveries.

It's a unique mode of combat. The infantry launches attacks, never knowing exactly what they will amount to and what will follow the operations in which they go to annihilate the enemy forces. It's the same for the marines. The route they take depends on the forces they encounter. The commanders often modify the initial plans. Ships change course according to the other boats and enemy planes present in the zone. The men aboard cruisers or destroyers stay in this artificial environment for long periods of time. They can't just go outside and find themselves in civilian life when they get leave. Very strange, the lifestyle of a bomber pilot. A fixed target. You go there and you have to come back.

At the moment, Phil is absorbed in his life outside the airbase. He quickly forgets the war when he is on leave. He is very interested in Victoria, who is becoming increasingly important to him. He often thinks about his family in Meknes, but without anxiety, because he knows that they are safe. That allows him to put his family life on hold. Victoria is the first woman that he has really liked since his arrival in England. She is beautiful and mysterious, and he would like to know her better.

The previous two days were rainy in Gaitford, but the weather is fine this Saturday. A few sparse cumulus clouds render the sky less monotonous, without obscuring the azure. Phil leaves towards noon, on his bike, with a sandwich, an apple and a flask of water. He stops at the edge of a small wood about two miles from the base, hides his bike behind some brambles and walks among the fir trees and oaks, which gradually become denser, until he reaches an unlikely sunlit clearing. The ground is dry and covered in grass, ideal for a picnic. This place is isolated and ideal for the daydreams of a solitary hiker who wants to focus for a while on himself and those he is close to at the moment.

He asks himself several questions. Will Victoria tell him a bit more about herself? She said that she lived with an old lady. Is she a relative? Or is Victoria a sort of servant, looking after a patient? Phil can't really work out Victoria's social position. English isn't his first language. He can speak it well now, as he has been using it every day for eight months, but he still can't distinguish a local accent with more rustic intonations indicative of a more humble origin. Does the house he is supposed to go to belong to Victoria? And what does Victoria do all day in the English countryside when she isn't fishing? Why did she refuse to dance with him when he first met her, whereas she was happy to speak to him straight away the following day?

These questions remain unanswered and maintain the mystery surrounding the current heroine of Phil's world. He gets back on his bike towards 2 o'clock and has only a quarter of an hour to pedal to reach Gaitford, which he now knows very well. He takes the Yale road, which heads north, and, attentively, he scrutinizes the houses at the edge of the village, but none of them correspond to Victoria's summary description. Phil continues to pedal and, three hundred yards further on, after a bend in the road, he catches sight of an imposing brick building, probably dating from the last century, surrounded by beech trees that have clearly been pruned but are nevertheless very tall. The place is deserted. Effectively, there is a narrow dirt track to the right of the house. Phil follows this track and immediately spots a narrow gate serving a small building, providing access to this building without the need to pass by the main entrance. Probably built to house someone working for the people in the main house, a caretaker or gatekeeper maybe.

Phil enters the courtyard with no problem and, with his heart beating furiously, he knocks discreetly at the door. He hears footsteps. Victoria opens the door.

"Hello Phil. You're right on time. Did you have any trouble finding me?"

"Your house is easy to find. It's quiet here."

Phil plants a kiss on her cheek. He is astonished by her appearance, because she is wearing a shapeless, cream-colored pair of pants spotted with paint stains of different hues, mostly yellow and green. Her light blue shirt is also stained with multiple colored projections. Phil looks at her with an amused expression on his face.

"Are you painting your house? Do you want some help?"

"No, you'll understand soon enough. Follow me."

Phil follows her into a corridor, which ends in a vast, highly cluttered room.

"Welcome to my kingdom, my studio. I spend my time painting. I want to show you my latest works."

The room is very bright. Light enters via the windows, which look out onto the garden. Victoria has hung four brightly colored canvasses on the walls. Phil studies the paintings carefully and finds it hard to work out what has been painted.

"You'll have to explain them to me. I can't see what you were trying to convey."

"I like abstract art. You draw shapes without meaning, just because they are pretty in themselves. You put several of them together. They should be in harmony with each other. You paint them to make large blocks of color. You shouldn't look for a representation of reality. Just nice shapes and pretty colors."

"I'm not sure I get it, but you can keep on explaining it. I'll be an attentive pupil."

Now Phil understands why she asked him if he liked painting. She seems passionate about it. She wanted to show him her paintings, and he wants to know more.

"Tell me how you started painting and why you chose this style It's unusual, particularly in the country."

"I'll explain everything over a cup of tea."

Victoria starts by showing him around her little house. After the studio, there is a good-sized kitchen with a table that can seat five. She shows him the door that leads to a bedroom that she can rest in when she gets tired, but she doesn't open it. Her real bedroom is in the main house. Phil rapidly finds himself seated in the kitchen, drinking tea. They are facing him. She offers him some delicious Scottish shortbread.

From the window, Phil can see the back of the main house. Four high leaded windows on each floor. Eight in total on the façade of this two-storey building. The first floor isn't level with the ground and there are steps up to the entrance. A building in the Georgian style, built in the 1840s. The small house is more recent, dating from just before the Great War.

"Have you been painting for long?" Phil asks. "Have you always painted like that or did you paint in other styles before?"

"I didn't say so before, but I spent two years in India and then two years in Paris. I can speak French, although I've forgotten a lot."

Phil is surprised and says in French "*Vous êtes une cachotière.*

C'est la quatrième fois que nous nous voyons et vous ne m'avez pas dit que vous parliez le français. Mais c'est bien, nous allons pouvoir alterner les langues."[3]

She replies in French, with a light British accent that he finds charming, *"A Paris j'ai fréquenté des peintres de Montparnasse comme André Lanskoy, qui m'ont initiée à l'abstraction. Avant, j'avais suivi des cours de dessin et de peinture à Londres. Depuis que je suis petite, j'ai envie de devenir peintre."*[4]

She gets up and comes back with a watercolor showing the interior of an apartment, a living room, with a fireplace, two armchairs and a seated woman doing some embroidery.

"That's what I used to paint before I got into abstract art. You see. It's very classical."

Phil likes this painting and realizes that Victoria is talented at both drawing and painting. She hasn't chosen abstract art because she can't hold a pencil or a brush.

"Has your work been displayed anywhere?"

"No, I was preparing an exhibition when the war broke out. I've been living here ever since. I paint a lot. It's my only distraction. I need it. Life isn't much fun around here! But I don't want to talk about me today. Tell me about your week first. Where have you been dropping your bombs?"

In France, the day before yesterday. A flying bomb depot again, not far from Paris. Isle Adam. A forest where I used to go collecting lily of the valley with my parents on May 1st. I doubt there will be any of its delicately perfumed little white bell-shaped flowers

---

[3] That was sneaky. It's the fourth time we've seen each other and you never told me that you speak French. But it's a good thing. Now we can switch between languages.

[4] In Paris, I used to hang out with the painters in Montparnasse, like André Lanskoy, who introduced me to abstract art. Before that, I took drawing and painting classes in London. I've wanted to be a painter ever since I was small.

next year. It was a massive bombing. More than a thousand planes. Can you imagine the fireworks? I've also had a lot of organizing to do. There were some repairs to be done, damage caused by fighters. Two new bombers were delivered. We had to carry out technical flights to check everything. We also have some sick airmen that we need to replace. The men are starting to get tired. Our planes are not comfortable. We often fly at altitude, at 16,000 feet, and we get cold. Personally, I always put a layer of old newspapers under my jacket. That keeps me warm. It's all soft! So you know Paris well, and the Montparnasse quarter. I lived near there before the war. At the start of rue Lecourbe, near to the overground Metro line. Do you see where I mean?"

"Yes, I know it well. One of my painter friends had his studio round there. I remember that there was a café on the corner, at the intersection of rue de Vaugirard and boulevard Pasteur. We used to go there to eat oysters. The French taught me to appreciate oysters."

Victoria and Phil continue to talk like that about Paris, about the cafés, taverns and restaurants that they might both know. She continues to divulge nothing about herself. Why was she in Paris? What did she live on? Why always so mysterious? Phil can't help but remark sardonically "I know a bit more about you now, but you still haven't told me anything very personal. Do you like to shroud yourself in mystery Victoria?"

"You don't say much about yourself either Phil. But that doesn't stop me from liking you. Quite the contrary in fact. Actually, you now know more about me than I know about you. I showed you my paintings, and that's a part of my life. All I know about you is your current life as an airman. That's it. You must be about forty so you must have a past. I'm thirty-five, and I also have a past. You wanted to know what I'm doing in Gaitford at the moment. I can explain that."

"Yes, please do!"

"I'm looking after a relative, an old lady who had a stroke four years ago. She hasn't got much family, she is paralyzed down one side and she can't speak anymore. I wash her, feed her and keep her company for part of the day. Fortunately, she sleeps a lot. She's having a nap at the moment, like she does every day. When I can't take it any more I get a woman from the village to come and look after her for a few hours. Not exactly a bundle of laughs, my life at the moment!"

"I understand. It's not much fun. I lived for three years in Meknes in Morocco before I came here. I was glad to leave, even though it meant leaving my children behind."

That triggers curiosity in Victoria, and she wants to know more.

"So you've got children?"

"Two, a boy called Paul and a girl called Claire. Fifteen and thirteen."

"And you were pleased to leave Morocco and come to England?"

"Yes and no! I really didn't want to leave my children behind. It was my mother who was the problem. When my father died, before the war, I was obliged to look after her. I'm an only child. My mother came to Morocco with us. She looks after my kids, but she interferes too much and she was making my life a misery. It was like I'd gone back to being her little boy! It was like a breath of fresh air being sent to your country!"

"And your wife?"

"I was widowed seven years ago. My mother came to live with us because my father died, leaving her without an income, and I needed someone to help look after my children every day."

"I'm so sorry Phil. I didn't want to stir up painful memories."

"Don't be sorry. Since I've been in England I feel like I've been on a long, exciting holiday. It's paradoxical. I loved the training period. Several months. Lots of flying hours. Discovering Scotland. Parties with the WAAFs. Things are a lot more hectic now. Over the last two months, we've been taking part in Bomber Command missions. There have been a few losses, but not too many as yet. It doesn't really feel all that dangerous. We have to do about 30 missions. And then we are relieved of duty. But I'm a long way from that."

Victoria can't resist asking a more personal question.

"And haven't you met any pretty girls to your taste and impressed by a handsome French officer since you've been in England?"

"Only a little shepherdess in the mountains near Loch Ness. But she was too young, almost a child compared to me. I behaved correctly, although it was difficult because she was so fresh, funny and charming. I think she liked me. But she didn't deserve to be taken advantage of."

"So you know how to control yourself?"

"Too well, possibly!"

"That's pretty impressive, and not very common. Men often think only of their immediate pleasure and do a great deal of damage."

"I've undoubtedly found it hard to get over the death of my wife. But I think I'm making progress. It's about time!"

Victoria glances at the clock. She's always pressed for time.

"It's time for you to go now. I've got to go and look after my patient, but I would like to see you again. Do you think you could come next weekend? For another cup of tea? I'll be a bit more loquacious next time."

"I don't know if I can get any time off next week. I'm being replaced until tomorrow night. Don't you have any free time tomorrow?"

"Come at 2 o'clock, like today, for another cup of tea! Be discreet when you leave please. I don't want people to know that I have men coming here!" she says jokingly.

He wasn't expecting that. Maybe this beautiful woman is interested in being more than just friends!

He stays for another five minutes, lost in his contemplation of Victoria's paintings, and then he leaves the house discreetly, without encountering another living soul. He has some time to think about the pretty painter and decides, on a whim, to go for a bike ride. He continues along the road to Yale, a small town about ten miles to the north. Phil is starting to get answers to his questions, but he still knows little about Victoria. He knows that she is not a servant and that she is talented, even if he doesn't really understand the essence of abstract painting. He knows that she has traveled and spent time in India and in France, but under what conditions, he has no idea. Victoria is opening up, but only very gradually. Why? Is she reserved? Does she have something to hide? Maybe he will find out more tomorrow. But what is sure is that she has bewitched him and is increasingly in his thoughts.

Phil doesn't go all the way to Yale. After three miles, he takes a road on the left and decides to follow the sun, so as to complete a loop and return to his starting point. The road in question rapidly transforms into an increasingly narrow dirt track. The calm of the countryside is periodically disturbed by the roar of military planes, Halifaxes and Lancasters, filling the sky. There are many bases in this part of England and not all the planes come from Gaitford.

The track ends in a large meadow where a herd of cows is grazing, huddled around a superb walnut tree. Phil decides to continue cross-country, pushing his bicycle and praying that there aren't any bulls in the herd. During his childhood, he spent some holidays with his cousins, at their farm, and he knows that you have to be careful in such circumstances. It's not just German flak that you have to avoid! With bulls, so long as you move slowly and don't wear bright colors, accidents are rare, but they are nevertheless not totally impossible. Phil has no desire to die in an English meadow. He passes at some distance from the animals. They don't seem to be interested in him. Reassured, he reaches a wheat field just as immense as the meadow before it. He walks along the edge of the field so as not to damage the future harvest, still heading west. He comes to another dirt track and then a winding road heading off to the left that brings him back to Gaitford.

Back at the base, Phil relaxes in his little home-sweet-home, which is not very cozy, but at least no-one comes to disturb him. He eats a quick dinner in the officers' mess, plays bridge for an hour and then goes to bed.

Phil is punctual the next day. The surroundings are still just as deserted when he arrives at Victoria's little house. The front door is ajar. He enters without knocking, finds no-one at home and tells himself that his hostess will be back soon.

Effectively, Victoria arrives a few minutes later. A different woman from the day before. She isn't in her painter's outfit, but is instead wearing a very elegant spotted dress with short sleeves, revealing a pair of attractive plump arms. She has put her hair up in a particularly neat bun and has made up her eyes. She is wearing a beautiful pair of simple golden hoop earrings. Around her neck are two rows of pearls. Phil admires her even before he greets her.

"How elegant! Is all that in my honor?"

"Of course it's for you. I don't have any other dates this afternoon" she replies gaily.

"I hope you're going to devote all your free time to me. You're always pushed for time when we see each other. After an hour, all of a sudden, it's time to go. I want more of you. We've got so many things to say to each other. We need some time to get to know each other properly" adds Phil, smiling.

"I'm happy to chat, provided I can have a cup of tea."

Phil follows her into the kitchen. He admires the curve of her hips, apparent from the shape of her very fitted dress. When they are once again sitting opposite each other, it's Victoria who takes up the conversation.

"If I've understood you correctly, it's my turn to tell you more about myself today. I was putting it off because my situation isn't an easy one. Nine years ago, I married an army officer. I was twenty-six. Malcolm was forty-two. I found him very attractive. Sixteen years might seem like a large age gap to some, but it didn't bother us. Soon after our marriage, he was posted to Bombay. We discovered India together. I found the atmosphere of the country fascinating and life was easy. Lots of receptions. We traveled around the country together. Afterwards, Malcolm was promoted to military attaché and posted to Paris. A wonderful life again. I painted a bit in India. In Paris, I worked much harder at it and I hung around with a set of very creative artists. They were carefree and funny. They drank a lot and were seductive and seducers. Malcolm and I found ourselves living on two different planets. We didn't have any children. I often came home very late after parties at which the alcohol flowed freely at *la Coupole* or *la Closerie des Lilas*. Some nights I didn't come home at all! Malcolm was unhappy and didn't understand. He wanted me to change my lifestyle. I refused. I got better at painting. We'd just started talking about divorce when the war broke out and we went back to England. Malcolm was promoted to colonel. He went to fight in France and, in May 1940, he was taken prisoner at Dunkirk. For the last four years he has been held in an *oflag* in Pomerania."

All this leaves Phil stunned.

"So who is the lady you look after?"

"In June 1940, his mother, my mother-in-law, had a stroke. She's a widow. There was no-one else to look after her because Malcolm is an only child. This house belongs to my mother-in-law. We came here together and I look after her. It's even more difficult because she doesn't like me very much! Malcolm had already told her about our marital problems. There, you know much more about me now. I didn't want to tell you all that straight away."

Phil understands better now, although he's a bit disappointed by what he has just heard. Victoria has a husband. An officer on Her Majesty's Service and, what's more, a prisoner of war in a German camp. It's unfortunate, but he doesn't feel he has the right to seduce the wife of an English colleague who has been suffering in a German prison camp for four years.

"I would have preferred to hear that you were single. Are you still in contact with your husband?"

"Yes, I write to him once a month. I send him parcels via the Red Cross. His life is very difficult there. Not enough to eat, and some of the prisoners die from typhus. Very harsh reprisals when someone tries to escape. Malcolm is always on the receiving end because he is one of the highest graded officers there. I suspect it may be even more difficult than he says it is in his letters."

"Was it because of your situation that you refused to dance with me when we met that first time at the restaurant? You didn't want to be seen with another officer while your husband was a prisoner?"

"Yes, that's it exactly. I've been living here for four years and lots of people in Gaitford know me and my history. Out of respect for Malcolm and his mother, I'm always very careful. Tongues wag you know!"

"It's true, your life isn't easy and it can't be much fun. You've won a sort of artificial freedom. I'm sure you don't deserve all that, and that your husband doesn't either. I really enjoy being with you, Victoria. We're two casualties of life, you and me. We can be friends if you like. I understand that we can't go any further. It's a shame, because I find you really attractive. But no, it's not possible for me to court you. I wouldn't be able to look myself in the face. I would be ashamed. Would you like us to remain friends though?"

Victoria responds cryptically, "I really like seeing you too. Let's just see what the future has in store for us. We've met twice on the river bank and twice in my studio. Where shall we meet next do you think?"

"I don't know. We need to be able to correspond occasionally, discreetly. I noticed that there is a letter box on your gate. There aren't many people around here. Maybe you could write letters to me and put them in the letter box, and I could do the same for you. I could come by and check the letter box without disturbing you every two or three days or so. What do you think?"

"Great, it's very romantic! Do you think we could see each other next weekend, or some other time?"

"I'm afraid not. I think I'm going to be very busy over the next couple of weeks. But I have an idea. There's another French base under RAF command at Badvington, about 70 miles away from Peterborough, to the east of Sheffield. They're going to have a very big party, with 500 people, to celebrate the progress of the Allies.

They've invited all the officers from my base from the rank of lieutenant-colonel upwards. There are four of us going and we can each take a date. I would like you to come with me. Do you think that you could get away for a few hours? We'll travel in a little military bus. We'll leave at six in the evening and we'll get back during the night, about two in the morning I think. I don't know the exact date for the minute, but I should know more in a week or so."

"I'd love to! It would be wonderful to go with you, to drink and to dance with you. I'm not sure yet how to get someone to replace me as my mother-in-law's nursemaid in my absence, and what excuse I could use, but I will think about it. At least there would be some fun to look forward to! It's been so sad around me for so long. And at least there, no-one would know me!"

Victoria and Phil carry on chatting for a quarter of an hour or so. She tells him more about her life in India and her travels around the country. He then leaves quickly because she thinks that she can hear noises from the main house. They exchange tender, melancholy gazes before going their separate ways.

14

ABOVE THE NORTH SEA AND GERMANY, AUGUST 1944

Phil is in a good mood on August 7. He has just learned of the liberation of Rennes a few days previously. It's the first large town to be taken back from the Germans and it will certainly not be the last. How wonderful it would be if Paris could be freed from its invaders and their sick ideology. Hopefully in a few more days or weeks! Optimism is essential.

Phil realizes that he can't stop thinking about Victoria. He finds her interesting, cultivated. She likes to read and to paint. He doesn't really understand her very abstract style of painting, but there is a certain harmony to the paintings on display in her studio. And what's more, she's very pretty. She's the sort of woman that doesn't leave you indifferent. She is tall but shapely, with such femininity in her curves. But she is married. Her husband, a prisoner of war, will return to England when the war ends. A fact he cannot ignore! It wouldn't be right to try to seduce the wife of a captured allied officer!

He does, however, feel authorized to cultivate their friendship. Phil sees no reason to break off all contact, provided that they respect the limits they set themselves.

If they are to continue to see each other, they will need to be able to organize meetings. Phil wants to test the communication system they have developed. He writes a note on a sheet of writing paper, which he then folds to serve as its own envelope.

Dear Victoria,

If we want to cultivate our friendship, we need to be able to communicate easily to fix meetings. That's why I am writing this note to you today. Tell me if you found it. I'll come looking for a response in three days' time.

Look after yourself. I'm glad to have found an English friend who speaks my language and knows how to use colors so well.

Your friend,

Phil.

Thursday is the day on which Phil will go and look for a response. Fun and games in prospect with these discreet exchanges of letters!

On Wednesday, Phil and his crew are on alert. They will take part in a nighttime mission provided the weather conditions are suitable. The weather is poorer than it has been of late on this August 9. The sky is covered with thick cumulus clouds. It's gray and depressing, with scattered showers. Phil thinks that the mission will be cancelled but, towards 8 p.m. the loudspeakers around the base resound with a request for all the crews concerned to go to the briefing rooms.

Many of the airmen called up for this mission have blank expressions on their faces. They know that they are going to risk their lives, die or possibly come back injured. Most of them stop talking. They don their flying suits and leave their corrugated metal huts. They take their bicycles and go first to the stores, where they collect their parachutes and inflatable vests, which they will have to put on if they have to bail out in midair.

After separate meetings for each type of airman, they all get together for a final briefing towards 9.30 p.m. The briefing officer holds up a large map. A certain stupor is evident on the faces of the airmen when they realize that their target is Berlin. Phil frowns. This is not going to be an easy mission! The anti-aircraft defenses must be particularly strong around the capital of the Reich. But, even if some of the airmen are very worried, they are all proud to be part of this adventure. It's the first time that the airplanes of Gaitford have been called upon to wear down the morale of the Germans, who believe themselves to be invincible and out of reach in their capital. Seven planes from the base, including three from the Aquitaine group will be involved. Forty-nine airmen are going to risk their lives. In total, 232 bombers from Gaitford and the other neighboring bases will be going to Berlin. A mass bombing designed to neutralize chemical factories and to destroy administrative buildings, so as to weaken the confidence of German troops and citizens in their leaders.

Phil is very attentive during the description of the flak they are likely to encounter and he carefully studies the detailed maps with their targets. Everyone receives the essential materials they might need if they are shot down: a map of Germany, food, a compass, some medical drugs. Phil doesn't like anything that brings to mind the dangers they face, but he is very good at filtering out any information that might destabilize him. Like the others, he has brought his papers with him, together with his most personal effects. He must sort them and put them in two large envelopes, one that will be destroyed if he doesn't come back, the other to be passed on to his family. They go through the same ritual every time they leave on a mission and it only serves to heighten the fear felt by many of the airmen at the start of the mission. Phil stays calm, but, for an instant, he thinks of his mother and his children, but also of Victoria, the woman from whom he hopes to find a letter in a day or so.

The airmen then go to their planes, which have already been prepared by the ground staff, who do not fly. They have an impressive load of bombs, some of which weigh over a thousand pounds. Lots of fuel, of course, to reach such a distant target. More than 10 hours of flying, there and back. Bullets too, cartridges for the gunners, who will have to fire on the German fighters when they approach to attack. More than 26 tons when fully loaded.

The motors start up at the appointed hour. The hum is deafening. The planes begin to advance majestically and move towards the runway, passing in front of the control tower for identification. Phil gives a thumbs-up sign to indicate that all is well. All the pilots use this signal as a way of affirming their determination.

At four minutes past eleven, the seven planes start to take off and adopt a formation in the night sky over the base, respecting to perfection for the timing they have been given.

The navigator indicates the coordinates that Phil must follow to meet up with the bombers from other bases and form an impressive stream. They initially fly at a very low altitude in the darkness of the night, with all the lights switched off, for two hours, to escape German radar. The navigator occasionally notices a little light escaping from a neighboring plane and indicates the proximity of this other plane to Phil, to avoid a collision.

At thirteen minutes past one, Phil sees the sky light up for a few seconds and glimpses the sea. Two planes have hit each other and exploded. Fourteen airmen have just died!

Phil must start to climb close to the island of Düne, eventually reaching an altitude of 23,000 feet. The entire crew puts on the oxygen masks essential for survival at such altitudes. Close to Hamburg, Phil spots the powerful projectors trying to detect them. There's nothing they can do to avoid detection. They are rapidly spotted and the flak starts up almost straight away. The night is disturbed by the explosion of the shells fired by the anti-aircraft defenses and their twinkling lights. Phil tells himself that it's a good thing they are so high up and that flak is very imprecise. Once they get past Hamburg, they have orders to change direction and head south for about 60 miles, to distract the enemy and conceal their true objective. They then turn north-east again.

Unfortunately, the sky clears about 60 miles from Berlin. No clouds to hide them. The beams of the German projectors light up the sky in search of bombers. In front of him, Phil sees two planes on fire, hit by flak and diving towards the ground. The German fighters will soon be in action again.

Berlin is coming into view. A real firework display, with sound effects in the form of the crackling of shells exploding in the sky. Buildings on fire. Projector beams frenetically searching for enemy planes. Phil can see several green lights on the ground. A sort of highly luminous Bengal fire that the English pilots, the pathfinders, have just released to mark the targets. Another two minutes and it will be time to go back. These minutes seem to last forever.

"Bombs away!" comes the victorious shout of the bombardier via the plane's intercom.

"Well done, now get the photos" replies Phil, pleased with the success of this first part of the mission.

Once the usual photos have been taken, the crew members begin to relax. They must carry on flying at high altitude for an hour on the way back before they can descend and fly lower.

Phil follows the coordinates indicated by the navigator. For a fraction of a second, he thinks about the little outing he has planned for the following evening, to search for a reply from Victoria. Then he concentrates on flying again. The time drags past.

"Arrival at Bremen in two and a half minutes," indicates the navigator.

At this precise moment, they both feel an enormous jolt due to the explosion of a shell. But it's not as bad as they fear. The plane doesn't seem to have been hit. Immediately afterwards, the darkness of the sky is replaced by the intense light of a flare. They have been identified. Two minutes later, Phil sees clearly a Halifax in flames, rapidly disintegrating into two pieces.

The mid-upper gunner reports two enemy Junkers three hundred yards above them and starts to fire at them. These light German bombers, used as fighters, execute a maneuver to place themselves directly behind the plane, to get it into their sights. The rear gunner understands what they are up to and informs Phil via the intercom. Phil then follows a special corkscrew trajectory that they have practiced hundreds of times during training. He manages to get away from the fighters.

Twenty minutes later, they leave Germany close to Cuxhaven and fly west over the sea. They begin to breathe more easily. The worst is behind them. Phil wasn't really frightened, despite the density of the flak around Berlin.

Four minutes later, the sound of the motors is masked by that of numerous projectiles being fired behind them. A German fighter has got into the stream and is picking off planes. Phil can see a light coming from his right wing. His external motor is on fire. He tells the flight engineer to fix it. The flight engineer cuts off the fuel intake and starts the extinguishers. He also tries to modify the angle of the propeller blades to reduce drag. This calms the fire, but doesn't put it out altogether.

Phil thinks that he can carrying on flying in these conditions but, just to be on the safe side, he tells his men to put on their parachutes, just in case. The risk is that part of the wing will become white-hot, heated by the fire, and detach from the plane.

They fly at about 6500 feet. Phil examines the external motor, which still has small flames escaping from the exhaust. The plane should hold together until they can reach an emergency runway very close to the English coast, but that means another three quarters of an hour flying like this!

Another deafening hum and some crackling. This time it's the left external motor that is on fire. Another fighter has come to finish what the first one started. Unlucky. Phil tells himself that they still have two working motors. He can keep the plane flying if they can get the fire under control. But the flames are getting bigger and bigger. They are increasingly impressive, extending right to the tailplane.

The situation is critical. Phil has no choice. He cannot expose his men to the risk of probable death, and he gives the order for the rest of the crew, including the navigator to leave the plane.

The navigator signals their position by radio.

"Plane A for Able. Three fifty-nine. Two motors on fire. Fire not under control. 152 miles from the coast. Evacuating."

The men don't have to be asked twice to bail out and they jump via the hatches behind, in the center and close to the cockpit.

Just before he jumps, the navigator shouts to Phil "It's your turn Sir. Jump now. Hurry up."

Phil wants to continue to fly as well as he can towards the English coast, but doesn't really believe he has any chance of making it. If he wants to stay alive, it's now or never. Phil makes his mind up, jumps from the hatch at the front and opens his parachute after an interminable 10 seconds, just as he has been taught to do. As the parachute opens, he feels an enormous jolt to his shoulders and loses consciousness.

In the starry sky, illuminated by an almost full moon, a

parachute descends slowly, transporting a French lieutenant-colonel fighting for his country's freedom down to the sea. He loves life, particularly since meeting a very attractive English woman. This officer wants to know what happens next in his own life story. It wouldn't be fair for it all to end suddenly at the end of this night in August 1944. The parachute descends at a rate of 26 feet per second, and he has almost 5000 feet to fall. The descent takes about three minutes.

Phil comes to his senses and sees the starry sky and the sea lit up by the moon. Above him, he can see the reassuring canopy of his parachute, which will take him down to the sea. He knows what to do in such a situation. He pulls the toggle on his Mae West, his life jacket, which immediately fills up with gas, swelling up around his chest so that he will be able to float easily. He'll have to splash around in the water for a while, but he hopes to be picked up rapidly by Air Sea Rescue. He looks at his aviator's watch. It's eight minutes past four in the morning, and in August that means it will soon be dawn. Phil reckons that he should be picked up towards eight o'clock. He thinks about all the members of his crew, who are undoubtedly already in the water, and he does a quick calculation. They are about 125 miles from the English coast. It'll take a speedboat about five hours to get them back. Then he will have to find a way to get back to Gaitford. He might be able to get there by the end of the evening and have time to see if there is a reply in Victoria's letter box!

The water is getting nearer. It's a shame, because he is enjoying this descent, in total silence other than the murmur of the air in his parachute. Only a few more seconds to go. Phil lands gently in the sea, without going under, his life jacket proving very effective and allowing him to float easily. The water isn't cold and he's wearing enough layers of clothing to ensure that he doesn't feel chilled much anyway, at least at first. He detaches his parachute but keeps it near him, so that it forms a white patch on the sea, making him easier for the rescue team to find.

Phil has been waiting in the water for almost an hour now. It's nearly light. He can't hear anything and there is no-one in sight.

Six in the morning. He's still in the water. He can see a plane flying at high altitude, but he can't identify it. It passes over him and then flies away. No sound other than that of the sea, which is fairly calm.

Half past seven. Phil is starting to find the time long. He thinks he can hear a sort of purring noise in the distance that might be the rescue boat. The sound lasts two minutes, and then dies away. He hasn't seen anything on the horizon.

Nine o'clock and Phil is starting to worry. He has a bottle of water in one of his pockets. He takes it out and drinks a little. He eats some of the food from his survival rations. Towards half past nine, his morale improves considerably. He sees a boat approaching in the distance. Phil thinks he touched down in the sea fairly close to where the plane must have crashed. The planes are equipped with transponders that indicate their position when they sink.

After a few minutes, Phil is sure that it really is a rescue boat coming to pick him up. He is rapidly hauled aboard. He is given dry clothes and is reunited with five members of his crew. Phil is relieved, but the airmen don't look happy. Duclos, the flight engineer is the first to speak.

"Sir, there's been an accident. Vincenot, the rear gunner. They found him. But one of the straps of his parachute had got caught around his neck. Maybe he opened it too soon. The shock must have been very violent when the parachute opened. The rescue team found him dead. Broken neck in all probability. His body is in the back of the boat."

Phil is distressed. Since jumping from the plane, he hadn't for one second imagined that things might turn out badly. Vincenot has three young children. His wife lives in Burgundy, near Chalon-sur-Saône. How terribly sad!

Phil moves to the back of the boat, where the body of Warrant Officer Vincenot lies. He realizes that he is finding it hard to walk. He can feel a sharp pain in the buttocks, continuing down the thigh and the rear of his leg. He finds Vincenot laid out on a stretcher, still in his flight suit. Phil remains silent with his thoughts for some time next to his colleague's remains.

It dawns on him that he might himself die during a future mission. Strangely, until now, he hadn't really dwelt on the risks he was running. He had been saddened by the death of others, but didn't feel directly concerned himself. Today he has come face to face with the lifeless body of one of his own men. They might all have died if a shell had exploded close to their plane or if the fighter's bullets had hit the cockpit rather than the motors.

But Phil pulls himself together and refuses to give in to these morbid thoughts. The rescue boat has turned towards the English coast. He asks its captain when they will arrive and is told that they might get back for two in the afternoon. A nurse tends to all the survivors, trying to establish their state of health and their morale. Phil says nothing about the pain in his leg, which is getting worse.

Clearly marked on the hull of the boat is the emblem of the Air-Sea Rescue Service, marking it out to the Germans as a sort of "ambulance boat". Despite a number of protests to the International Red Cross, such boats have been targeted by machine-gun fire on a number of occasions. One hour into the journey, a German JU88 squadron passes overhead, but it doesn't try to attack them. The rest of the journey is uneventful. At around quarter past two, they land at Grimsby, 80 miles north of Peterborough, a port specializing in the elimination of sea mines in the North Sea that was heavily bombed by the Luftwaffe in 1943. They have to wait until six o'clock for a coach to take them back to their base.

There is a warm welcome at Gaitford. The crew had been declared "missing" and everyone had been pessimistic about their chances of survival. Nevertheless, sadness takes over when the death of Warrant Officer Vincenot is made known. The crew is taken to a debriefing room, where, over the course of almost an hour, each member recounts the circumstances of the accident.

They are then taken to the infirmary, to be examined by the airbase doctor. Phil is starting to get annoyed. It's almost nine o'clock in the evening and he is desperate to be able to take his bike and ride to Victoria's gate to collect the letter that should be waiting for him.

Phil insists on being examined rapidly. The doctor complies and carries out a thorough clinical examination. When he moves Phil's leg, Phil can't stop himself from crying out in pain because it hurts so much. The doctor suspects a problem with the lumbar vertebrae and wants to keep Phil under observation for two days. Phil feels sick to the stomach, but has to lead by example and do what he is told.

15

BADOCK, TO THE NORTH OF LONDON, UNITED KINGDOM, AUGUST 1944

John has the whole month of August off before taking up his post as an instructor at Lossiemouth in the north of Scotland. He decides to start by spending a few days with his parents. He will see how he feels after that.

They live in Badock, a small town of four thousand inhabitants about 30 miles north of London. That's where he grew up and his father has been the vicar there for 32 years.

He hasn't been able to inform his parents of his imminent arrival, due to the lack of communications. It's an emotional moment when he knocks on their door on August 4. They are very proud of him and congratulate him enthusiastically for his medal, the Distinguished Flying Cross. John rediscovers his childhood bedroom, which has remained unchanged since he left to study at Oxford.

He is invaded by a feeling of emptiness on the day after his arrival. He has been away from his parents for several years now and he feels that they don't understand him. His childhood friends have all left Badock to follow their various destinies: emigration to the United States, a prisoner-of-war camp in Germany, active service in the army like himself, and medical services, like surgery, for another.

Happily he has a younger sister, Mary, who is 22. She is married and lives at Badock, and she has an 11-month-old son who is just starting to walk. They weren't very close in the past, but John can see that his sister has grown up a lot since.

She invites him to lunch two days after his arrival. She tells her brother that her husband is away at the moment. He's an engineer in a company that makes nautical equipment and he had to enroll in the technical services of the army, which are currently refining their defenses against flying bombs in the south and east of London. The capital is bombed every day. You never know how long it's going to last. The V1s are launched and haphazardly directed towards the city from France or Belgium, but with no precise target. The idea is to make people panic and to kill as many civilians as possible. The British are developing an unusual form of defense against these engines of death, in the form of steel cables held in position vertically by balloons inflated with helium. Mary's explanations make John curious to see what such a defense might look like and what happens when a flying bomb runs into one of these cables. He decides to have a look before his departure from his parents' home.

John is captivated by Arthur, his nephew, an energetic ginger-haired little boy who clings on to chairs to raise himself up onto his feet and then falls straight down, eventually sitting on the ground when the effort becomes too much for him.

Mary asks her brother to tell her about his time in the Royal Air Force. He is uncomfortable with the idea that she thinks of him as a hero. But Mary is insistent, and wants to know why he was awarded the DFC.

So as not to disappoint her, he explains very simply what happened to him.

"It was at the end of May 42. Our target was Cologne in

Germany. A night bombing. There were more than a thousand planes. I was flying a Lancaster bomber, a plane with four motors. A German fighter managed to hit me about 125 miles from the town. One of the motors was hit and caught fire. I decided to keep going to the target, a railway station. The plane held out. We completed our mission. Getting back was difficult. The cockpit had been damaged by shrapnel. We ended up doing an emergency belly landing. Not on the runway at our own base, but on an emergency landing strip close to the English coast. The plane caught fire, but the firemen were able to put it out rapidly. The rear gunner suffered burns, but nothing too serious. That's it really. I didn't even have time to get frightened. Too busy trying to fly the plane, to keep it heading in the right direction. It wasn't easy with three engines. The flight engineer was remarkable. He was the one who adjusted the engines with the utmost precision. You see, Mary, it's nothing to make a fuss about, really."

"Well if I'd have been you I would have died of fear! I would have been paralyzed, incapable of doing anything. I'm very proud of you, big brother."

"And I'm proud of my nephew. He'll be an athlete when he grows up, I'm sure of it!"

Playing with his nephew keeps John occupied and calms him, stopping him from thinking about what he feels so guilty about. He stays at his sister's house the whole afternoon. He talks to her about their parents, their childhood. They both agree that they have good parents, loving and affectionate, although a bit limited in their exchanges with their children. Always one obsession in mind, to make good Christians of their children. Brainwashing, every day. Grace before the evening meal and prayers before bedtime. Both of them had gradually lost their faith during their adolescence, but neither has dared tell their parents. Mary still goes to services on Sunday, so as not to upset them. John managed to escape that ritual when he left for Oxford.

The next day, John accompanies his father to the church to help out. It's not about religion today, but about helping people who have just lost everything during the London bombings. The vicar has organized a collection of food and clothing for these families temporarily housed in empty houses in and around the town.

John spends the day sorting and packing clothes, making up batches of clothing appropriate for the size of each family and the number of children. His father is grateful for his help and thanks him. John is glad to have pleased his father.

At the end of the first week in August, John's sister invites him over for afternoon tea. Afterwards, at about 7 o'clock, they go to their parents' house for dinner.

The door of the vicar's house is ajar, which is unusual. John calls his parents, but no-one replies. Mary says nothing. The living room door is closed. John is worried. The house seems strange. He opens the living room door and, dumbfounded, catches sight of about 20 people of all ages, who start shouting "Well done!", congratulating him and launching into a rendition of "God Save the King". His parents are there, smiling. They've organized a party for him.

John is annoyed. He recognizes people from his father's parish and realizes what is going on. All these people are here to celebrate his commendation with a prestigious medal. John can't help thinking that if only they knew what he was really like and what he was capable of, they wouldn't even be here!

But John feels obliged to play along, out of respect for his parents. Once again, he has to recount in detail the reasons for which he was awarded his medal. He speaks quietly and is asked to repeat several sentences that his audience fails to catch. After his story, the guests toast his bravery, but all he really wants to do is escape from the room and go somewhere a long way away, where no-one knows him.

Happily, the cocktail party then takes a different turn. Friends of his parents have come with their daughters, some of whom are of a similar age to John and have husbands who are elsewhere because of the war. John runs into Lisbeth MacErlean, who sang with the choir that his mother ran when he was about twelve. She's two years younger than he is and is already a widow, her husband having been killed in France, during the German advance in June 1940. She wasn't married long enough to have children. She teaches math at the local secondary school and that provides them with a ready subject for conversation.

The party lasts an hour and a half. The guests leave, one after another, but not without taking the time to congratulate the hero a second time. John is relieved when the last guests leave. He nevertheless thanks his parents for organizing this party, which actually only served to wind him up and embarrass him!

The days pass. John continues to help his father. He feels a need to redeem himself if he is ever to be at peace and be able to look himself in the face again. Self-esteem is important, and John has lost his.

One day, an idea comes to him that he finds superb. Once he has finished his period as an instructor at Lossiemouth, if the war continues, he will apply to become a pathfinder. He will be one of those pilots sent to release luminous signals over targets telling the bombers exactly where to drop their bombs. It's dangerous, but oh how very useful! He will place his life in danger during every mission but will know that it is worth it. It will be like a therapy for him. He will start organizing things as soon as he arrives in Scotland.

16

GAITFORD, UNITED KINGDOM, AUGUST 1944

Every day, at the end of the afternoon, Victoria checks her letter box, hoping to find that the missive she wrote the day before has been collected by its recipient. The contents of her letter are as follows:

Dear Phil,

I'm also pleased that our paths have crossed. I like our meetings and your visits. We have lots to talk about. If your invitation to the party at Badvington still stands, I think I can get someone else to look after my mother-in-law. I would be delighted to dance with you this time. Let me know.

Love from (if that's allowed!),

Victoria

Every evening, she is disappointed to find the letter that she wrote still there. Her friend Phil isn't coming back. Victoria is worried and sad. She's scared that something might have happened to him. All day she hears aircraft noise, reminding her of the war and the dangers to which the pilots are exposed. Sometimes, other thoughts enter her head. She asks herself whether knowing that she is married hasn't put him off completely. But she can't do anything but wait.

Time passes slowly. Nothing on August 13, 14 or 15! She keeps a lookout and goes to the letter box several times during the afternoon. But it's difficult for her to leave her mother-in-law on her own for too long.

Towards 7 p.m., she goes back one last time. There's nothing OK waiting for her. Still no response! She turns around slowly, vexed. She wants to see Phil again and the prospect of going to a dance at a French base a long way away from Gaitford has made her as excited and impatient as a young woman going to her first ball. Victoria thinks she hears the screech of bike brakes behind her. She retraces her steps and comes face to face with Phil, who bursts into a broad smile, his face lighting up when he sees her.

"I'm so happy to see you. I was really worried about you! Do you have a few minutes? Why don't you come in?" she asks him.

"I've had a few adventures. I'll tell you about them if you like."

Victoria opens the door to let him into her studio and can't resist the temptation to hug him, chastely.

"Oh Phil, you're actually here! I was so scared that you might be dead. I've been having really dark thoughts."

Phil looks at her, moved that she has been so worried about him.

"They were almost justified. I could have died. We got shot down coming back from a mission over Berlin. The whole crew had to parachute out of the plane. Over the North Sea. We all got soaked. Fortunately, your rescue services were very effective. I spent a few hours in the water, but it's not a major problem in this weather! Unfortunately, one of the crew was killed. What a tragedy! He was such a nice man. He was from Burgundy and had three young children. I hurt my back a bit, but it turned out to be nothing serious.

But that's why I couldn't leave the base sooner. I can start flying again tomorrow."

"Let me get this straight: you were hit by a fighter, you had to parachute out of your plane over the sea and you're still talking about flying again tomorrow? Aren't you scared?"

"Let's talk about something else. As we're always saying, those are the risks of the job! We'll be luckier next time. And now I'm going to read your letter."

Phil opens the envelope and reads with pleasure that Victoria should be able to accompany him to the party at the Badvington base. He's recently found out more about this party.

"I'm glad that you can come. I will be very proud to have you by my side. Do you have a ballgown? Even if you don't, it doesn't matter, so long as you are there and on my arm!"

"I don't have a ballgown, but I intend to make one. I can sew you know. I had to learn when I was living in India. It proved useful."

"Perfect. The party is likely to take place on August 27th. Is that OK for you? It's the 15th. That leaves you 12 days to sew your dress! I'll confirm the date and the time at which we will come and collect you from here. Is that alright? Unfortunately, I can't stay longer. I have to go. I said I would only be out for half an hour and I'm on duty."

"Take care! Now I've got a ball to go to, I need a partner in good shape!" adds Victoria, joking to lighten the atmosphere, but with a heavy heart all the same.

Victoria watches Phil wistfully as he mounts his bicycle, and briefly prays that nothing serious will happen to him.

Phil soon arrives back at the airbase, happy in the knowledge that he will have a pretty date for this party. He had liked the way that Victoria looked scared when he had told her about the problems during his last mission. Maybe she cares about him more than he thought?

Back in his room, Phil finds two letters. The first envelope contains the response from Mrs Dumaine to the letter of condolence that he had sent her during his leave at Foyers, close to Loch Ness. This letter must have taken several months to reach its destination.

Letter from Françoise Dumaine to Lieutenant Colonel Philippe Destivel

Sir,

Thank you for taking the trouble to send me your condolences. Please excuse my tardiness in replying. I found it very difficult to manage after my husband's death, but I have to go on living and I have my three children to bring up.

I hope to be able to return to France soon, because I feel very alone here. I would be delighted to see you again if the occasion should arise.

Yours sincerely…

The second letter is from Maggy and is not unconnected to the first.

Letter from Marguerite Destivel to her son, Philippe

My dear Phil, prepare to be amazed. You'll never guess who I've just seen. I invited someone round for dinner tonight, a very nice woman who lives in Algeria. We met by chance at the airbase. It was Françoise Dumaine, the widow of Captain Dumaine. We spent a very pleasant evening together. She said that you had met and that you had sent her a letter of condolence from England. You little sneak! She's very brave and doesn't complain about anything. I thought she was very nice and I hope to see her again in France when we go home. I'll invite her round one Sunday for lunch so that we can meet her children, if she comes to Paris. Our money problems have been sorted out…

Phil smiles at these two letters, which arrived together, and at the initiative of his mother, who is managing, even at a distance, to interfere with his private life. He also thinks for a few moments about this young widow, whose children are still small and who doesn't have her mother around to help her look after them. What will she do when she returns to France? It's not easy to find a new husband when you have three children.

Victoria is radiant, happy to find that Phil is not dead as she had feared and delighting in the prospect of their forthcoming escapade. She hasn't had so much to be happy about since the start of the war.

In the next few days, she spends her time making her ballgown. Searching among her mother-in-law's things, she finds an organdy evening dress that is very old-fashioned, but made of a lilac material that has retained all its freshness. She gets to work, without delay, on the transformation of this dress, working relentlessly whenever she has a few spare moments.

17

LONDON, UNITED KINGDOM, AUGUST 1944

John has good days and bad days. His morale is less than solid. He often wakes up sad, with a low opinion of himself. The education he received from his father was focused on morality, sacrifice and giving. It has marked him for the rest of his days and is exacerbating the feelings of guilt that have invaded him. The enthusiastic welcome he received from his parents and their friends has only strengthened the feeling that he is a usurper who doesn't deserve to be called a hero. It was only to please them that he agreed to tell them about the precise circumstances in which he was awarded the DFC. He is finding the days long after three weeks at his parents' house and he needs a change of air, for a few hours at least.

He is intrigued by the anti-V1 defenses that have been set up in the south-east of London and decides to visit them, after a trip to the center of the capital. Flying bombs are launched every day and kill large numbers of people, even if it's now being said that many V1s are destroyed before they get to the city.

On August 20, a Wednesday, John tells his parents early in the morning that he needs to go to London to finalize the details for his posting to North Scotland, which is scheduled for September. He uses this excuse to stop them from trying to dissuade him from taking unnecessary risks by going to sites that are regularly bombed.

He arrives at the station at 8 o'clock and takes a train to the center of London. There are many stops along the way and it takes three hours to cover the 30 miles or so to King's Cross station.

John is amazed to see that the streets are teeming with people. He starts by walking south east down Farringdon Road. He occasionally hears a noise high above him in the sky that might be a flying bomb. He arrives in front of St. Paul's Cathedral and feels a need to go inside. Many Christians are already praying in this beautiful building fortunately spared by the succession of bombings since the start of the war.

John regrets having lost his faith. He would have liked to be able to pray to God and ask to be forgiven for his responsibility for the death of his navigator, which has become an obsession. But how can you pray to a God that you haven't believed in for years?

John leaves the cathedral and walks at random towards the west. He doesn't notice his surroundings and moves around like a robot for half an hour. He returns to reality when he reaches Trafalgar Square and passes in front of St. Martin in the Fields. John enters this church, attracted by its calm reflective ambiance, so like the atmosphere that had so seduced him at St. Paul's. He walks around slowly, regarding the church and the people in it. The parishioners seem very fervent. At the back of the church, on the left, there is a small, dimly lit room in which he can see a young man sitting next to a vicar and engaged in discussion with him. Maybe he's making some sort of confession? John watches the pair of them for a moment. He waits for about ten minutes, until the young man finally gets up and leaves the church looking relieved after receiving the advice and benediction of the vicar.

John sees the vicar get up slowly to leave the room. He isn't young and he seems tired. John hurries to join him and asks, feverishly, "Excuse me Reverend, I would like to talk to you. Do you have a few minutes to spare?"

"Yes, of course. I'm here this morning to talk to anyone who feels the need for my help or advice."

They sit down next to each other.

"So how can I help you?" asks the vicar.

"Reverend, remorse is eating me up. A few months ago I did something terrible that feels to me like a murder. I regret it enormously. I can't stop thinking about it and need to get it off my chest and tell someone about it."

The vicar, somewhat astonished, looks at him and says "Then I think you'd better tell me all about it!"

John tells him about his life as a pilot, his last mission, the period of amnesia and the recovery of his memory. He tells the story as if he were talking to a doctor rather than a clergyman and concludes by saying "Right now, my navigator should be with his wife and children. The pilot is supposed to be the last to leave the plane. I was completely in the wrong and I feel guilty."

"Yes, but you panicked. You didn't want to kill him deliberately. It's fine to regret what happened, but you shouldn't feel guilty about it. We are not necessarily masters of our own behavior in such circumstances. Your navigator was not in control of himself either. He shouldn't have blocked the way. God will recognize your merits. You have done well to recount this terrible episode in your life to a clergyman. Personally, I see you more as a courageous soldier than as an assassin. Be at peace my son."

John gets up, thanks the vicar and goes to sit quietly for a few minutes among the other parishioners in the church. He goes over the kind words of the vicar, a man like his own father. John feels lighter, as if a weight has been lifted from his shoulders. He leaves the church.

He walks, looking at the crowd around him, to Piccadilly Circus, where he spots the entrance to the Trocadero Hotel on the corner. He hasn't had anything to drink since early that morning, and he decides to go and quench his thirst in this superb environment that he has already heard much about from other airmen.

He goes in and finds the bar, sits down on a stool and orders a pint of lager and a sandwich, as he hasn't had any lunch. There are other members of the Royal Air Force here. He recognizes their uniforms. He is in civilian clothing, having not yet rejoined the ranks of the military. John thinks about his plans for the rest of the day. He must absolutely see these anti-V1 defenses in the south of the capital and he needs to find a way of getting there. It might take a long time.

An officer comes and sits down next to him. He's dressed in the uniform of another country that John cannot identify. He was wearing a forage cap when he arrived. He also asks for a beer. His accent is a bit difficult to place. John is intrigued and starts up a conversation.

"You're not British are you? Which Commonwealth country are you from? I'm having trouble guessing."

"That's probably because I'm not from the Commonwealth! Let me give you a clue. I'm from a country that the Allied forces are currently liberating? Does that make it easier?"

"Belgium? No? You must be French then?"

"Yes, French! My name is Philippe Destivel and I'm a bomber pilot from the Gaitford airbase."

"Oh, French! That's good. I didn't know there were French airmen in the RAF. My name's John Luxley. I'm a pilot too. Same job as you. Except that I've finished my tour of operation. I'm on holiday at the moment. Let's drink to the liberation of France and the defeat of Germany."

John is happy to be speaking to someone who isn't English.

"I've come to London for the day," Phil explains. "Business to take care of at the headquarters of the free French forces. To do with promotions, medals and salaries that haven't been paid. It was getting too complicated to do all that by post. I thought it would be easier to come and discuss our problems directly with the general concerned. I've just got out of the meeting. It went pretty well."

Phil and John get on well and are soon on first-name terms. John asks Phil lots of questions about where he is from, his family, his life in France and his time in Morocco. He seems to be more interested in Phil's civilian life than in his current activities. Phil asks him if he is a career military man and is surprised to learn that he is talking to a top-flight mathematician. John looks at the clock. It's one o'clock. He needs to hurry, but he has just had an idea.

"Phil, why don't you come with me to South London, to take a look at the anti-V1 defenses. I've heard they're spectacular."

"I wanted to spend some time in your capital, which I don't know very well. I've only been here once before, to talk to the RAF about a Bloch plane in 1935. But I'm not in any hurry. I'm staying till tomorrow, so OK, I'd like to come with you. How do we get there?"

"I've checked it out. We can take a commuter train from Victoria Station, close to here, all the way to Oxted in Surrey. The anti-V1 barrage balloons are located around there apparently. How does that sound?"

"Fine. Let's go!"

They walk rapidly to Victoria Station, where they find that there is a train leaving for their destination in twenty minutes. They sit on a bench in the station and wait. Phil is curious about John's past as a pilot.

"So you've just finished your tour of operations?"

"No, I actually finished a few months ago."

"Did you have any problems during your missions?"

"Yes, several times. The worst was the last one, which completely traumatized me."

John looks Phil in the eye and says "I'll tell you about it. It will do me good, but please don't judge me."

John then tells Phil precisely what happened. The end of the mission with the navigator who didn't want to jump, his period of amnesia, his nightmares and the hypnotherapy. At the end of his tale, he remains silent, waiting for Phil to say something. But his French colleague remains dumbstruck, so much so that John has to ask "You despise me, don't you?"

Phil stays silent for a moment longer and then says softly, "This war places us all in extreme situations. What matters is our long-term commitment. At any given moment, we do what we can. We all have a strong instinct for self-preservation. We can't do anything about that. You're still very young and you didn't hesitate to put your life at risk for a cause that you believed in. I don't see any reason to despise you. I just admire your commitment. The military is my career, my job. It's normal for me to fight a war. It's not like that for you. So where did the RAF send you at the end of your missions?"

"I've been working as a mathematician at the Bomber Command research center."

"What kind of work do mathematicians do there?"

"Several things. But it's mostly confidential. I'm a probability specialist and they asked me to think up a fairer system for determining when a tour of operations should end. You know, the thirty missions."

"Ah, that's interesting! It seems to me that no-one I know really knows how to evaluate the dangers we face. We don't talk about it much either! They tell us that, on average, the losses during each mission are about 3%. That's a pretty low risk. So how do you calculate the overall risk for 30 missions?"

"Would you like to know? Really?"

"Yes, really. Don't worry, I'm a natural optimist. Maybe if you explain it to me slowly I'll be able to understand! You know, I always worry about the others, but not really about myself. Probably just not aware of the dangers!"

"OK, let me explain. The calculation is simple. If you carry out one mission, your probability of coming back alive is 0.97. Are you with me so far?"

"Yes, that makes sense. Carry on."

"If you carry out two missions, the probability of remaining alive is 0.97 times 0.97. For thirty missions, you simply multiply 0.97 by itself 29 times. You can write that as 0.97 to the power of 30. Do you see?"

"Yes, that's clear enough. But what does that actually give, 0.97 to the power of 30?"

"0.4"

"And what does that 0.4 mean exactly?"

"It means that you have only a four in ten chance of still being alive at the end of a tour of operation."

"A four in ten chance! But that's less than a fifty-fifty chance of surviving! It's like putting six bullets in a revolver that can hold 10 and playing Russian roulette. Is it really that dangerous? Why don't they ask the crews to carry out fewer missions?"

"Too few trained airmen. You know, when there are more than a thousand planes converging on a target, there are 7000 airmen and about 200 deaths during the mission. You already need to replace those 200 men!"

John hasn't added an ounce of sadism to his detailed explanation of his calculations. Phil asked for an explanation and he has given one, as clearly as possible, without considering the potentially harmful effects on the morale of his French colleague.

For Phil, it's as if he just received an uppercut full in the face. In the space of just a few seconds, the magnitude of the risks he runs has come home to him. Risks that his superiors are fully aware of but don't want to talk about. He feels like a patient hearing from his doctor that he has a serious disease and a less than one in two chance of surviving! Pale, he loses his usual cool and starts to sweat, very ill at ease.

"Are you OK Phil? You look a bit funny? Is it because of what I just told you? Didn't you have any idea?"

"No, I didn't know! It's a bit difficult to take! It's alright for you, you've already finished. I'm still in the first third of my tour of operation and I've got two kids who have already lost their mother."

"I have finished my tour of operation, it's true, and for a few months I'm going to be an instructor. But after that, I'm volunteering as a pathfinder pilot."

"But that's even more dangerous! You're so young! And you've already given so much!"

"I need to expose myself to the risk. I want to make up for what I've done. That's just how it is and I can't do anything about it.

But come on, we need to get on the train now."

The train departs on time, gradually leaving the center of London and heading towards the south-eastern suburbs. Along the way, every half mile or so, they see gutted houses, rubble and still-smoking ruins. Some of the shops no longer have windows and the shopkeepers have replaced them with an assembly of wooden planks. At one point, four flying bombs pass over the railway, still high in the sky, leaving a trail of smoke in their wake. The racket they make resembles that of fighter planes and is not drowned out by the noise of the train. These V1s continue on their way to their murderous end some distance away.

The train stops at Oxted station and they get off. They ask the way to the best place to see the barrage balloons. They walk for half a mile and stop at the top of a small hill, from which they can see the impressive spectacle.

They can see more than a hundred large balloons inflated with hydrogen, suspended in the air more than 6000 feet above the ground. They are linked to the ground by steel cords, forming a line of defense against the flying bombs. When the wing or body of a V1 hits one of these cables, it rapidly explodes or changes trajectory, such that it is directed towards the least populous zones of London. When the clouds pass overhead, the balloons disappear from view, and all they can see is a forest of cables that seem to be standing upright in the air as if by magic. It's a surreal sight.

"Let's get a bit nearer. We'll be able to see better," suggests John.

They walk through open countryside, in the direction of the balloons. They are still about five hundred yards away when the sirens go off again. John is enthusiastic.

"It's our lucky day. We're going to see some fireworks!"

A couple of minutes later, they hear the growing rumble of the flying bombs and catch sight of several that will soon reach the barrage. Two V1s barely touch the cables and are deviated, continuing their flight in another direction. Another arrives at low altitude and passes the barrage unhindered, continuing to fly in their direction. They hear its motor stop suddenly, the sign that the V1 is about to dive, exploding as it reaches the ground. Phil understands the danger and cries "It's very dangerous here. Come on! Let's run!"

Phil runs with long strides into a field. John stays put and continues to watch the scene, fascinated, with his arms by his side, as if he is exposing himself to a redeeming force. A formidable explosion occurs. Phil is flung to the ground by the blast and is hit by some rubble flung into the air by the machine that has just exploded nearby. He remains on the ground, stunned, for a few moments, and then comes to his senses.

"John, John, where are you? Say something!" he cries at the top of his voice.

Thick smoke, burning debris where the bomb has smashed into the ground. Phil approaches carefully and sees a bloody body, immobile and lying on the ground. He quickly recognizes his friend, who does not answer him and displays no signs of life. Phil takes his pulse, first at the wrist and then at the neck. Nothing. John's heart is not beating. He must have been killed instantly.

Phil is shocked. If John had followed him, he would still be alive. Why did he stay rooted to the spot watching? It's as if John had wanted to expose himself to the danger and to die. What an enormous sense of guilt he must have!

Phil returns to Oxted and reports the accident that has just happened. Whilst walking, he spots another group of flying bombs overhead in the sky and, two minutes later, he hears the sirens. When he reaches the village, he encounters two WAAFs in uniform and he tells them what has just happened. Someone will have to retrieve the body and try to identify it. Phil can only remember the airman's first name. The WAAFs are not part of the health service and there is no nurse available. They go to find an ambulance that the eldest WAAF drives herself. Phil goes with them to direct them to the site of the incident. Phil's diagnosis is not called into question. Faced with the inanimate body of John, Phil imagines himself in a coffin. The younger of the two WAAFs explores the pockets of the victim and finds his dog tags, identifying him as an RAF pilot. The body will be easy to identify.

On his return to Oxted, Phil has to go to the town hall to give a report of the circumstances in which the accident occurred. He signs it, after providing all the necessary information about his identity, post and address.

At the end of the afternoon, he finds a train that takes him back to Victoria Station. He is stunned by the events of the day, which have taken him by surprise. Death has made two appearances in the proceedings. His new friend was killed in front of his very eyes and he has the impression that his own days are numbered. How long does he have left? A few months? Or, more likely, a few days? What a funny day this August 20, 1944! It has opened his eyes. He knew the risks associated with each operation, but he had not previously realized that, when you considered all the operations together, the 30 missions they were asked to complete exposed the airmen to such a high level of risk! None of his colleagues are aware of this either!

The war is no longer an impassioning experience like his training in Scotland. Will he still be able to enjoy the beauty of the seas of cloud under the light of the setting sun that he loves to discover a few minutes after take-off? He feels like a prisoner condemned to death awaiting his execution.

In his hotel room that evening, Phil thinks a lot about his

children. What will they do when he is dead? What will their life with their grandmother be like? Where will they live when they go back to France? This war is horrible. It shouldn't last much longer. But will he still be around to celebrate the victory? Probably not! But at least the sacrifice of his life might help to improve the world. In any case, there is no other way to halt the barbarism of the Nazis.

Phil finally falls asleep. His night is punctuated by dreams of the war. But, in the early morning, his dreams are sweeter. He is at home in Paris. He hears the doorbell, opens the door and sees Victoria. They throw their arms around each other and embrace, remaining entwined in each other's arms for a long time. Phil wakes up and thinks about the ball he is going to go to with Victoria. At least that's something pleasant to think about in the short term.

But Phil is no longer the same. He now wants to live his remaining days to the full. Every day counts and none of them should be wasted. Being really alive, that's what's most important to him now!

18

GAITFORD AND BADVINGTON, UNITED KINGDOM, AUGUST 1944

Gaitford airbase is in a frenzy on August 23. The BBC has announced the liberation of Paris, but has provided very little detailed information. The news becomes official on August 25, when General von Choltitz signs the documents surrendering Paris to the Allies. De Gaulle is in Paris. Phil is over the moon. The party at the French airbase at Badvington will be wonderful.

He passes by Victoria's studio in the evening. Phil hasn't been back to see her since his trip to London. She hears him arrive and lets him in.

"I heard the good news. Paris has been liberated. That must mean a lot to you."

"Ah, it's extraordinary. Paris has been occupied for four years. I must kiss you. I can die happy now!"

Phil approaches Victoria, hugs her and kisses her on each cheek.

"No, you mustn't die. What an idea! Have you been having morbid thoughts?"

"I went to London for a couple of days. I'll tell you all about it.

But, basically, I learned that I have little chance of still being alive at the end of all these missions. I already feel like a dead man walking. I see life differently now. I'm more focused on the present and I want to make the most of things!"

"Would you care to explain?"

"No, not now. I have more important things to talk about. Our ball is going to happen. I've organized everything. I thought we were going to go with two other colonels, in a little military bus with a driver. But I've found an alternative solution. I have some English friends that I often go to see at weekends. They belong to an association that is trying to maintain the morale of foreign airmen. They've offered to lend me a car and I've accepted. So, I will drive you there, if you still want to go. It will be more private. We'll have time to chat. Can I come and pick you up here at about six in the evening on August 27th? It will take us just under two hours to get there. We'll leave at about 11 and you should be back here for about one in the morning. Is that OK? And have you found yourself a ballgown?"

"I've been sewing like a maniac these last few days to do you proud! Six o'clock should be fine. Even a bit before if you like. The lady who's coming to look after my mother-in-law should arrive at about five o'clock. I'll leave in my normal clothes and I'll put my ballgown on when we get there. I'm very excited. I love dancing! And it's so long since I've had the chance!"

Phil prepares to leave. Before he goes, Victoria asks if he has any bombing missions before their escapade. Happily, he doesn't, and that reassures her. She didn't like his pessimism when he had spoken of his chances of being killed.

The next day, the day before the ball, Victoria thinks a lot about Phil and asks herself how much she means to him. He seems to like her, but he has always been very reserved or respectful. She wonders whether knowing that she is married, and to a colonel held prisoner in a German camp, stops him from thinking of her as a woman that he could get closer too. She also thinks about his widowhood. Have there been other women in his life since his wife died? At least they will have much more time to talk to each other during the journey.

August 27th rapidly arrives. Victoria makes herself beautiful. She perfumes herself with a little leftover *Vol de nuit* perfume from Guerlain. It makes her think of Phil, the name of this very Parisian perfume. She finds a big suitcase, which she fills with her ballgown, taking great care not to crease it. It is a sunny day, agreeably warm without being too hot. Victoria has found some high-heeled leather sandals. For the journey, she is wearing a straight floral-print dress that highlights her curves, and she doesn't forget to take a woolen cardigan for the evening, when it might be a bit cooler. She has tied her hair up in a chignon, which makes her look very attractive.

Phil arrives at quarter to six. He is in his lieutenant colonel's uniform and is wearing his medals, the *legion d'honneur* he received last year after the Tunisian campaign, and the *croix de guerre* he received recently, after the Berlin mission. When Victoria comes out to greet him, her beauty takes his breath away. Victoria is also swept away by Phil's appearance, when she sees him get out of a superb Triumph Dolomite. Each finds the other well turned-out and they compliment each other.

They carefully lay Victoria's suitcase down flat on the back seat and then set off rapidly. They look good together. They could be husband and wife, leaving on a trip. About 70 miles to cover, a bit under two hours as they will have to cross several villages. They feel great in their luxurious car. For a few hours at least, they will be far from the war. Phil is the first to speak.

"It's good to have some time to relax. I haven't had that in ages, several years in fact. Some moments to savor. It's good of you to come with me. There should be a good atmosphere at this French base. I've heard they've made some superb decorations for the occasion. Paris is liberated. That's highly symbolic. The war shouldn't last much longer. The Germans have no chance of winning now. I really hope to see their total defeat, but I'm not sure that I will."

"Why? Have you really become so pessimistic about your own fate?"

Phil tells her about his day in London, his meeting with John, the simple calculation of the risks run by the bomber crews, their walk near the barrage balloons and John's death.

"You know, Phil, you might have been born under a lucky star. You might be protected. Almost a one in two chance of surviving 30 missions you said, and how many missions have you completed already?"

"Nine."

"So, you've got just over 20 left. Your chances of staying alive must be greater now. Imagine your last mission. You'll only have a 3% chance of dying in that mission. Be more optimistic."

"OK. I'll try to think about other things. Tell me about your parents, your childhood, your family. I want to know more about you."

Victoria tells him about her birth and childhood in Cornwall, her parents, well-off shopkeepers, and their accidental deaths at sea when she was twelve. She's also an only child. Her teenage years, living with an aunt in London, one of her mother's sisters, a nice woman, but severe. And then her marriage, no doubt much too young, to a handsome officer.

The road is empty and in a fairly good state. Very few people, mostly farmers finishing their harvest. Arriving at a crossroads, Phil has to pile on the brakes because a horse-drawn hay cart pulls out in front of him unexpectedly. Instinctively, he places his left arm in front of Victoria to stop her from banging her head against the windscreen. She takes his hand, squeezes it and gently kisses it to thank him. He looks at her, smiling.

Phil then tells her about his problems with his mother, since she moved in and started looking after his children. He adds a large dose of humor and makes Victoria laugh.

"You're lucky to have children. We weren't able to have any. That didn't help matters. Maybe if we had had children, things might have been different. The doctor we consulted said the problem was with me, but the war would have made things even more complicated!"

Phil feels at ease in the intimacy of the car. The time flies past. At 7.30, they are nearing the base at Badvington. Only another five miles, Phil tells himself.

"There are lots of woods around here. Would you like to stop so that I can go and change somewhere, without anyone knowing?"

Phil turns left down a deserted dirt track heading into the undergrowth. He pulls over to the edge of the track and stops. An ideal changing-room. He helps Victoria to take her things out of the suitcase and walks a bit further away so as not to be in the way. When he comes back, he sees a princess. Her lilac organdy dress is perfectly cut and she's wearing a little tiara on her head that lends her a royal air.

"Am I going to this ball with a queen, then? I'll have to do my best to be worthy of you."

They set off again and, ten minutes later, they enter the Badvington airbase. People are arriving from everywhere. They park the car where they are told to and then go to the officers' mess, where the party is to take place. Lots of uniforms. Mostly French, but some British and Canadian uniforms too. Women are well represented. WAAFs and guests like Victoria, some of whom have come all the way from London. Victoria doesn't know anyone and that suits her just fine. She is beautiful, so alluring. Everyone is looking at her. Phil looks good too and his arrival in such a fancy car did not go unnoticed.

Victoria gives Phil her arm as they enter the corrugated metal hut that serves as the mess. The colonel who commands the base and the leaders of the two groups of bombers greet them. Phil knows them well. They are colleagues he knew in France and then in North Africa. Victoria speaks to them in French and tells them how happy she is to be at the party, especially now that Paris has been liberated. She seems to have worked her magic on them too.

On entering the mess, which is usually quite spartan, they are astonished by the sight that greets them. Refined decorations, wall hangings. They first pass through a bar, a replica of an airmen's bar from the First World War. There are several caricatures of officers hanging on the wall. The top-graded officers from the base are easily recognizable and the artists have not been kind to them! Under the drawings, someone has written a humorous comment: "Do not confuse grade and competence."

The next room houses a running buffet and the paintings on the walls are of landscapes and scenes from Morocco. The town of Meknes, an oasis with palm trees, renders some of those who have come from North Africa nostalgic. In the middle of the room, tables loaded with mountains of food. More than five thousand sandwiches to feed the guests! Little cream cakes, and, to top the whole thing off, an enormous *pièce montée* in the form of the Kasbah of Marrakech. Such marvels in wartime, when rations are limited. And, to quench everyone's thirst, 25 barrels of beer, prodigious quantities of whiskey, gin and French wine.

After the buffet, another room has been transformed into a

winter garden, with well pruned hedges, fountains of colored water and lighting effects.

Finally, two rooms for dancing, decorated with paintings. The first evokes Paris. A veritable artist has represented the *Place du Tertre*, with the restaurant of *Mère Catherine*. Another painting portrays Paris by night, as seen from the *Sacré-Coeur*. Victoria is enthusiastic about these paintings, which remind her of her time in Paris and she vaunts their pictorial qualities. They were painted by one of the pilots from the base. The other dance room is decorated by paintings summarizing the history of clothes through the ages, beginning with Adam and Eve, passing through the eras of cavemen and the wigged courtiers of Louis XIV, and ending up with the outfits of a bomber crew.

There must be almost five hundred people at this party. The musicians amongst the airmen at the base have formed a band that is playing in one of the dance rooms. In the other, there is a record player hitched up to an amplifier and some speakers.

At 8 p.m. on the dot, the commander of the base gives the signal for the party to begin. He starts by warmly thanking the British general under whose orders he works, Air Commodore Walton, who is present. He then announces that he has no intention of giving a speech and launches rapidly into a rendition of the *Marseillaise*. All the military men and civilians present who know the words begin to sing. Their enthusiasm is infectious, driven by the formidable hope born out of the highly symbolic liberation of the capital of France. Berets and military caps fly among the crowd. At the end of the national anthem, everyone yells *"Bravo!"* and *"Vive la France!"* The din lasts a good five minutes, until the band starts playing *"la Java bleue"*, a waltz that everyone knows. The sound of the accordion has everyone wanting to dance. The dancefloor rapidly becomes crowded.

"Would you like to dance with me this time, Madame?" Phil asks Victoria.

"Yes, this time I would love to, Colonel! In fact, I couldn't wait for you to ask. I love waltzing."

They start to waltz, each discovering the talents of the other as a dancer. Phil is very good and Victoria enjoys letting him lead her, with her complicit eyes gazing into those of Phil. They dance several waltzes and then go to get a drink at the bar. Both drink beer. Phil presents Victoria to his old friend, Lieutenant Colonel Viénot, who commands the Gascogne bomber group at this base. Victoria carefully observes this very pleasant man, who is not very tall, smiles a lot and has very little hair, but has piercing blue eyes and bucket loads of charm when he talks. They chat for a few minutes and then Phil and Victoria return to the dance floor.

"Your friend is no Apollo, but he's extremely charming. Shall we go back and talk to him?" teases Victoria.

Phil doesn't seem to be amused and does not respond.

"I'm only joking! You're even more charming Colonel!"

He looks at her tenderly. They walk hand in hand to the second dance room. The style is different there, more jazzy.

"It's a boogie-woogie Phil. I bet you don't know how to dance that!"

"That's where you're wrong. I learnt in Morocco, come on!"

Effectively, both of them dance very well to these North American rhythms, with a rapid alternation of fast and slow numbers, during which they sway to the music enfolded in each other's arms.

Several blues numbers like "There will never be another you" and "You don't know what love is" follow, bringing them even closer together.

The evening continues to be wild and warm. The luckier

airmen have come with their girlfriends. Others are drinking with their buddies. No sooner is a glass empty than it is refilled with whiskey or gin.

But, at a military base, the war is never too far away. Many will be back in the air fighting, the next day or shortly after. At 11 p.m. precisely, the Colonel announces the end of the party. The orchestra and the record player fall silent. Phil says goodbye to a number of his French colleagues and then returns to his car, with Victoria on his arm, to take the road home. It's still warm outside. The sky is clear. They can drive without headlights, using the full moon as their only illumination.

"I've never been to a party with such an atmosphere before. Thanks for asking me to come with you. What a breath of fresh air to liven up my otherwise dull life! I didn't want it to end," says Victoria.

"I was very proud to have such a beautiful partner on my arm. My friends were very flattering about you. They said that you were even more beautiful than this car! Some of them were a bit jealous and wanted to know if we were lovers."

"What did you tell them?"

"We've all spent some time in Morocco. I just said '*Inch Allah*'!"

Victoria doesn't understand this last phrase very well, but Phil prefers not to enlighten her. After a few minutes in the car, her eyelids become heavy and she yawns several times.

"All that dancing has worn me out Phil. You won't be annoyed if I have a little nap, will you?"

"Of course not. Rest your head on my shoulder, you'll be more comfortable."

Victoria falls asleep almost immediately, snuggled up against her driver who, fortunately, is not at all sleepy and makes the most of this moment of intimacy with his beautiful friend.

Rather than 'having a little nap', Victoria falls into a deep sleep that lasts until they arrive at the village of Gaitford.

"Oh, we're here already! I didn't notice the time pass. You were such a good pillow!"

Phil soon arrives at Victoria's house and parks in a field close to the entrance to her studio. He takes his partner's suitcase and opens the door for her. She gets out of the car, still just as magnificent in her ballgown, takes the hand of her driver and, without a word, they both enter the little house, her private kingdom.

Phil enters first and doesn't switch on the light. He places the suitcase on the floor, turns around and finds himself face to face with Victoria. He puts his arms around her neck, watching her intently in the shadows. They approach each other slowly and kiss properly for the first time. Passionately, their lips unite, their tongues meet, giving and receiving. Their kisses transport them, igniting a desire to explore their bodies. Phil carefully undoes Victoria's ballgown, while she takes off his tie and undoes the buttons of his shirt to reveal the skin of his chest.

Victoria is no longer wearing her dress and Phil is in his pants. They are still standing, pressed against each other, kissing and caressing. He strokes her generous but firm breasts and then undoes her bra, passing behind her to hold her breasts in his hands, caressing the nipples that have become hard, kissing her neck, there where the arteries are throbbing. He then runs his hand very slowly down to her abdomen, descending until he reaches her pubic hair, the sensation of which excites him beyond measure.

Face to face again, Victoria begins to rub her hand against Phil's pants. She undoes them and wraps her right hand delicately around his erect manhood. Phil takes off his pants. They find themselves naked, their bodies touching. She leads him to the bedroom, where a large bed awaits them.

They lie down side-by-side, facing each other, discovering each other first with their hands and continuing with their kisses. Phil lies Victoria down on her front, caressing her round buttocks. He turns her onto her back, exploring her erogenous zones, pressing gently. Phil is on his knees next to her body, which arches, stiffens and undulates. She is breathing rapidly and she is impatient for him to penetrate her. He realizes this and slowly eases into her, brushing against the inner lips. He slides into her easily because she is so excited, almost in a trance and very moist.

Phil remains inside her for a long time, his body covering that of his lover, almost coming out of her to burrow into her again ever more deeply. He fingers her clitoris, which has become very firm. Victoria rapidly explodes in pleasure, animated by endless spasms of joy. Phil ejaculates, whispering words of passion.

They have wrapped themselves up in the sheets. Victoria is lying with her head on Phil's shoulder. They talk about how good it was. The tension decreases and they are bathed in tranquility. They sleep with their bodies snuggled against each other until early in the morning.

Victoria wakes up first. The room is subtly lit by daylight, allowing her to watch Phil, who is still asleep. She finds him very handsome and lifts the sheets to contemplate his body. She doesn't know whether he will have to leave in a rush to get back to his planes or whether they will be able to linger and make love again. She gets up carefully so as not to wake Phil and goes to quench her thirst, wash her face and brush her hair. She puts on a nightdress, goes to her studio and retrieves some drawing paper and charcoal. She deftly sketches her naked lover, thinking that he is still adrift in a sea of dreams, without realizing that kindly eyes are observing and admiring him.

Later, Phil opens one eye, and then the other, and sees his lover with a tray, two cups of steaming tea and some scones. He sits up in bed, smiling, wide-eyed at the sight of his ravishing and attentive Victoria.

"For a few seconds, I forgot where I was and that life could be so good. You're not going to throw me out just yet are you? Do we have a bit more time?"

"I'm free until tonight; what about you?"

"The same. Incredible!"

They drink their tea. But they soon put their cups down to lie down again and recommence their caresses. Their desire rapidly increases and they make love again, happy to rediscover the warmth, curves and sensations of their bodies.

Victoria runs a hot bath. Naked, without embarrassment, they sit facing each other in the bath, playing with the water and splashing each other like children. Phil leans towards Victoria, bringing him closer to her so that he can caress her breasts and her thighs under the water, stroking her skin right up to the pubic hair. He is excited and his penis becomes erect. They stand up and wash each other, with water at first, and then with soap, rubbing against each other. Victoria caresses Phil's manhood, which she has covered in foam, and she rubs it against the palm of her hand. She crouches down, washes off the bubbles with some water, and voraciously takes his penis into her mouth. They have both been starved of love for so long that their desire shows no signs of abating. They go back to bed. From time to time, naked, they like to look at each other, their hands continuing to discover and stroke their bodies. Then, covered with no more than a sheet, they talk about love and kiss.

Towards 11 in the morning, they start thinking about going out somewhere. Phil still has the car and suggests that they go and eat lunch at a country inn about 15 miles away that he has already been to with his English friends. Victoria agrees. Very few Gaitford natives should be there, particularly on a Monday. They go and it's open. They receive a warm welcome and have lunch in the garden, in the shade of a weeping willow.

They talk more about their childhood and youth. Victoria never talks about her husband, who seems to be definitively out of the picture. Phil doesn't talk about his family either. They are both living like single people with no constraints.

After lunch, they don't leave straight away, instead walking hand in hand in the surrounding forest. They walk for a long time and then, tired, they lie down in the grass under a lime tree a little out of the way. Victoria is sprawled out over the grass with her head on Phil's stomach.

"It feels good to be with you. I'd forgotten that kind of happiness. I don't want it to end. I wonder what the future will bring?"

"Me too. I want to stay with you for as long as possible. I like you a lot Colonel! Let's make the most of the here and now! In a country at war it's difficult to make plans. Anything can happen from one day to the next."

The two lovers remain snuggled up together on the ground for a long time, without talking, concerned about what might happen in the future. Towards 5 p.m., they have to return to Gaitford. They get up and retrace their steps back to the car. Both of them want to know when they will be able to see each other again. Phil doesn't think he will be able to get any time off before the following Sunday. Six days! That seems like such a long time. When they get back to Victoria's house, they say goodbye with a lingering kiss.

Victoria is glad to have met Phil, a man she finds charming, often funny and very handsome. She feels that she is in love, even though their relationship has only just begun. He seems so decent, and that reassures her in her very chaotic life. But the war complicates everything. If the Germans lose, and that seems very likely in the near future, then her husband will be released and will come home. Victoria has no bad feelings towards her husband, but she doesn't want to live with him anymore. She is still young and she loves her freedom. They don't have children and she has wanted to leave him for several years. But it's impossible for the moment. She can't do that to someone who is likely to come back very weak after four years in very difficult conditions in a camp. The months following the end of the war are going to be a trial, because she will have to look after a man that she no longer loves while longing to spend time with her lover, who is free, even if he does have major family responsibilities.

For the moment, all she can do is make the most of the moments she can steal with her lover, who risks his life on a daily basis. It's much better than not having a lover, but it's extremely stressful knowing that the person she cares most about in the world might leave in great shape in the evening and not come back the next day, because it was his turn to die. Curiously though, she doesn't want the war to end too quickly, because that would hasten the return of her husband and the probable departure of Phil.

She goes back to her mother-in-law in the main house and relieves the lady who has been looking after her for the 24 hours.

On the way back, Phil reflects that life is good with Victoria. To hell with the rest! Phil blanks out completely the existence of her husband, a high-ranking officer and prisoner of the Germans. He is less than enthusiastic to find himself back at the airbase after returning the car to his friends. It now feels him with dread: death's waiting room! Oh, if only this war could stop right now! Why don't the Germans capitulate? They must see that they are being pushed back on all fronts. They've lost in Russia. They were unable to invade Britain. The Italians, their only allies in Europe, have been beaten.

They've been chased out of North Africa and the Allies have landed in Normandy. All they can do now is retreat back eastwards. They've already lost Paris.

Phil goes to bed early and sleeps straight through the night, without being awoken by the planes making their way to join the stream heading towards the Ruhr valley. He gets back into the swing of things the next day. British High Command asks him to get 10 crews ready for August 30, and another six for August 31. He volunteers himself for the mission on the last day of the month.

19

MEKNES, MOROCCO, END OF AUGUST 1944

Maggy is delighted to hear that Paris has been liberated. She had lived there until the German advance of June 1940 and her belongings are still in the apartment in *rue Lecourbe* that she had had to leave in such a hurry with the children before going first to Bordeaux and then to Vichy, where she found herself in the middle of nowhere for a whole year. It had been very difficult to live in three hotel rooms for 12 months. But the departure for North Africa had been exciting, because she had never left France before.

Now it's high time for her to go back to the country of her birth. It's the end of August. It should be possible to go back by mid-September. She is in a hurry and can't see any reason to fester any longer in such a hot country. She needs to talk to her friends about it, or at least those who were living in France before the war. They must also want to go back to the mother country. Maggy decides to go and consult with those she knows best the next day. On August 28, before going to bed, she takes a pencil and paper, prepares for battle and draws up a list of all the people she will contact. The wives of high-ranking officers. Their support will add extra weight to her arguments.

Maggy gets up early. She has asked her friend Slimane to act as her driver. Paul and Claire are still at scout camp, so she is free to go where she likes, when she likes. She starts by getting Slimane to drive her to Germaine's house. Germaine is the wife of Squadron Leader Vigard, who is also at the Gaitford airbase. She is a bit taken aback to see Maggy arriving at 8.30 in the morning. Maggy wastes no time getting down to business.

"Hello Germaine. I've come to see you early because I want to get our return to France organized as quickly as possible now that Paris has been liberated. I'm afraid we're going to have our work cut out twisting the arms of the men in command here. Things might go a bit faster if we work together. What do you reckon?"

It's undoubtedly a bit direct, but Maggy is a woman of action and not one to encumber herself with oratory convolutions.

"Maggy, you've caught me a bit off guard. I haven't even thought about that. Like you, I was living in Paris until the surrender in 1940. But I don't know what's happened to our apartment and I can't see myself going back without my husband. The war isn't over yet. The army is looking after us here, we're getting money. Our children are going to school. I think you're getting ahead of yourself. I'll write to my husband to find out what he thinks about it."

Maggy is disappointed. Germaine has said that she will write to her husband. But the post takes at least three weeks to get to England from Morocco. A month and a half to get a reply. What a joke! She can't possibly wait that long!

"Why do you need to write to your husband? This is about you! I'm certainly not waiting for the post to go backwards and forwards between me and my son to get things moving. It's my business much more than my son's. Think about it! If you carry on doing nothing, you'll still be here in a year. Let me know if you change your mind. Afterwards it will be too late. If there's enough room for 10 people in the plane, there won't necessarily be enough for 12 or 13. I'd better be on my way. Goodbye!"

Things haven't started as well as Maggy had hoped. But she isn't really all that surprised. She had always found this woman a bit spineless. After Germaine, she goes to see Thérèse, the wife of Captain Jopet, Phil's deputy at Gaitford. Same speech from Maggy, but an even more pessimistic response, almost moralistic even.

"But Maggy, the war isn't over. The Germans aren't beaten yet. There are even rumors doing the rounds that they might have secret weapons. We're safe here. You can't put your grandchildren at risk. Think of Paul and Claire! Your son would never agree. He's a reasonable man."

Maggy is furious, but still determined, when she leaves. It is dawning on her that any collective action is doomed to failure. It will be better for her to handle things on her own, but how? She thinks about it for the rest of the day and develops a strategy. Why not leave Meknes with the children, get herself driven northwards, to a port like Tangiers, find a boat and then go to Spain? It's a short crossing. Afterwards, with a bit of cash, it would probably be easy to get back to France, and then to Paris. She just needs to have enough ready cash on her for this little adventure. The principal problem worrying Maggy is the roadblocks on the roads in Morocco. You can't go more than a dozen miles without running into a military patrol stopping cars and asking for identity papers. The obvious solution is to hitch a ride to the Mediterranean in a military bus, to get round all the controls.

Maggy has an idea. She liked Warrant Officer Fieschi who had helped her solve her financial problems a while ago when Phil's salary wasn't being paid. She will go and see him and get him involved in her plans. He won't refuse to help her if she argues her case properly and diplomatically slips him a few banknotes.

The next day, she asks Slimane to drive her to the airbase. At the gate, she laboriously argues that she should be let in on the grounds that she is the mother of a lieutenant colonel. This approach eventually pays off. They let her car in after Warrant Officer Fieschi agrees to see her without an appointment.

Fieschi remembers her. He had been moved by her account of her son leaving for England while she looked after her two grandchildren.

"I would like to return to France as soon as possible now that Paris has been liberated. All my family is in Paris and the suburbs. I don't want to be left rotting here for months. I can't stand it anymore. I've come to see you to get your help. I need to be driven to a Mediterranean port, with my grandchildren, in a military vehicle. I need you to arrange that for me."

Maggy brazenly pulls out a bundle of banknotes that she places on the warrant officer's desk. He looks wide-eyed in amazement.

"That's for you and your colleagues taking part in the expedition. Yes, I insist, it's only right!"

The warrant officer is alarmed but nevertheless takes the money, which he slips into an envelope.

"Come back at 10 o'clock tomorrow morning," he says, "I'll see what I can do."

He sees Maggy out quickly, claiming that he has a mountain of administrative tasks waiting for him.

Maggy is jubilant. She understands human nature and she knows that people can't resist her charm and her banknotes for very long. She goes home. There's a lot to do because her grandchildren will return soon from their scout camp and she will have the laundry to sort and wash.

During the night, she dreams of Paris, a town she will see soon, Bois-Colombes, her friends and her cousins. All that is very exciting and her son will have to congratulate her on her decisiveness. The next day, she prepares for battle early, to go and see the warrant officer.

Fieschi makes her wait in an office for almost an hour, which annoys her. You shouldn't make the mother of such a highly graded airman wait that long! She will give him a piece of her mind. The warrant officer finally comes to get her, looking a bit on edge.

Maggy is thrown off her stride by the appearance of the colonel commanding the base at Fieschi's side.

"Mrs. Destivel," he says, "Warrant Officer Fieschi has told me a rather strange story about you. I do hope he misunderstood you. It seems you wish to leave Morocco incognito, of your own volition, with your grandchildren, to go back to Paris, and you need a military vehicle. This is all rather awkward. Out of respect for your son, whom I hold in the highest esteem, I won't waste too much time remonstrating with you. But you must know that your approach is rather odd. You must remain here with your son's children for the moment. The war is not over yet, unfortunately. Be patient and follow your son's instructions when the time comes. No going it alone. Got that?"

Maggy is ashamed to have to submit to the remonstrances of an officer little older than her son. She needs to find a way of saving face.

"Yes Colonel. Maybe I got a bit carried away, but I have a sister in poor health in France and I wanted to help her. But I understand what you are saying. I'll bear it in mind. Thank you Colonel."

The Colonel shakes her hand.

"Goodbye my dear lady. Come and see me if you have any problems and don't forget what I said."

The colonel passes her the envelope containing the banknotes that she had given to Warrant Officer Fieschi the day before. Maggy blushes to the tips of her ears and looks daggers at Fieschi as he accompanies her out of the office. He can't help smirking as he says, "I think it's better like this. Your safety and that of your grandchildren is at stake. Look after them. Goodbye, Mrs. Destivel."

20

GAITFORD, UNITED KINGDOM, END OF AUGUST 1944

It occurs to Phil that if something happens to him during a mission Victoria wouldn't know about it. This last weekend has created a bond between them. He feels very attached to Victoria. She has become his lover. It's not reasonable to leave things to chance. He needs someone to confide in, someone discreet that he can tell what to do if anything should happen to him!

The colonel wouldn't be a good choice. He's not someone with whom it would be easy to talk about private matters, although he was at the Badvington party and spoke to Victoria for a moment. He is not very jovial and many of the airmen hate him.

Phil comes up with the idea of talking to his deputy, Captain Jopet. They never fly the same missions, because he is responsible for replacing Phil if Phil is not available or if he should die. He hasn't met Victoria and it's probably better that way.

On Wednesday August 30, Phil enters the officers' mess at lunchtime. There are a number of airmen listening to Lieutenant Perrin, who is playing the Warsaw concerto on the piano, as is his wont. This short but grandiose work by Addinsel has become familiar, almost a refrain, to the ears of the airmen, because Perrin plays it so frequently. Phil spots Jopet and asks him to come to his quarters after coffee.

The captain is punctual and knocks on his door at 2.30 p.m. Phil gets straight to the point.

"Thanks for coming. I want to talk to you about something personal. I have a charming lady friend, an Englishwoman I met here by chance. If anything should happen to me, someone will need to tell her about it, whether I am dead, missing, injured or a prisoner. Do you see what I mean? I thought that you might be the ideal person. Would you do that for me? Of course, I would need you to be discreet."

"Of course. I understand entirely. I won't say anything to anyone. You just need to tell me how to get in touch with her, her name, her address."

"Her name is Victoria Miller. She lives in a big house, on the right of the Yale road, about three hundred yards to the north of Gaitford. When you're facing the house, you can see a smaller building on the right. You have to take the little dirt track on the right, running along this smaller building. It brings you directly to a gate with a letterbox. You can leave letters in the letterbox. It's also possible to open the gate and knock at the door of the smaller building. Victoria spends her time there. She's a painter and it's her studio. But I do hope you won't need to go there."

"I've memorized what you just told me and I'll write it down, just to make sure. This woman, is she the one that went with you to the party at Badvington? I've heard that she was really magnificent, looking like a queen, at the ball. How did you meet her?"

"A lucky catch. I went fishing and caught her as well!"

"So is she free, this lady friend of yours?"

"Not really. I'll tell you a secret. She's married to an older man, a colonel, who is currently being held prisoner by the Germans. I initially saw that as an insurmountable obstacle, but I've recently become aware of the risks we run and how unlikely we are to get out of this situation alive. That taught me to see my life differently. I realized that since the death of my wife, seven years ago, I've only really been half alive. It's time to change all that. Victoria has brought me back to life and the time I spend with her is fabulous. No future, no plans, just the here and now. That's enough for me. There you go, now you know everything!"

Phil thanks his deputy, who returns to his own occupations. Relieved to have prepared the ground in advance, just in case, he can now participate in the bombing mission planned for the next day without worrying.

On Thursday August 31, thirteen planes from the Aquitaine group go to destroy V2 storage sites in the north of France. Phil is one of the airmen involved in this mission, which is taking place in broad daylight. There is a lot of cloud cover. It's difficult to see the targets. Only three planes manage to release their bombs after several passages, taking advantage of holes in the clouds to get a glimpse of the ground, to determine exactly where they are. Phil isn't one of the lucky ones. The master bomber asks those who still have their bombs on board to give up and return to base. They will have to drop the remaining bombs over the North Sea. There is a lot of German flak and several planes have been hit. Nothing too serious, fortunately. All the airmen of the group manage to make it back to base, safe and sound.

On their return, after the debriefing, Phil counts his missions. Ten, he has carried out ten missions. Only 20 left, provided the rules stay the same. Phil doesn't realize it, but things are improving. He now has more than a one-in-two chance of surviving! He has crossed the Rubicon.

At the end of Friday afternoon, he cycles to Victoria's studio to place a letter in her letterbox, asking her at what time he can come on Sunday and explaining that he doesn't have any missions programmed for the next few days after Sunday. She's not at home. He comes back the next day to look for a response. He finds a short letter that she has written for him, in French.

[5]*Mon chéri, j'ai tellement envie de te revoir. C'est dur d'attendre toute une semaine en craignant pour ta vie. Viens vers 18 heures, je serai dans mon atelier et si je n'y suis pas, patiente quelques minutes. Je nous préparerai un dîner. J'espère que tu pourras rester longtemps. J'ai trop hâte de te voir. Victoria.*

These sweet words, words of love that he hasn't heard since he was engaged to Anne, make Phil very happy. He is pleased to see that she uses the "tu" form when writing to him. He will call her "tu" as well, when they see each other.

Phil has a lie-in on Sunday morning, dozing and thinking about his lover, reliving the tender and intense moments of the preceding weekend, during and after the Badvington party, where she was like a princess.

The weather turns and it rains during the afternoon. But the sky clears towards five o'clock and rays of sunshine reflect off the wings of the planes, glittering as they leave their hangars.

Phil is punctual and arrives at 6 o'clock. He knocks discreetly at the door to the studio. No-one comes. He goes in and finds the house empty. There is a package and on the table in the studio, together with a note that reads "Open it, it's for you. A present from an admirer! I'll be there as soon as I can."

---

[5] My darling, I so want to see you again. It's hard waiting a whole week and worrying about you all the time. Come towards 6 p.m. I will be in my studio and, if I'm not, wait for a few minutes. I'll cook us dinner. I hope that you can stay for a long time. I can't wait to see you. Victoria.

He unwraps his present and finds a small painting showing a man asleep in a large bed. He is partly covered by a sheet, but his shoulders are exposed. His face is depicted in profile. His eyes are closed. Phil has no trouble recognizing himself.

"It will console me when you're not here."

He hadn't heard Victoria come in.

"I drew a sketch in charcoal while you were asleep early last Monday morning. I added some color during the week. Do you like it?"

"I prefer you!"

They soon find themselves standing, entwined in each other's arms. Their lips find each other. Their tongues spice up their kisses. They fell a need to embrace. Phil escorts his girlfriend to the bedroom. For the time being, that's all she asks. He undoes her blouse, button-by-button, and slides in the palm of his hand to support and caress her breasts, which excite him so much. They soon find themselves naked, lying down and eager to devour each other. She strokes his manhood and places it in her mouth while his hand strays to her pubic hair and the jewel it contains. They take their time and slow the rhythm to prolong their pleasure. But their excitement becomes unbearable, leading them to endless spasms of pleasure, accompanied by moans and words of love. They remain snuggled up against each other for a long time, without speaking. Phil gets up first and comes back with the painting of him asleep.

"I like what you've done. I'm glad it's not an abstract painting. Can I take it with me?"

"It's my first gift to you. Lovers should surprise each other by giving each other presents from time to time. Don't you think?"

"I get it. I'll cover you in presents! I wanted to say that I like it when we speak French, because we can say "tu". It's a shame that there isn't a distinction between "tu" and "vous" in your language."

Victoria then gets up, naked and unembarrassed. Phil admires her feminity, her slim waist, the cute dimples at the base of her back, her abundant pubic hair and her firm buttocks. Victoria wraps herself up in a sheet, which makes her resemble an Ancient Roman in a toga. She tells Phil to rest while she prepares dinner. He dozes for a few minutes, takes a shower and then he appears, also draped in a toga.

"I managed to find a salmon. Do you like salmon?" she asks.

The salmon reminds Phil of his lunch with Lily, the little shepherdess. He has already told Victoria about it, but now he talks about the episode in more detail.

"But didn't you want to jump on her when you were lying side-by-side in the grass?"

"Yes, I did, but I restrained myself. She was no more than a child, all alone in the mountains, and I had to leave her an hour later! Not all men are animals you know!"

"Really? I thought you were all great beasts!" she exclaims, laughing.

"Yes, all except me!"

"I love you even more for that, my angel!"

They eat their dinner in the togas they have fashioned from their sheets. They have opened a bottle of white wine.

"A bottle of Corton-Charlemagne 1939 that I swiped from my mother-in-law's wine cellar. Do you think it will still be good?"

"Probably. It's one of the best white wines of France."

Effectively, it is wonderful and it goes very well with

Victoria's salmon. Their dinner is joyful. They continue to talk about their childhood and adolescence, but avoid talking about their marriages. Phil doesn't want to provoke memories that will make him sat, and Victoria is trying to conceal her ambiguous position as the wife of a colonel held prisoner by the Germans. They both count their futures in minutes, or hours, but don't think any further ahead than that. They don't know what the future holds for them and they cannot even begin to guess.

When the time comes to taste the apple pie that she has cooked, Phil gets up and teases her, tugging at the sheet covering his lover. She is amused and doesn't stop him and, once she is completely naked in her kitchen, she does the same to Phil's toga.

"Come on, let's go take a break in the bedroom. The pie can wait."

"We're like Adam and Eve. But I hope there's no forbidden fruit in the pie?"

"You'll see."

They are like two sweethearts, laughing and impatient to rediscover the pleasures they have missed for so long.

Desire soon gets the better of them. They are beginning to know their bodies and their reactions better. It makes their caresses even more exotic. Their antics lead them to the shower, where they soap each other, enjoying each other's forms and muscles, whilst continuing to kiss passionately. Their aquatic delights are followed by the tasting of the apple pie. They then fall asleep in each other's arms. At midnight, Victoria wakes Phil up.

"I have to go look after my mother-in-law. It's a pain, but I don't have the choice. Will we see each other again soon? Don't forget to stay alive, Phil! I can't live without you now! Do you think that we will be able to carry on seeing each other?"

Phil doesn't answer because he doesn't know what will happen in the future. They hug each other very tightly. As she leaves, Phil says very tenderly, "I think I love you, Madame!"

Victoria walks out of the room smiling, but moved, her eyes damp.

21

GAITFORD, UNITED KINGDOM, SEPTEMBER 1944

Lieutenant Colonel Destivel is in a hurry to finish the operations underway on Saturday September 9. He has spent a lot of time organizing the three missions this week, but his girlfriend has been ever-present in his mind. She is with him all the time in spirit, even when he is flying his plane. Victoria has arranged to be free at lunchtime and for the few hours immediately afterwards the next day.

Thirteen planes from the Aquitaine group are leaving to destroy German positions this afternoon. Phil is going along on this mission, which should take him over Le Havre, where the German resistance is still fierce. The Allied landings in Normandy took place more than two months ago, but the town of Le Havre is still in German hands. Allied high command wants to finish the job and has increased the number of bombing missions over enemy positions. Almost three hundred planes are going to converge on the town.

The planes leave towards 1.30 p.m., after the usual briefings. This mission is taking place in broad daylight, but the weather is not great. A few drops of rain here and there. A strong wind. But the cloud cover is an advantage too, as it should hide them for longer. Phil thinks that the mission will be abandoned, but the weather forecast for the target must be better than those at Gaitford. He takes off last.

An hour and a half to reach the target. No German fighters over the Channel. In a few minutes, Phil will have to order the release of the bombs his plane is carrying. The ground is very difficult, if not impossible, to see. Let's hope that there aren't any French civilians in amongst the enemy positions!

The master bomber transmits the following message over the radio:

"Mission abandoned. All bombers to return to base. Cloud cover too heavy. Bombs to be released over the sea during the return journey."

The airmen are disappointed. They don't like being stopped in the middle of their bombing runs. They were almost there! What a waste!

A quarter of an hour later, they are over the sea. Phil asks his bombardier to release all the bombs in the hold. They can immediately feel that the plane is much lighter. Five tons less. Another hour and they will be home. They haven't run into any fighters and there was no flak.

For the first time, they have red, white and blue cockades marked on the fuselage and wings of their planes. It was only yesterday that the British authorized the use of French markings. They certainly took their time!

Phil can see the Gaitford airbase. His navigator has directed them perfectly. He receives permission to land on the main runway. He concentrates hard, as it is important for him that his landings are perfect. He isn't group leader for nothing and he must lead by example.

He decreases speed and, satisfied, approaches the start of the runway, only some feet from the ground. He descends again and lifts the nose of the plane slightly. The landing gear scrapes the ground and Phil decreases the gas further. Suddenly, he is deafened by an enormous explosion. He doesn't know what is happening. The plane is no longer responding!

He loses consciousness for a few instants. When he comes round, groggy, he can see flames licking the cockpit in front of him, very close to where he is sitting. The intercom is dead. He understands the danger and realizes that the front of the plane is crushed and gaping wide open. He wants to get up, but he can't. He tries again. Impossible! Is he paralyzed? He realizes that he is still wearing his safety belt. He unclips it, gets up from his seat and sees that he is only a couple of yards above the ground. He can jump, but everything around him is on fire, and there are flames on the ground too. Never mind, he has no choice. He jumps into the inferno. He hasn't noticed that he has lost a glove and that his hand is injured.

He lands safely on the ground and starts running in the flames to get as far away from the plane as possible. He hears the sharp and piercing sound of the machine gun cartridges set off by the fire. Ambulance sirens signal the arrival of help. Phil is picked up by the ambulance men, who transport him to their vehicle on a stretcher. Disorientated, he loses all sense of time and finds himself at Peterborough Hospital.

He isn't dealt with immediately. No fractures, or, apparently, internal injuries, but he has serious burns. The doctor tells him that he is going to be transferred to Rauceby Hospital, which specializes in treating the injuries of RAF airmen.

Rauceby is about 40 miles away. When he arrives, after traveling for an hour and a half, he asks about the other members of his crew. He is told that they will soon be arriving too. Phil is undressed. His right hand looks odd. Blackened flesh, not very pretty. Certain parts of his face sting, as do his back and legs. A photographer arrives and takes pictures of the affected parts of his body. He is then bandaged and transferred to a bed. He is given a sedative injection and falls asleep straight away.

Phil remains unconscious until the next morning. He has difficulty waking up and asks what happened to him. He is told that a bomb that had gotten stuck in the hold under the right wing had exploded on landing.

He goes to pieces when he learns that he is the only survivor of the accident. All the other members of the crew were killed on the spot, blown apart by the shards of the thousand-pound bomb. He had been protected by the protective shielding behind the pilot's seat. There is no copilot in a Halifax, making the protection of the pilot, by means of a thick sheet of metal, paramount. Phil is in tears. He has been flying with the same crew for several months. They supported each other, they knew each other well and they were always joking. No tension. Almost like a group of buddies, even if most of them were ten or 15 years younger than he was. Six deaths!

He remains prostrate in his bed all morning, indifferent to his burns and not asking about his state of health. He is in a room with four beds. Two of the beds are empty and the remaining bed is occupied by an English airman in a coma who dies towards the end of the morning. Third degree burns over too large an area. Seventy per cent of the surface area of the body destroyed. He had no chance of survival.

A doctor comes to inform him that he will have to take his first burns bath, and that he must be brave. He is transported to a treatment room, in the center of which is a bath filled with lukewarm water and antiseptics. The nurse starts to remove his bandages. First the face and the head, then the right leg, which is not pretty. Finally, gently, she exposes his right hand. It's far from enjoyable, but Phil grits his teeth and puts up with it without flinching. The sight of his hand, grilled on both sides, repulses him. He asks for a bowl as he needs to be sick. He also has extensive burns on part of his back. Once he is in the bath, they meticulously remove small pieces of dead skin and flesh. When these operations are complete, the nurse calls the surgeon, a Dr Archibald McIndoe.

"Dr McIndoe is still young, but he's our major burns specialist. A star from New Zealand," she tells him. "He works wonders. You'll be safe in his hands."

At which, the surgeon arrives and examines Phil thoroughly.

"There's a lot of work to be done, but you've been pretty lucky. On the face, skull and back, the burnt areas are quite large, but only first or second degree. Well bandaged, those areas should heal all by themselves in a few weeks. Your right hand is more of a problem, but we'll be able to sort it out. Maybe in two steps. Do you have any questions?"

"Yes, how many days will I need to stay here, Doc?"

"Days? More like two or three months. It will feel like ages no doubt, but you won't suffer. If your right hand is just too ugly and you're uncomfortable with it, then we might carry out a skin graft on that hand, not straight away, but in a few months. We'll take a piece of skin from the thigh."

What he has just heard is not exactly music to his ears, but he has seen so many guys completely deformed and disfigured in the corridors of this place that he doesn't feel he has the right to complain.

What upsets him is thinking about Victoria, who must be waiting for him. It's Sunday. They were supposed to meet. Jopet must have had to go and tell her. She must be as disappointed as he is. How will they communicate now. She can send him letters, but he can't write back, unless he can find a scribe among the injured at the hospital. She doesn't have a telephone. Two months without being able to see her! That's just too long! What kind of shape is he going to be in, in two months' time? Will he be presentable? Or repulsive, with a damaged face and a healed but horrible-looking hand?

It's six in the evening at Gaitford. Captain Jopet is returning from a problem-free mission over Octeville in Normandy. Good visibility, precise bombing, no flak, no fighters. The Germans are losing strength in this region. Le Havre is on the point of falling. There is talk of the last hangers-on of the Wehrmacht still there surrendering. But the town has been almost entirely destroyed. The captain has taken over command of the Aquitane group since Destivel's hospitalization.

Jopet thinks about his group leader. What bad luck, poor old Phil! But, he'll be OK. And the missions are over for him. At least for a while. He's out of danger. Unfortunately, we're not!

The captain suddenly thinks about what Phil asked of him. To go and see Victoria Miller if anything happened to him. He'll go on his bike after the debriefing, which probably won't take long. None of the planes were hit. Everyone returned safe and sound. Fortunately! Six deaths already, the day before, those of Destivel's crew, for whom there will be military honors at the Harrogate cemetery in three days' time. That will be really hard. Everyone liked those guys. They were one hell of a team.

After the debriefing, he gets changed and cycles out to the village. He has no trouble finding a house matching Phil's description and he glimpses the small building next to it that must be the lady's studio. He follows the instructions Phil gave him, opening the gate and knocking on the door of the smaller building. He hears a female voice.

"Come in darling, I'm in the kitchen. You're late, an hour late. Did you run into problems? I've been worried to death about you."

The captain enters the house and announces his presence.

"Excuse me, I'm one of Colonel Destivel's colleagues."

Victoria arrives, pale-faced, prepared for the worst.

"Captain Jopet. I'm Philippe's deputy. He asked me to come and tell you if anything happened to him.

Victoria takes her head in her hands, afraid of the news she fears she is about to hear.

"No, don't worry! Philippe is alive. He had a serious accident on his way home from a mission yesterday, but he's alive. He's not in any danger. He's at Rauceby Hospital, an RAF hospital. He has a badly burned hand, but we've been told that he will be fine."

He continues his explanation, recounting the explosion of the bomb and the deaths of the other crew members. It was a miracle that he had escaped.

"I was so scared!" she says, breathless, very emotional after what she has just heard. "I really believed you were going to tell me that he was dead. But, sit down for a bit. Can I get you a whiskey. I'll have one too. I need it! Just this once!"

They sit down in the kitchen. Victoria is glad to have someone there who knows Phil, someone she can talk to about him.

"Do you think he will be able to fly again?" she asks. "How long will he have to stay in the hospital?"

"I don't know whether he'll be able to fly again, but they say that he will have to stay in hospital for two or three months."

"As long as that? So it's really serious then?"

The captain reassures her and explains that they have to wait until the skin grows back, which takes a long time.

"At least he's out of danger," he concludes. "He won't get himself shot down by a Messerschmidt! That's the up side. Not everyone is that lucky!"

The captain thanks Victoria before leaving, adding "You can send Phil a letter by post. I'm sure he would be delighted to hear from you. Those months are going to feel like forever to him. The address of the hospital is easy enough to find."

He leaves Victoria sad and alone. She was initially relieved to know that her lover was alive and not too badly injured. Now she is disappointed that he isn't with her and that they won't be able to be together for such a long time. Three months until she can see him again, that's a hell of a long time! She doesn't know if she can get away or whether he will want to see her at the hospital. She will write to him soon.

22

GAITFORD AND RAUCEBY, UNITED KINGDOM, SEPTEMBER AND OCTOBER 1944

Letter from Victoria Miller sent to Lieutenant Colonel Destivel at Rauceby Hospital on September 17 1944

My darling Philippe,

I hope that this letter reaches you rapidly. I was scared to death when the captain, your deputy, came to tell me about your accident, but he soon reassured me that you would pull through. I keep imagining you in your hospital room, with bandages everywhere. I hope the treatment isn't too painful, but I'm sure you're one of the strong and silent types that tolerate pain without complaining.

I was told you'll be in hospital for three months. Is that right? It's such a long time! For you, of course, but also for me because I miss you so much. Life is so absurd. It feels so right when we're together. Would you like me to come and see you? Please answer that question honestly. I don't know if I can get away, but I'll do my best to manage it.

I'm trying to console myself for our separation by telling myself that at least you won't have to carry out any more of those sinister war missions, risking your life each time. Your life means a lot to me you know, my darling!

Love from your English lady friend, who cares about you so much.

Victoria Miller

Yale Road,

Gaitford.

Phil receives this letter on Monday September 25. It's the first letter he has had since his accident. His right hand is in no fit state for him to write back at the moment. He's been hospitalized at Rauceby for almost two weeks now. Time drags past, but he is lucid and he quickly realizes that this accident will keep him out of harm's way for several months. He has already moved on from an imminent fatal accident to a more normal life in which he can make plans for the future, even if he has bandages all over. He has been able to dictate a letter to his mother and children, telling them about his accident, his hospitalization and the good prognosis for his burns. At least they won't have to worry about him dying anymore. Claire had recently written to tell him that every time they received mail from England she was terrified by the idea that she might learn of his death.

He is overjoyed to read Victoria's letter. It arrived shortly before a bath, an experience that he still finds terrible. But this time at least he is not apprehensive, as his spirits are high after reading Victoria's message. He finds plenty of warmth in the words from his lover and, obviously, wishes to see her as soon as he is more presentable. He has bandages on the face, back, legs and hand. The surgeon has told him that his first- and second-degree burns are healing well and that in about a fortnight, only his hand should still be bandaged. He can ask Victoria to come in three weeks' time, to be on the safe side.

Phil now shares a room with two other men. Two young RAF officers who, like him, are not too badly burnt. He talks to them a lot in English for part of the day, improving his knowledge of the language all the time. One of the other two officers in his room has an undamaged right hand and writes a letter than Phil dictates to him on September 27.

My darling Victoria,

I received your letter, which took eight days to get to me. It's such a shame that my accident has separated us. How terrible, to be the victim of your own bombs! How stupid! My right hand is bandaged and Winston, one of my two room-mates, is writing this letter for me.

Of course I would like you to come to see me! I don't really think I'm presentable at the moment. If you can, please come here in two or three weeks. My surgeon says that by then I should only have a bandaged hand and my face will have healed. Nothing could make me happier than to see the one I can't stop thinking about. I have so many sweet nothings to say to you and I want to hold you tenderly against me.

Our love story is so beautiful. I really don't want it to end. As I'm no longer risking my life with each mission, perhaps we can start to think about our future. Please answer soon. I can't wait to hear from you.

With lots of kisses,

Phil

The post is working a bit better now. Phil tells himself that if this letter takes four or five days to arrive, he should be about to have a reply in about 10 days or so. It's a long time, but he will just have to grin and bear it.

The days continue to pass slowly. Phil reads a lot, plays cards with the other patients, and goes to the hospital cinema, where they change the film every two days. After six days, Phil is overjoyed when the mail is being handed out and he receives an envelope bearing writing that he recognizes as Victoria's. It's lunchtime. Phil decides to prolong the pleasure, placing the letter in his pocket to read later, when things are a bit quieter. He wonders when he will see his darling and can't resist talking to his friend Winston about it.

"It's my girlfriend. She's replied. I haven't opened the letter yet, but I think she will be coming to see me soon."

He manages to wait until the end of the meal and goes to the hospital garden, where he sits down on a bench to find out what Victoria has written.

Letter from Victoria Miller to Lieutenant Colonel Destivel at Rauceby Hospital, September 27, 1944.

My dear Philippe,

The army has informed me that Colonel Miller has managed to escape from the camp where he was being held and cross the front line. He is now on his way back to England. That's great news for him, but a bit odd for me!

I'm going to have to look after him, at least for a while, and I won't be able to come to see you. I'm terribly sad and disconcerted by this turn of events, but none of that can stop me from loving you. I don't want to lose you.

Victoria Miller

Letter from Lieutenant Colonel Philippe Destivel to Mrs. Victoria Miller at Gaitford, October 2 1944:

Victoria
The letter you sent me on September 27 depressed me. I so wanted to see you again. I can't see any room for me in your life anymore. What a disappointment! Let me know how things work out. We must continue to write to each other. When I get out of hospital, I think I will go and see my children and my mother in Morocco for a couple of weeks. After that, everything depends on the state of my hand. If I can get enough mobility back in my hand and the war hasn't finished, I'll go back to being the leader of the Aquitaine group of bombers at Gaitford. But I doubt it. I'll probably be sent back to headquarters in Paris and we will have to wait a while to see each other again, unless your situation changes. I'm impatient to hear from you again…

Letter from Victoria Miller to Lieutenant Colonel Destivel at Rauceby Hospital, October 30 1944

My dearest Phil,

My mother-in-law had another stroke two weeks ago and died last week. Fortunately, she lived long enough to see her son, Colonel Miller, who has arrived at Gaitford to recover after all these years in captivity. He is worryingly thin, and he coughs up blood. Tuberculosis probably.

We are going to leave Gaitford to go and live in London so that he can get the best possible care in a military hospital. I'm afraid it will be difficult for us to write to each other. Carry on writing to me at Gaitford. We'll get the post sent on. Tell me about your health. I'll send you my address in London as soon as we are settled. I'm glad you are going to be able to see your children. I want to cover you in kisses. Please don't forget me, my darling.
Victoria

Phil receives this letter on November 10. He is sorry that Victoria is leaving Gaitford with her husband. It was already difficult to stay in touch, and now things will undoubtedly get worse. However, from what she has told him, Colonel Miller is not in good health. Will he live long? Who knows? Phil is ashamed of these thoughts and tries to suppress them, but he can't. The colonel's death would change everything!

Life is monotonous at Rauceby. Every day is the same. It's autumn now, gray and rainy. Phil wants to reply to Victoria, but he doesn't know where to write to her. He feels blocked by the presence of her husband. Every day, he keeps a close eye on the mail in the hope of hearing from his beloved. At the end of November, he decides to dictate a letter to Winston for Victoria, to explain how he feels. Why hasn't she sent him her address in London? Having no news of someone you love makes you very anxious.

Letter from Lieutenant Colonel Philippe Destivel sent to Mrs. Victoria Miller at Gaitford, November 29 1944.

My darling Victoria,

I'm worried and sad not to have had a letter from you telling me where to write to you in London. My life has no meaning without the hope of seeing you again. I hope nothing bad has happened to you. The burns on my face, back and legs have healed. My right hand is getting better. The days drag by here and I can't wait to be released. I'm still planning to go to Meknes for Christmas.

With lots of love,

Phil

Every day, Phil checks the post, and each morning he is disappointed to find that there is still no letter. He doesn't eat much and loses weight, leading his doctors to worry that he might have an infection. Nevertheless, his wounds heal and he leaves Rauceby Hospital on December 13 1944, eaten away by Victoria's silence. His right hand doesn't look good and functions poorly and he wears a glove to conceal it. Tendon retraction limits his mobility. For the moment, there is no chance of him flying a plane.

23

MEKNES, MOROCCO, DECEMBER 1944

Phil first goes back to his base at Gaitford, where his colleagues give him a warm welcome. His closest friends have prepared a party for him in the officers' mess. At Rauceby, strong liquor, beer and wine weren't a part of his everyday life. The glasses of whiskey he enjoys make him see the bright side of life. During the party, whilst talking to Jopet, who has become the commander and leader of the Aquitaine group in his place, he expresses his surprise at the absence of a few people he knew well.

"Where are Captain Aramis and Captain Trinchot? I don't see them here. Are they out on a mission?"

"I wish they were! Sadly, they're both dead. Brought down by Boche flak during the same mission over the Ruhr a month ago. And they weren't alone, unfortunately."

Jopet then reels off a long list of names, mostly young men, about 25 years old, who have made the ultimate sacrifice.

Phil had often played bridge with the two deceased captains. They had known each other since his time in Chartres before the war. They are dead and he is wounded, but at least he is alive and probably out of danger. In the cocoon of the hospital, Phil had forgotten that the war was continuing without him.

Now he needs to get back to Meknes. The next day, he boards a Halifax taking several airmen on leave to spend some time in Paris. He is very moved when the plane lands at the military base at Villacoublay that has only recently been restored to working order. During its occupation by the Germans, it had been badly damaged by several Allied bombings. He left Ile de France four and a half years ago and has not been back to the capital since! A taste of freedom regained!

But his final destination is Morocco. His travels have only just begun. Luck is on his side and the very same day he manages to find a place in a military transport plane on its way to Marseille. He arrives in the afternoon, spends the night in the barracks and remains stuck there for two days before finding a place in a plane that takes him to Algiers. Another day of hanging around and then the final stage of the journey that takes him to Meknes. Five days of traveling to get from Britain to Morocco. That's not bad going considering they are still at war.

The colonel in charge of the airbase at Meknes, who knows him well, is surprised to see him get out of the Lockheed P-38 two-seater in which he has traveled as a passenger, with his little suitcase. Phil tells him about his life in England, the repeated bombing runs, his accident and his stay in hospital. He doesn't mention the names of the airmen who have died in combat. The colonel finds him a jeep and a driver to take him home. His family aren't aware that he is on his way. He rings the doorbell at about 5 p.m.

His "little" Claire isn't so little anymore. She opens the door and almost faints in his arms when she realizes who he is. She pulls herself together and throws herself into his arms, crying "Dad, it's dad! He's back! Quick, come and see him!"

She is nearly 14 now. Teenagers grow fast and Phil has

trouble recognizing her. She is very pretty, with her blue eyes. And she's not a child anymore. She's grown just over three inches in the space of a year.

Maggy can hardly believe her eyes.

"Phil, how wonderful! What a surprise! You should have told us you were coming!"

Phil is very emotional at this reunion. It's been more than a year since he last saw them. Paul is well on the way to becoming a man, and Claire has also hit puberty now. Maggy is proud of her tall son. For the dinner, she manages to improvise a festive meal with a local rosé wine, some pan-cooked lamb and fried potatoes, and an orange salad. Phil spends his time listening to his children talking about their holidays and their friends. They also assail their father with questions about his life at Gaitford, the missions, bombing techniques and the dangers. Paul seems to be particularly interested in his father's work as a pilot, whereas he never spoke about that before. Claire asks, jokingly, if he has met any pretty Englishwomen. Maggy

"Your father has had so much on his plate that he won't have had time to meet anyone!" Maggy answers.

Phil takes advantage of Maggy's temporary absence to see to something in the kitchen to whisper to his daughter "I'll tell you when we're on our own."

Claire is delighted with this complicity with her father. Over the next few days, they celebrate Christmas together, as a family. This interlude reminds Phil of his paternal responsibilities. His children enjoy telling him all about the things that have happened in the year that he has been away. He goes through their school reports, which are pretty good. Paul had had some difficulties in math for a while, but he seems to have improved. Phil tests him by setting him some algebra problems.

One evening, after the children have finished eating and gone to bed, Maggy serves her son a glass of wine and starts a discussion with him. She raises the subject of a possible return to Paris.

"It looks like the war is almost over. It must be time to go back to Paris now. What do you think?"

Phil plays the diplomat and leaves things open.

"If I'm sent to Paris we will be able to think about it, but I don't know where I'm going yet. Military headquarters in Paris is a possibility. I can't fly anymore, with my hand. But it could be in England too. I'll find out more in January."

Maggy doesn't push the subject and Phil is astonished by her lack of pugnacity. He hasn't been told about her attempted escape yet!

Instead, she changes the subject, saying "The dinner I had with Françoise Dumaine was very pleasant. Do you remember? I told you about it in a letter. She's a very nice young woman."

"I barely know her, you know. Just a dinner with her and her husband. He was really unlucky and she has been too. A widow with three children!"

"She's still young. She's pretty. She won't have much trouble finding a new man, will she?"

"I'm not so sure. Three kids to bring up. Who's going to want to take on a woman with three kids?"

"Maybe someone with his own kids to bring up, who could understand? You should go to see her when we get back to Paris."

Phil can't help but smile. That's the old Maggy he knows so well, bossy and unable to stop herself from organizing her son's life for him. He doesn't want to start an argument so he concludes by saying "I'll try and get in touch with her when we return to Paris, if I haven't fallen in love with an Englishwoman by then!"

Maggy is not amused by this last comment.

"Why do you say that? I hope that you have been behaving yourself with the women in England this last year!"

Phil isn't looking for a fight but reassures her, with a mocking smile on his lips.

"I've been very busy you know!"

Phil leaves for England on January 2nd 1945. Once again he hitchhikes from plane to plane in the military airports. The first plane takes him back to Algiers, where his is astonished to find that the famous white city is even whiter than usual due to some rare heavy snowfall. Then back to Marseille and Paris, all in the same day. He has a little free time and spends two days in the capital, during which time he pays a visit to his old apartment on *rue Lecourbe*. He hasn't set foot there in more than four years. Everything is fine, but it's very dusty. He also visits his family. He has some cousins at St. Maur who are astounded to see him and welcome him warmly. Then, back at Villacoublay, he finds a Halifax from his base that takes him directly to Gaitford.

24

RAUCEBY AND GAITFORD, UNITED KINGDOM, JANUARY-FEBRUARY 1945

Back in England, Phil first returns to Rauceby for a check-up. Still no word from Victoria! He is terribly disappointed, but has had time to put things into perspective.

Doctor MacIndoe examines him and, as previously suggested, proposes further surgery in a few months. He promises Phil a first-class functional and esthetic result. Phil is reassured about the future, but less than thrilled with the prospect of having to come back and spend another three months at Rauceby.

He returns to the base at Gaitford because his superiors have asked him to wait there for his posting, which should arrive soon. He can't fly anymore due to the current state of his right hand. In mid-January, he is promoted to commander of the base, replacing Colonel Maillard, who has been sent to headquarters. It's a major responsibility and no walk in the park because the airbase has more than two thousand staff, the airmen from the two French bomber groups responsible for carrying out military missions and the ground staff, mostly English, responsible for maintenance, plane repair and logistics. His colleagues are pleased with his promotion. At least he knows what it feels like to bomb enemy territory.

At the same time as this promotion, he receives a letter informing him that he has been awarded the grade of officer of the *Légion d'Honneur*. The text is emphatic and makes Phil smile.

"Commander of a heavy bomber group of exceptional value, possessing the most noble and effective virtues characteristic of a leader; brilliant executor of missions, organizer and exceptional administrator. Leader of his unit for more than two years, he has obtained magnificent results. Led his group in combat personally in the Tunisian campaign (1943) and was then sent to Great Britain with this group to fight in four-engine planes. Lieutenant-Colonel Destivel has personally carried out many daytime and nighttime missions as a pilot, over the occupied territories and Germany…..was seriously wounded during a war mission."

Phil also appreciates this promotion to director of the base, which enables him to remain at the heart of the war effort, but he is sad about Victoria's silence. He doesn't understand why she hasn't contacted him and he doesn't know how to reach her. The letters he sent on his return from Morocco have gone unanswered. Concerned and melancholy, he explains the situation to his former deputy Jopet, without concealment and asks his advice. Jopet is the only one he has told about Victoria.

"I don't suppose you have a brilliant idea to help me find out what has happened to Victoria Miller by any chance?"

"Finding out what has happened to her would be difficult, but maybe you could find out what happened to her husband, the colonel, through our English friends."

"You're right, that is a good idea. Thank you. I'll go and talk to Walton. I see him at least twice a week at the moment."

As commander of the Gaitford base, Phil is under the direct command of a young general, Air Commodore Walton, who coordinates several bases. He is pleasant and always positive with the airmen, and he often calls them by their first names. Phil wastes no time explaining that he would like to know what has happened to a certain Colonel Miller that he says he once knew and who seems to have managed to escape from Germany. Walton tells him that he will do whatever is required to find out what has happened to him. If he has indeed escaped from Germany, it shouldn't be difficult for Walton to find out more.

Phil wonders how long it will take to obtain any information from his English superior. Time passes slowly.

On January 30 1945, Air Commodore Walton tells Phil that Colonel Miller died the week before. Phil is relieved. He didn't know Victoria's husband, but his existence greatly complicated his relationship with Victoria. At least she is free now, and he hopes to hear from her soon, unless she has had problems herself. Phil waits impatiently for the post, but the days pass with no letter from his beloved.

On February 2, Air Commodore Walton asks Phil to mobilize 12 Halifaxes. The planes take off towards 6.30 p.m. for a night mission to destroy a synthetic petrol factory near Dortmund.

Once the planes have left, Phil can leave the base and he says that he will be away for two hours. He wants to do some exercise, to tire himself out, and he leaves on his bicycle, pedaling fast through the English countryside. He first pedals to the village of Gaitford, where he finds himself in the grip of an irresistible desire to go to Victoria's house. On the Yale road, at the edge of the village, he is submerged by his emotions, reliving the intensity of the passion he experienced in the painter's studio. He contemplates the large Georgian house, imposing but austere in the late afternoon light, sad with all its shutters closed. He gets off his bike and walks towards the studio, where he sees with sadness the letterbox they had used to exchange messages and to organize their meetings.

Phil opens the gate and listens at the door of the studio. He thinks he can hear the sound of someone inside. He knocks at the door and, effectively, hears the footsteps approaching. There is someone inside. The door opens. Phil is stupefied to find himself face to face with Victoria, wearing a blouse that is much too large for her splattered with paint stains.

"You're here! I came on the offchance. I hadn't heard from you but I found out that your husband died recently."

"Come in. I arrived early this afternoon. We need to talk. Do you have time now?"

Victoria lets Phil past and tells him to go into the kitchen. They remain silent for a moment, just looking at each other, full of emotion. Victoria is the first to speak.

"You can't see anything. No scars on your face. You're as handsome as ever. Just your right hand. You're wearing a glove? Are you still flying?"

"No, my hand doesn't work very well at the moment. They're supposed to operate on it again in a few months. I can't fly any more. I'm in charge of the airbase at Gaitford now and it's no picnic. It's a huge responsibility. There are more than two thousand people at the base. But how about you? How are you? Why didn't you stay in touch?"

"My husband's return was really hard for me. He was very ill. His chances of survival were slim and he knew it. I think I looked after him well. I couldn't cope with nursing him through the end of his life and nurturing other very strong ties at the same time. It was complicated. I felt guilty. But now I'm starting to find my peace of mind again."

"I was sad and worried. I didn't know whether you were alive or dead. I couldn't understand what was going on. And now, were you intending to contact me?"

"Probably! I wanted time to think about it. But tell me about the end of your stay in hospital. Did you get to see your children at Christmas?"

Phil rapidly describes his trip to Meknes, his surprise arrival, his daughter who has grown up so much, his son too, and Maggy, who hasn't changed an iota. Phil gets up, walks around the table and arrives behind Victoria. He lifts up her hair and kisses her tenderly on the neck. She doesn't stop him and simply says "Oh Phil. I've missed you so much too!"

Then Victoria stands up and faces him. Gazes of infinite tenderness. The thrilling kisses of an unexpected reunion.

"Come, our sheets are still on the bed. It's a bit cold. There's no heating in the house. But I have some spare covers."

Two bodies are soon uncovered in the bedroom, with the shutters closed. Their clothes fly off. Two sets of skin seeking and finding each other. And two mutual desires, sighs of love and thigh and abdominal muscles tensing. Victoria gets up briefly to go to the sink. Phil can barely make out her silhouette in the half light. She seems to have slightly more accentuated curves than before. She asks him, in French, *"Tu me trouves plus ronde qu'en septembre?"*[6]

"Maybe, but I like it!"

They return to their sheets. Phil seeks out and finds the curves his lover was talking about. Victoria is more tender than sensual, but she receives him inside her with ardor. Together they experience spasms of pleasure that invade them and appease them. Victoria rests against Phil's shoulder for several minutes before he hears her sobbing quietly and feels her tears against his skin. He looks at her beseechingly.

------

[6] Do you think I look fatter than in September?

"You're crying! Why, my sweet love?"

"It's very hard for me, but there's something I have to tell you. I'm not quite sure how to go about it. I didn't want to talk to you about it, but I don't want to have to hide it from you anymore. I'm expecting your baby Phil. I'm five months pregnant. I saw a gynecologist in London and he confirmed it. I thought I couldn't have children, but it must have been my husband who was sterile. I was very surprised at first, but so happy. I always wanted to have a son. But I'll be delighted if it's a girl too."

Phil is dumbstruck. It had never occurred to him that their relationship could result in a baby. Becoming the father of a little English child when he already has two older children in Morocco and a complicated family life! But, on the other hand, he is so emotional to see the love of his life again and to know that she still loves him that the present is what counts most to him.

"I'm so happy to see you again. Without you in my life I feel very alone. I just need to get used to the idea of having a big family!"

"I'll be in Gaitford for a week or two. I'm in no great rush to go back to London. I hope we will be able to see each other again soon. We'll both have time to think about things. It's a difficult situation. I don't want this child to be considered the fruit of an extramarital affair while his father was a prisoner of war. As things stand, he's the heir of Colonel Miller, who was far from poor."

"I see what you mean. I need some time to let things sink in and to find solutions. I can't stay long tonight, Victoria. I can see from my watch that it's already time I was getting back to the base. I have a day off next Wednesday. Can we talk about things, about our future, then?"

"Yes, of course. I've got the main house to sort out. Please be discreet when you come here. I haven't been a widow long, and certainly not long enough to be a merry one!"

She leaves the room for a moment and returns with the painting of Phil asleep that she had rapidly completed after the party at Badvington.

"Do you remember? You can take this painting if you want. Would you like that?"

"Oh yes! Thank you. Such a beautiful memory!"

Phil gets dressed and kisses Victoria slowly. He leaves a bit concerned, but very happy. That night, in his bed, he finds it hard to get to sleep. The situation is complicated, but it's no great disaster that Victoria is carrying his baby. This child will tie them together forever. He is aware of how important she has become to him. He hadn't even dreamt that he might see her today. Their reunion was completely unexpected.

But he can't imagine returning to his family and announcing that he has had a third child during his stay in England. Victoria doesn't want her son to be considered a bastard and herself a slut who got herself pregnant while her husband was a German prisoner of war. He quickly comes to the conclusion that Victoria could come to France with her child once the war is over. She could go back to her life as a painter in Paris. They could pretend that they had just met and then get married and Phil could adopt the child. It's a convoluted scenario, but at least it's realistic. He promises himself that he will talk about it with Victoria the following Wednesday and ends up falling asleep.

Towards three in the morning, he is awoken by the hum of the first Halifax returning from the mission. Moments later, a distraught Captain Jopet arrives.

"Come quickly. There's a problem. A large number of German fighters seem to have got into the stream. Intruders. On the way back from the mission. We just got the news over the radio. Our planes are being rerouted to other bases. The secret services were aware of an operation called Gazela, but they didn't know exactly what it was about. Unfortunately, we know now."

"OK. I'll get dressed as quickly as I can and then I'll be there. I'll see you in the control tower."

Phil understands the danger and considers the situation carefully while putting on his uniform. German fighters have managed to enter the stream of planes, which would have extinguished their lights on the way home from their mission. The German planes would have remained invisible in the dark. They plan to follow the bombers to their airbases and then open fire on them as they land. The best thing to do is switch off all the lights at the base. Darkness will be the best protection.

He rapidly makes his way to the control tower. He sees a Halifax preparing to land. As it touches the ground, it is immediately targeted by a German Junkers that was following close behind. The plane is hit and quickly catches fire, stopping in the middle of the runway. The crew members evacuate the plane rapidly. The flames light up the ground, providing the enemy with a reference point. There are now another two fighters making low-level passes and firing at the crew, the planes on the ground and the hangars housing the planes. Phil orders the fire trucks to put out the fire in the Halifax on the runway as soon as possible, but with the many passages of the fighters, other fires have broken out, providing additional, easy-to-identify targets.

One of the fighters is coming back. It really seems as if the pilot is determined to risk his life, almost skimming the ground, at night, to increase his precision. Thirty seconds after his passage, a large glow lights up the English countryside a few miles from the base. Maybe the fighter has been wiped out nearby?

Calm returns. The German fighters, which have a limited autonomy, have rapidly turned back. But their attack has taken its toll. Three bombers out of action. Five airmen and three mechanics from the ground staff dead. Plus about 20 wounded.

Towards six in the morning, Phil is informed that one of the German fighters crashed. Undoubtedly flying too low, it had hit the branches of a tree, which had knocked it off balance, and it had ended up crashing into the roof of a house at Gaitford, which had then collapsed. Phil gets a driver to take him out in a jeep to see for himself.

When they arrive in the center of town, they are told that the accident happened on the outskirts, along the Yale road. Phil's heart skips a beat when he begins to imagine what he might find. The road they are told to take is exactly that leading to Victoria's house. They are guided by a halo of black smoke rising up into the sky. Phil is sure that his heart is about to explode when they leave Gaitford. There is only one house on the edge of town. His pulse is racing when he arrives at Victoria's house and finds that it is indeed the house into which the German plane crashed.

"Look, Sir, one of the trees in front of the big house is half out of the ground. The Junkers must have hit it and then crashed into the little house next door and demolished it."

Phil gets out of the jeep and approaches the remains of his beloved's studio. There is nothing more than a pile of rubble, and some half-carbonized beams that are still smoking. The air close to the ruins is difficult to breathe. About 50 yards away, the remains of the plane are visible. It had ended up in on the path and in the ditch alongside the house. If Victoria had been in her studio, she must have been killed instantly. There are no signs of life in the vicinity.

Phil, distressed, runs to the big house. The door is ajar. He goes in and finds himself in a dark hall leading to a staircase providing access to the upper floors. He calls out at the top of his voice.

"Victoria! Victoria! Are you there? Are you OK?"

No answer. Running up the stairs, he sees blood stains on the steps and fears the worst. The red marks stop in the corridor leading to the rooms on the first floor. He isn't familiar with this house and doesn't know where to look. Increasingly worried, he continues up the stairs to the second floor, where he sees a new trace on the landing, in front of a door with another red stain on the door handle. He opens the door, goes into the room and sees Victoria stretched out on a bed, sobbing, with her right hand wrapped in a white cloth covered with scarlet stains. In a nightshirt, numb from cold, she is sobbing and seems to be in a state of shock.

Phil is relieved. She is alive and doesn't seem to be badly hurt. He sits next to her, places his hand on her shoulder and speaks to her gently.

"Are you hurt?"

The sight of him brings Victoria out of her torpor.

"Oh! I'm glad you're here. I thought I was going mad. It was horrible. There was a humming noise and then an enormous explosion, like an earthquake. I'd just left the studio where I dozed off. But it was too cold and I decided to finish the night in my room in the big house. A few seconds later and I could have been killed! I went back after the accident and that's where I cut myself. The studio is completely destroyed. All my paintings! Everything I painted since I came to look after my mother-in-law. All gone up in smoke. There's nothing left! I'm devastated! My hand will be fine. It's a light wound, but it bled a lot."

Phil looks at her hand and sees that the palm is grazed, but there is no serious injury. He realizes that his beloved has had a great scare and sees the loss of her paintings as a catastrophe. All her work over the last four years. Phil tries to calm her down and holds her in his arms. Between sobs, she murmurs "I can't take any more. I don't want to stay here. I'm scared I might have a miscarriage. I'm going to go back to London!"

"My next leave is in a week. I'll come to see you."

"Yes, please come as soon as possible. You're all I've got left Phil and I love you."

Victoria is like a defenseless child, overwhelmed by the events that have shaken up her life.

"I thought that maybe you could come and live in Paris after the birth, when the war is over. You can start painting again. You must have a few friends left there. We can see how things work out for us afterwards. All I want is to make sure I don't lose you."

"I don't really want to make any plans yet, but yes, why not come to Paris to be close to you and continue to paint? There's nothing keeping me here. Why not start from scratch, essentially, just with your baby?"

She smiles at him, at which the driver enters the house and climbs the stairs.

"Sir, don't you think we should be getting back to the base?"

"I'll be down in a few minutes. I'll see you at the car."

Phil doesn't want to leave Victoria too quickly.

"Clean up that wound with some antiseptic. You mustn't let it get infected. Are you really going to leave today?"

"Yes, if I can find a train or bus. I don't want to stay in this sinister house. I need to rest. I'll give you my address and I'll write to you at Gaitford. From now on we'll stay in touch!"

"I have to go. Our base was attacked last night by enemy fighters who did a lot of damage on the ground. We have dead and injured to deal with. The Germans aren't beaten yet. I can't stay long, but it breaks my heart to have to leave you!"

Victoria leaves the room briefly and comes back with her address in London written on a piece of paper. They then go down to the front door together. Victoria is in tears and clings to Phil, who holds her close. A kiss and such a tender embrace. Her final words on parting are music to Phil's ears.

"Come and see me soon! There are no obstacles to our love now!"

25

GAITFORD, UNITED KINGDOM, MAY 7 1945

On the morning of May 7, Phil starts by writing a letter to Victoria, who is due to give birth in three weeks' time. At the start of April, he had been able to take two days' leave to go and see her in London. Phil found her blooming, very happy to be having his baby after believing herself to be sterile for so long. Despite her swollen abdomen, she had started painting again, having been able to get hold of the minimum amount of material required, a palette, an easel, some tubes of paint and a few brushes. More very abstract paintings, similar to those she had shown Phil in her studio in Gaitford. Pretty, elegant forms, in mauves and lilacs. Phil can sense that she is still passionate about her art. In his letter, he passes on reassuring news about the advance of the Allies and asks about her health. Twice weekly they exchange letters, repeatedly telling each other how impatient they are to meet again.

Once he has completed his letter, Phil goes to his office, where a tedious task awaits him. Each month, he has to carry out an evaluation of the technical incidents, breakdowns and accidents of the last 30 days for his superiors. The aim is to find corrective measures that could be applied to render the planes of the base as reliable as possible. His secretary, Mary, enters the office while he is deep in thought.

"Sir, I've just had a call from security. A lieutenant, an English pilot without an appointment, wishes to speak to you for a moment. He refuses to reveal his identity to anyone but you. He's very insistent apparently. What should I say?"

"Tell them to let him in. I'll see him in half an hour. I've got something to finish first. Make him wait in the small waiting room. I'll go and find him when I'm ready."

Phil continues his calculations. Fewer deaths during the April missions. March had been an awful month, with five planes and 35 airmen lost. The German defenses seem to be less effective now. Maybe the end of the Reich is approaching? If only! Phil takes almost three quarters of an hour to finish his report and then goes to meet his visitor.

"Good morning, Lieutenant. Please come into my office."

The lieutenant follows him, walking with some difficulty, with the aid of a cane.

"Sit down and tell me what brings you here. I don't believe we've met and you haven't introduced yourself."

The lieutenant looks at him for a moment with a smile on his lips before replying, "Are you sure you don't recognize me Sir? We spent a day together a few months ago. We had a long chat in a London pub and then we went to see the anti-V1 defenses. Do you really not know my face?"

Phil looks at him carefully, suddenly very ill at ease.

"You are speaking of someone I saw die before my very eyes. It can't be! Did they manage to save you? Tell me if I'm wrong. Surely you're not the English mathematician hit by a flying bomb? You can't really be John can you? John who explained and demonstrated to me mathematically that I only had a one-in-two chance of getting out of this war alive?”

“Yes Sir, the very same, John Luxley. But don’t worry, I haven’t been resurrected from the dead. When they transported my body to the hospital, the medical examiner who was supposed to give permission to bury me noticed that I was still breathing. Weakly, but breathing nevertheless! I was in a coma for more than a week. Miraculously, I survived. Several operations, a broken femur and pelvis and an internal injury to the liver due to shrapnel from the bomb and the blast from the explosion. While I was bed-ridden, I often thought of you and our conversation that morning. But I have trouble remembering exactly what we did and said that afternoon. It’s all a bit vague. Several days in a coma doesn’t do the memory any good. I can remember your first name, Phil, but not your surname, and I remember that, at the time, you were not the commander of this base. I had trouble tracking you down after I left hospital, but I finally picked up your trail a couple of months ago. I wanted to see you again to thank you. If you hadn’t been there, you wouldn’t have raised the alarm and I really would have died.”

“I’m stupefied, John. What a miracle! I can hardly believe it! But do tell me, there is something that intrigues me. I’ve often thought of it. When we saw the flying bombing coming straight for us, you didn’t move. It was as if you exposed yourself to the risk voluntarily, like a sort of suicide. Why didn’t you run away like I did?”

“I really don’t remember what happened at the moment of the explosion. It’s news to me that I didn’t run. I don’t know why I didn’t. I was a bit disturbed at the time, but I’m much better now. All these missions over Germany, all these deaths. I was traumatized. You never knew whether you were going to come back alive. I lost the plot for a while. I’ll tell you all about it if you have time.”

At that moment, the telephone rings in the secretary’s office. Air Commodore Walton wishes to speak urgently with Lieutenant Colonel Destivel. It is exactly 11.02 a.m. when Phil picks up the phone.

"Good morning Colonel Destivel. Listen, there is good news this morning, news we've waited months for. The Germans are beaten! The *Wehrmacht* signed an unconditional surrender today in Reims, in your country, France, at about three o'clock this morning. Jodl was present, and so was Eisenhower. It's the end of hostilities in Europe. I had the Air Marshal on the phone in person a few minutes ago. He asked me to tell some of the base commanders, including you. No more bombing runs. The ceasefire will come into force at about 9 o'clock tomorrow night. Spread the news. It's very unlikely that you'll be asked to supply crews for a mission now! I'll contact you again soon, but I should continue with my calls now. You'll receive further information from Bomber Command."

Phil, increasingly disturbed by the events of the morning, remains silent for a moment, lost in his thoughts. The emotion is intense. The war in Europe is over. Almost five years since the signing of the armistice in 1940. What terrible years! France was invaded and collaborated with the occupiers. Millions of dead and injured throughout Europe. Lots of French airmen from Gaitford lost their lives. Others were wounded, mutilated, burned. Young men had made the ultimate sacrifice to stop the horrors of Nazi barbarism. This German surrender justifies their devotion.

Phil looks at his visitor again.

"What a morning John! You coming back from the dead and now I've just been told that the Germans have officially capitulated. They signed the surrender last night. Not an armistice. An unconditional surrender. The Boche has been crushed. The whole of Germany is occupied by the Allies. The war in Europe is over. An outright victory. You're alive and so am I. How incredible!"

John is shocked and his own reaction surprises him. He should be happy and relieved. But the news has actually thrown him off balance because he had wanted to become a pathfinder once he had recovered. Planting luminous markers around enemy targets in the middle of German fighters at low altitude would be sublime, with a major risk of being shot down. Few survive, but for John, it would have been the price to pay to eradicate the remains of his guilt, still present despite his long months in hospital.

"John, you're pulling ever such a strange face. You are happy aren't you? The war is over! You do understand that? You're going to be able to go back to your mathematics research. You're alive. It's a miracle. You're young and at the start of a whole new life."

"I can't help but think about all those who died, those that we will never see again. I think it would do me good to leave England and go and work somewhere else. I need to forget."

Phil finds him strange, but nevertheless goes with him to the officers' mess, which he finds full to bursting. The two officers with whom he works most closely, Jopet and Vigard, are sat there, each holding a glass of beer. He asks for a pint of the same and starts speaking, loudly, so that everyone can hear him.

"Gentlemen, your attention please! I would like to raise my glass to, guess what? The Boche have capitulated. An unconditional surrender was signed at Reims during the night! Gentlemen, the war in Europe is over!"

There is great joy, that of victory, and emotion on the faces of these officers. They start shouting "Hurrah!", "Long live the Allies" and "Long live France". The airmen start singing the Marseillaise. They have never before sung with such enthusiasm. Phil then continues his speech.

"Gentlemen, a minute of silence if you please, for all those who died, young men who didn't come back from their missions. They left their lives in the hell of bombing and dogfights. More than half the airmen present here in Gaitford at the time of our arrival in

May 1944 have died. They were heroes. Don't ever forget them!"

The minute of silence is hard to bear. Everyone thinks about the comrades they liked, with whom they talked, played bridge and drank beers with in the pubs of Gaitford up until the fateful day they didn't return from missions and were declared missing. There isn't a dry eye in the room. This minute is long and oppressive. Happiness returns only after it has ended. The joy of victory gets the better of them. Phil ends his speech by providing a few additional details about the surrender.

The news spreads like wildfire across the airbase. Many come to celebrate with a drink in the mess. These men, for months, have been risking their lives on a daily basis. The hostilities have finally ended and now everyone is aiming to return to France, assured of coming out of the war alive, with their lives to rebuild.

END OF THE FIRST VOLUME OF "THE DESTIVELS".

The airbases at Gaitford and Badvington are fictional. There was only one French bomber base in England, at Elvington in Yorkshire. It housed crews of the Guyenne and Tunisie groups (squadrons 346 and 347). The father and brother-in-law of the author were pilots at this base.

The author consulted the various works and websites below to constitute the ambiance and functioning of these heavy bomber bases and the modes and sites of bomber pilot training:

Guy Fruchart. Squadron 346 Guyenne –Squadron 347 Tunisie. Les Français dans le Bomber Command. Grande Bretagne, septembre 1943-octobre 1945. Editions la Presse (2010).

Jules Roy. Retour de l'enfer. Gallimard (1951).

Lieutenant-Colonel Calmel. Pilotes de Nuit. Editions de la Table Ronde (1952).

Général Noirot. Les foudres du ciel. Editions France-Empire (1972).

Le groupe de bombardement Tunisie. Du 8 novembre 1942 à la victoire. Editions Berger-Levrault (1947).

http://halifax346et347.canalblog.com/ HALIFAX 346 et 347, Groupes Lourds Français Basés à Elvington en Grande-Bretagne 1944 – 1945 2/23 "GUYENNE" - 1/25 "TUNISIE" (last consulted February 2nd 2015).

A large party was held at the Elvington base on August 27th 1944, to celebrate the liberation of Paris. The author used this party as the inspiration for his description of the party at Badvington.

The author obtained information about the Operational Research Section located at the general headquarters of Bomber Command from the following site: http://forums.ubi.com/showthread.php/602999-Freeman-Dyson-operational-research-and-the-night-bomber-offensive-Forums " (last consulted February 2nd 2015).

Precise information about Bomber Command is available from the Royal Air

Force website:

http://www.raf.mod.uk/history/bombercommand.cfm (last consulted January 15th 2015).

There is a Halifax bomber on display at the Yorkshire Air Museum at Elvington (http://www.yorkshireairmuseum.org/). It is possible to visit the interior of the plane on demand. Close by, a few of the buildings from the airbase, including some with a half-barrel shape like those described in this novel, have been conserved. They house a museum associated with the Allied Forces Memorial dedicated to the various bomber groups housed at this base during the Second World War. A film shot during a night mission over Germany by one of the crews from the base can be seen. The control tower is still standing and resembles the descriptions of it from what is now more than 70 years ago.

ABOUT THE AUTHOR

James de la Boullaye is a scientist by training. This physician and researcher has, over the last few years, found great pleasure and freedom in the writing of works of fiction.